"There's no way I'll ever get married for real."

Although Sam had no intention of ever walking down the aisle again, Bridget's words surprised him. He wondered how she could make such a certain, sweeping statement.

Well, that was her business, he immediately answered himself. Not his. All he had to know about Special Agent Bridget Logan was that she was as dedicated to playing his wife, to getting the job done and to wrapping up this case as he was. He looked at her again, at the way the soft light filmed her hair in gold and made her skin glow and her eyes luminous. He noted the soft curves of her breasts and hips that even her baggy clothing couldn't hide. In her sleep-deprived state she looked soft and tempting and vulnerable.

Yeah, he thought. They *both* needed to dedicate themselves to wrapping up this case.

The sooner the better.

ELIZABETH BEVARLY

is a RITA® Award-nominated author of more than sixty works of contemporary romance. Her books regularly appear on the *USA TODAY* and the Waldenbooks bestseller lists for romance and mass-market paperbacks. Her novel *The Thing About Men* hit the *New York Times* extended bestseller list, as well. Her novels have been published in more than two dozen languages and three dozen countries, and there are more than ten million copies in print worldwide. She currently lives in a small town in her native Kentucky with her husband and son.

LOGAN'S LEGACY

New York Times and *USA TODAY* Bestselling Author

ELIZABETH BEVARLY

THE NEWLYWEDS

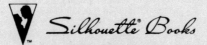

Silhouette Books

Published by Silhouette Books

America's Publisher of Contemporary Romance

If you purchased this book without a cover you should be aware
that this book is stolen property. It was reported as "unsold and
destroyed" to the publisher, and neither the author nor the
publisher has received any payment for this "stripped book."

Special thanks and acknowledgment are given to
Elizabeth Bevarly for her contribution
to the LOGAN'S LEGACY series.

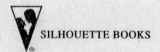 SILHOUETTE BOOKS

Recycling programs
for this product may
not exist in your area.

ISBN-13: 978-0-373-36356-8

THE NEWLYWEDS

Copyright © 2004 by Harlequin Books S.A.

All rights reserved. Except for use in any review, the reproduction or
utilization of this work in whole or in part in any form by any electronic,
mechanical or other means, now known or hereafter invented, including
xerography, photocopying and recording, or in any information storage
or retrieval system, is forbidden without the written permission of the
publisher, Harlequin Enterprises Limited, 225 Duncan Mill Road,
Don Mills, Ontario, Canada M3B 3K9.

This is a work of fiction. Names, characters, places and incidents are
either the product of the author's imagination or are used fictitiously, and any
resemblance to actual persons, living or dead, business establishments, events or
locales is entirely coincidental.

This edition published by arrangement with Harlequin Books S.A.

® and TM are trademarks of the publisher. Trademarks indicated with
® are registered in the United States Patent and Trademark Office, the Canadian
Trade Marks Office and in other countries.

Visit Silhouette Books at www.eHarlequin.com

Printed in U.S.A.

Be a part of

*Because birthright has its privileges
and family ties run deep.*

**Two FBI agents pose as newlyweds to expose
a black-market baby ring. With the mission
under way, this "pretend" couple finds the
idea of real marriage—to each other—
very tantalizing....**

Bridget Logan: While hunting down dangerous
criminals, Bridget secretly longed for a family of
her own. Being a special agent didn't offer her
much chance of true love until Samuel Jones
became her partner...and her husband!

Samuel Jones: When his ex-wife betrayed him,
Samuel vowed never to commit again. But then
Bridget, hardworking and earnest, stole his heart
and made him rethink his philosophy of love.
Would following his heart give him the happiness
he so deserved?

A wanted man: He was on the loose and no one
knew where he would strike next. Would his love
for a certain Portland General nurse calm his
vengeful soul?

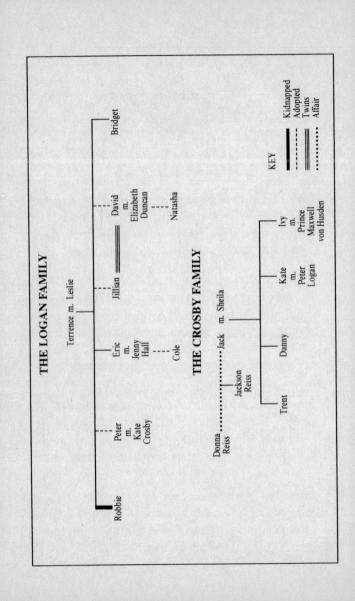

THE LOGAN FAMILY

Terrence m. Leslie

Peter
m.
Kate
Crosby

Eric
m.
Jenny
Hall

Jillian

David
m.
Elizabeth
Duncan

Bridget

Robbie

Cole

Natasha

THE CROSBY FAMILY

Donna
Reiss .... Jack m. Sheila

Jackson
Reiss

Trent

Danny

Kate
m.
Peter
Logan

Ivy
m.
Prince
Maxwell
von Husden

KEY

Kidnapped
Adopted
Twins
Affair

Because birthright has its privileges
and family ties run deep.

For all the great folks at Silhouette Books,
with many thanks and much affection.

One

Bridget Logan knew a lot of things about a lot of things. She knew the winner of every World Series since 1986. She knew how to speak Spanish, French and German. She knew pi to the twenty-seventh character. She knew how to make her whites whiter and her colors brighter. She knew the secret to beautiful skin. She knew all the lyrics to "Louie, Louie." Really. She even knew how to program her VCR.

She also knew how to bug a room so that nobody, but *nobody,* could tell it was wired. And she knew how to change her entire appearance with a few simple tricks and props that fit nicely into a nondescript handbag. And she knew how to disassemble and reassemble her .38 revolver, and how to hold it steady and shoot so that the bullet went straight through the white paper heart on the black silhouette at target practice.

But she didn't know nothin' 'bout birthin' babies.

Nor did she have any desire to learn. Because Bridget Logan was on the fast track in her career, a rising star at the Federal Bureau of Investigations. She had risen so quickly, in fact, that—as of a week ago, anyway— she'd been awarded a field assignment to a counterterrorist task force in Vienna, a plum appointment that even some veteran agents had been vying to win, and which would have boosted her into a very elite investigation group at the tender age of twenty-five.

And that would have put Bridget exactly where she wanted to be. She'd decided in junior high school that she wanted to pursue a career in law enforcement. Smart and driven and ambitious since her first day of school, she'd ultimately skipped two grades and graduated from high school at the age of sixteen. Then she'd left her hometown of Portland, Oregon, to move across the country, earning her bachelor's in computer science in three years' time at Georgetown University. Then she'd worked another three years for one of Alexandria, Virginia's premier private investigation firms. And then, once she'd fulfilled the three years of professional work experience required by the FBI, she'd gone after her dream. She'd entered the FBI Academy at Quantico, Virginia, when she was only twenty-two, and had become one of its youngest graduates. Since then, she'd put in three years for the Bureau, doing the usual grunt work all the newbies had to tolerate, then becoming a full-fledged field agent before she was even twenty-four.

She'd deliberately sought out the toughest cases, then had lied, begged, borrowed or stolen to be assigned to them. And she'd worked hard, with a passion that superseded anything she'd ever felt. She was still one of the youngest field agents working for the Bureau, yet she'd gained experience some of her older colleagues hadn't come close to achieving. She didn't have time even to think about a husband or family, because she gave everything she had to her job. The Vienna assignment would have boosted her into an even higher echelon, professionally speaking, and it would have been a hell of a lot of fun living and working in Europe.

Instead, two days after her arrival in Vienna, she'd been told she was being reassigned, effective immediately. And though she'd always had absolutely no interest in becoming a wife or a mother, she was now going to have to learn a lot about being both. Because for her new field assignment, Bridget Logan, G-woman and counterterrorist, was about to become Bridget Logan, trophy wife and mom wanna-be.

It was going to be the hardest role she'd ever had to play.

Especially since she hadn't met her husband-to-be. She wasn't even sure yet what the specifics of her assignment were, or why she had been selected for the job. She only knew that, a few days ago, she had been scheduled to be posing as a member of an obscure eastern European terrorist network, looking to score some stinger missiles from an American arms dealer working out of Germany, and today she was back in Portland. She'd gone into the Vienna office on Monday expecting to be briefed about her assignment before heading off to Zagreb, but had instead been told to turn around and pack her bags and head home, because she was needed for a "special assignment" she'd learn more about upon arrival.

Oh, and she'd also been told to spend her hours on the long flight home perusing the latest issues of *Vogue*,

Town and Country and *The Robb Report,* along with a variety of literature on clinical infertility. And because Bridget Logan knew a lot of things about a lot of things, she'd suspected right off that she'd been pulled from her work in Europe to go home—and to learn about clinical infertility along the way—because of her parents' involvement in one of Portland's most famous establishments: the Children's Connection. That could be the only reason why they'd taken her, specifically, off such an elite overseas assignment, one that would have pushed her even more quickly up the professional ladder, to travel halfway around the world for an assignment that could have gone to anyone.

Because the Logans of Portland, Oregon, were known—even internationally—for the work they did at the foundation that helped infertile couples adopt or conceive. Long before Bridget was born, her parents had suffered a terrible tragedy; their firstborn child had been kidnapped and murdered. Leslie and Terrence Logan had never quite gotten over the loss of their son Robbie, but eventually, they'd managed to heal enough to move on and start their family anew. Through adoption and conception both, the Logan children now numbered five, of whom Bridget was the youngest. That family had come about due in large part to Children's Connection, and Leslie and Terrence were so grateful to the organization for making it happen that they had virtually become a part of the organization, donating both considerable time and considerable money to help it thrive.

Before the Logans became involved, Children's Connection had consisted of a small orphanage that had been in operation since the early 1940s, and a fledgling fertility clinic associated with Portland General

Hospital. But through generous grants from the Logans, and very effective fund-raising events often orchestrated by Leslie Logan, Children's Connection had expanded over the years into a state-of-the-art fertility treatment center that included counseling for childless couples and support groups for single parents. Financial support—again, often provided by grants from the Logans—to orphanages in key cities around the world, especially Moscow, had, in recent years, also introduced foreign adoption as an option to prospective parents.

These days, Children's Connection had satellite orphanages all over the world, and they brought couples who were unable to conceive together with children who desperately needed homes. And their world-renowned fertility clinic had made conception a reality for couples who hadn't thought they stood a chance having biological children. Hundreds, even thousands of families had been born over the years, thanks to Children's Connection and the Logans. And thousands more would come about in the future.

Bridget utterly respected and admired her parents' dedication to the organization. Especially her mother's, as Leslie Logan was as committed to her volunteer work at Children's Connection as Terrence Logan was to his job as CEO of the Logan Corporation, the family's million-dollar computer software business. And Bridget's sister, Jillian, worked for Children's Connection, too, as a therapist. Her brothers Eric and Peter had followed in their father's footsteps, and both worked for the Logan Corporation. Well, she had to concede affectionately, Eric perhaps worked harder at being a playboy than he did at being VP of Marketing and Sales at the Logan Corporation. Or, at least, he had until he'd been auctioned off to his now-fiancée, Jenny. Jenny had had a rather humbling effect on Bridget's slightly older brother, something all the Logans had welcomed. And her adopted son, Cole, had had rather a wonderful effect on Eric, bringing out a softer, nurturing side of him that none of them had even known he possessed. That was something—and someone—all the Logans had welcomed, too.

Peter had recently married, to—wonder of wonders—Katie Crosby. The Vegas wedding had come as a surprise to all the Logans, because there had never been any love lost between the two families. Leslie and Terrence still blamed Katie's mother, Sheila Crosby, for the kidnapping and murder of their son Robbie, because Robbie and his friend Danny Crosby had been playing unattended outside when Robbie was abducted. Had Sheila been more alert and less neglectful, Robbie, to the elder Logans' way of thinking, would still be alive and well today. Still, it was good to see Peter and Katie in love and together, and maybe it was another step toward putting Robbie's memory to rest. Bridget had flown home briefly for a reception Leslie had hosted for Peter and his new wife, and the two had very obviously been devoted to each other—and to the baby they were expecting.

Bridget's interests and passions, though, like her brother David's, had lain somewhere other than the Logan Corporation and Children's Connection. David worked for the State Department and had until recently been on assignment overseas. In fact, he'd recently gotten engaged, too, to a woman he met while in Moscow. And he, like Eric, would soon be a dad, to Elizabeth Duncan's adopted infant daughter, Natasha. But that was where the similarities between Bridget and David ended, because she had no desire to find herself married and in the family way. Having cut her teeth on Nancy Drew and Harriet the Spy, Bridget had known early on what she wanted to do with her life. And she was doing it. Exactly the way she'd envisioned.

Well, except for being pulled off of a dangerous, high-profile foreign case to be assigned to a piddling, boring, domestic one instead. But then, no life, she supposed, was completely without bumps. She had to pay her dues at some point, didn't she?

After deplaning and collecting her two tailored leather suitcases from the baggage carousel, Bridget did her best to smooth the travel wrinkles from her beige linen trousers and white linen shirt. Knowing it was futile, but being tidy by nature, she tucked a few errant strands of auburn hair back into the no-longer-neat braid that fell to shoulder length. Then she finger-combed her thick bangs, grimacing when she noted how badly in need of a trim they were. She was exhausted from the twenty-plus-hour trip and what had seemed like hundreds of plane changes, and what she really wanted most was to go to her parents' house to shower and change and catch a quick nap. But she had work to do first. And for Bridget, work always came first.

She'd been told she would be met at the airport by someone from the Portland field office, so she resigned herself to make do for now with the few hours sleep she'd stolen over the last twenty-four, and with the airline peanuts and the bagel and cream cheese she'd consumed while changing planes in Chicago. Her stomach grumbled its discontent at her decision, and she grumbled back that it was the best she could do.

What time was it here, anyway? she wondered. She searched her tired brain, trying to remember what time her flight had been scheduled to land. Three-thirteen, she recalled. But was that a.m. or p.m.? Surely p.m., she told herself. Though, truly, she wasn't sure. It *was* the end of April, however, that much she did know, because it had been the end of April in Vienna, too. And spring-time in Portland, she recalled, meant rain. Lots of it. Of course, summer, fall and winter meant rain, too, but springtime seemed to be the worst for it. She just wished she'd remembered that *before* she'd packed her raincoat.

Popping a mint into her mouth, Bridget collected her things and made her way toward the exit, scanning the crowd of people beyond baggage claim before she realized she had no idea whom she was looking for. Unless maybe it was that guy over there who was holding up a hand-lettered sign that said Logan. Being a good agent, and knowing a lot of things about a lot of things, Bridget recognized a clue when she saw one. Even in her sleep-deprived state.

But she woke up a bit when her gaze wandered higher, and she saw the face of the man who was holding the sign. He looked plenty rested and was in no way rumpled, something that made Bridget feel even more disheveled than she already was. His hair was the color of imported milk chocolate, flecked with flashes of gold in the glare of the fluorescent lights overhead. Lights like that always made her hair look brassy, she couldn't help thinking. And instead of travel-worn and disarrayed locks like hers, his hair was expertly cut and styled, not a strand out of place. He was dressed in the sort of suit most field agents wore—dark, nondescript, the kind meant to draw no attention—with a white dress shirt and plain blue tie. In spite of that, the man had drawn quite a bit of attention, Bridget noticed, because a trio of women standing nearby were all gazing at him with something akin to longing.

Which wasn't exactly surprising, Bridget had to concede, since the man was, in a word, gorgeous, his features chiseled and powerful and jagged, as if sculpted by the ferocious hands of an irascible artist. Instead of making him look dull and inconspicuous, the blandness of his clothing only made more appreciable his virile good looks. But his eyes, she decided as she drew nearer, were without question his best feature yet, because they were seductively hooded and breathtakingly blue. But not the kind of blue one normally saw on people. They were a dark, midnight blue, reminiscent of a twilit sky, that silky mix of purple and sapphire that slipped in just before complete darkness overtook everything.

As she drew to a stop in front of the man, she noticed he was tall, too, something that came as no surprise at all. But at five-seven, Bridget didn't have to tip her head back to meet too many male eyes. For this man, though, she had to tip her head *way* back, because he easily topped six feet.

She told herself not to be intimidated by him—yeah, right—and did her best to sound efficient when she told him, "I'm Special Agent Bridget Logan."

He dipped his head forward in acknowledgment and gave her a quick once-over, the kind of appraisal any agent would give anybody, simply because it was in every agent's nature to do so. But Bridget couldn't get a handle on what kind of impression he formed about her, which was more than a little disconcerting since she had a real knack for reading people. It was something else that had benefited her in her quick climb up the Bureau ladder. As soon as he finished his silent assessment, he tossed the sign with her name on it into a trash can to his left, making the shot effortlessly without even looking.

"Sam Jones," he told her by way of a greeting. "Special Agent Samuel Jones," he then corrected himself, as if he needed to make the distinction. As if he needed her to *know* he needed to make the distinction. "I'm with the Portland field office. Welcome home, Logan."

His welcome was as warm as the rest of him—namely not warm at all—but that was just fine by Bridget. She wasn't all that pleased to be home, truth be told. Yes, she rarely made it back to Portland these days, but she spoke to everyone in her family regularly by phone. And although she missed them, she'd been too busy to feel homesick. It wasn't that she didn't like Portland. On the contrary, she loved being able to call the city her hometown. But she had things to do, places to go, people to see. She had a career to build. And returning here had been a giant step backward in that regard.

"*Special Agent* Logan," Bridget corrected his identification of her. She needed to make that clear to him, too. "So just what am I doing home, anyway?"

"You're needed for a job," he told her.

"That much I gathered," she replied, biting back the *duh* with which she'd almost punctuated the statement. Exhaustion, she told herself. She always got cranky when she didn't get enough sleep. "What I want to know is why me?" she elaborated patiently.

Instead of answering her, Sam Jones—or, rather, Special Agent Samuel Jones—bent to pick up the larger of her two bags, leaving the small one for Bridget. An equal opportunist, she thought. She liked that in a man. Not that she liked this man, mind you, she hastily backpedaled. But he clearly wasn't a coddler, and she respected that. She wasn't a coddler, either.

He tipped his head toward the exit doors. "Car's just outside. You'll be briefed on the assignment when we get to the field office. You're expected ASAP. I'm expected to be the one to get you there."

He was obviously no-nonsense, too, something else Bridget admired. Still, a little information up front would have been nice.

Without awaiting a response from her, Samuel Jones began to make his way to the exit, so she hastily retrieved her other suitcase and followed. Involuntarily, her gaze fell to the elegant expanse of his broad shoulders as he cut a swath easily through the crowd, and she noticed how much taller he was than everyone else. He turned his head once, to glance at something that must have caught his eye, and even his profile made her want to sigh wistfully. And seeing as how Bridget Logan didn't have a wistful bone in her body, that wasn't exactly a reaction she welcomed.

Fatigue, she told herself again. She was only acting like a boy-crazy preteen because she was tired and crabby and hungry. She hadn't been boy-crazy even when she *was* a preteen. She'd been way too focused on school, and way more interested in changing the world than in thumbtacking pictures of River Phoenix and Leonardo DiCaprio to her bedroom wall. Once Agent Jones dropped her at headquarters and took off again—and once she got some decent sleep and a decent meal—she wouldn't give him a second thought.

They walked in silence until Jones halted behind a

black, commonplace, four-door sedan—government issue, natch—and thumbed the key bob to open the trunk. He hefted her suitcase inside, reached for the one she held out to him and repeated the action, then thumbed the key bob again to unlock the car doors. He didn't stride to the passenger side to open the door for Bridget. And again, she grudgingly saluted him for it. He was obviously the kind of man who assumed a woman in her job could take care of herself. And she could.

So it made absolutely no sense that Bridget should feel slighted by his gesture. Or lack thereof. For some strange reason, though, she did. Boy, she really did need to catch up on her sleep.

After folding herself into the passenger seat and strapping on her seat belt, she turned to face Agent Jones again. "So how much do you know about this case I'm being assigned to?" she asked.

He looked over at her, his stony facade cracking just enough that she could see he thought she was nuts for asking such a question. "I know everything about it," he told her in a tone of voice that likewise suggested he thought she was nuts.

Or maybe he thought she was stupid. It certainly wouldn't have been the first time she'd received such a reaction from a male agent. Not that that made it any easier to tolerate now. She arched her brows in surprise and resentment at his tone, but before she could speak, he continued, this time sounding mildly disgusted.

"You think I'm just the errand boy they sent to pick you up, don't you?" he asked curtly.

"Well, aren't you?" she asked.

He narrowed his eyes at her. "How old are you, Logan?"

"Twenty-five," she told him crisply. Actually, she was mere months from her twenty-sixth birthday. Then, just as abruptly as he had, she asked, "How old are *you*, Jones?"

He clearly hadn't expected the rapid-fire retort. Nevertheless, he told her readily enough, "Thirty-two. I have ten years in at the Bureau. Seniority, one might say." And before she had a chance to remind him that seniority was earned by more than just years, he continued coolly, "Look, Logan, I know all about you, all right? Hell, it's been hammered home to every agent here in Portland how fast and furious the homegrown Girl Wonder rose through the ranks at Quantico. But I, for one, suspect a lot of that was due to Daddy Logan's influence, both in Portland and elsewhere. Must be nice having an old man worth millions pulling strings for you. Me, I wouldn't know. I earned my position the old-fashioned way—by working hard and fighting tooth and nail for it."

Now Bridget's eyebrows really shot up. The animosity she had sensed simmering just beneath his surface had boiled right up from under the lid, burning her with hisses and steam. This time she didn't battle anything except Jones when she replied. "My father had nothing to do with my progress," she snapped. "I earned my position, too, *Agent* Jones. By working my ass off, fighting a hell of a lot harder than you, and by making sacrifices you couldn't begin to understand. Don't you *dare* suggest otherwise. If anybody gets handed anything in this business, it's those of you who have a *Y* chromosome. We women get handed jack. We have to work twice as hard as any of you guys to get half as much."

He set his jaw tightly at her outburst, but he said nothing more in response. Which was just as well.

Bridget's animosity wasn't exactly cooling at the moment, and she hated losing control almost as much as she hated not being taken seriously. Jones cranked the key in the ignition then, turning his gaze forward. He said not another word for the rest of the ride, and that was just fine with Bridget. She wanted to be rid of the SOB as soon as possible. And until then, she wanted to forget he existed at all.

The Portland field office of the FBI was located in the Crown Plaza Building, a boxy white building downtown that housed a number of other organizations and businesses. The city itself was just as Bridget had seen it the last time she had spent more than a couple of days at home about seventeen months ago. When she'd come home for Peter and Katie's reception, she'd barely seen anything outside the Logan home. The only difference now was that when she'd been home two Christmases ago, for all of five days, a delicate whisper of snow had been falling—a fairly rare occurrence for the city. Now, a fine gauze of rain misted over the entire downtown, the product of fat slate clouds overhead. In spite of that, a strange warmth spread through her. Even though, under other circumstances, she might have been in Vienna at the moment, it really did feel kind of nice to be home.

Until she remembered her dour driver. Once she got rid of Agent Jones, she amended, *then* it would feel kind of nice to be home.

He parked the car on a lower level of the parking garage and, again without a word, unfolded his big frame from behind the wheel and began walking toward the elevators before Bridget's feet even touched the ground. Somehow she refrained from rolling her eyes heavenward.

Jerk, she thought.

But she hastened her stride to catch up with him. After all, she'd never been inside the Portland office. And since 9/11, a lot of new security checks had been put into place. She'd have to follow Jones's lead if she wanted to make this as simple and as fast as she could. So she doubled her pace, taking two steps for every one of his, so large was his stride with those long, long legs. And she did her best to keep breathing at her regular rate as she hustled along, because the last thing she needed to be doing was panting after this man, even if it was only because she was winded.

They rode in silence up to the fourth floor, then he led her down a hall to the field office and entered ahead of her. But he held the door open for her once he passed through it, something that frankly surprised her. Okay, so he had some latent sense of courtesy, she conceded grudgingly. That didn't make up for the way he had verbally assailed her in the car.

A secretary dressed in efficient gray snapped to attention at their appearance, and she greeted Agent Jones informally before saying, "He's expecting you. Go on in."

Bridget was surprised when Jones did exactly as the receptionist instructed. Okay, so he could take orders from women and not be put off by his inferiors, she further conceded, though still grudgingly. Clearly, it was just something about Bridget herself who put the guy off.

Her father's money and influence, she recalled, neither of which had she ever taken advantage as an adult. She'd earned academic scholarships to put herself through college, and had worked both on- and off-campus to pay for her living expenses. And although her new role would have her posing as a trophy wife, a lifestyle with which she should have been familiar enough, Bridget had never really been into the physical trappings of the Logan wealth. Yes, she'd grown up in a big, beautiful home in one of Portland's most desirable neighborhoods. Yes, she'd benefited from private schools and extracurricular activities a lot of families couldn't afford. But not once had she taken any of them for granted. And as soon as she'd been old enough to start making her own way in the world, she had.

Not that she'd bother to tell any of that to Jones. Within minutes, the guy would be out of her life for good. And good riddance to him, too.

For now, though, she followed him into the next room and found one that looked a lot like the offices of other Bureau heads she'd seen, painted an institutional off-white and furnished with institutional gray Berber carpeting, fake wood shelves, a fake wood desk and fake leather chairs. The man who stood behind that desk was very real, however, looking as much like a federal agent as Jones didn't. Average height, average weight, middle age, medium-brown hair and eyes. Average, middle and medium everything else, too.

"Agent Logan," the man said as he stood. "Welcome back to Portland. I'm Steve Pennington. Special Agent in Charge."

"Agent Pennington," Bridget said as she extended her hand.

He shook it once, confidently, professionally, then silently motioned that she should seat herself in one of the two chairs opposite his desk. She did, and was surprised that Agent Jones took the other one. That didn't bode well for his leaving, which was the one activity she would very much have liked to see him indulge in.

"I'm sure you're wondering," Agent Pennington continued, "why you were pulled out of Vienna to return home."

"It's crossed my mind," Bridget told him. "I'm assuming, because of the other information I was given about clinical infertility, that it's because of my family's involvement with Children's Connection."

"It is," Pennington said. "You probably already know about some of the problems that have been plaguing the organization for the past several months."

She nodded. "When I've spoken with my family, they've mentioned from time to time some of the, uh, setbacks the organization has experienced over the past year, yes," she said. "I know there was an attempted kidnapping of an infant adopted by one of their clients— mostly because my brother David was involved and will soon be that child's father," she added with a smile, still feeling strangely warm and fuzzy about the prospect of becoming an aunt so many times over so quickly. "And I know about a successful kidnapping of another infant that's still under investigation."

"Yes, it is," Pennington said. "What's not been made public, though, is that we have reason to believe both the attempted and successful kidnappings may be linked to some other kidnappings that have occurred in the city over the past year."

"I didn't know about the possible connection," she told Pennington. But she said nothing more, because she could tell by his expression that he wasn't finished yet.

"And what's also not been made public," he continued, "is that there was a mix-up not long ago at the Children's Connection clinic with some, uh, sperm," he concluded in a matter-of-fact voice, even though that last wasn't a word Bridget normally heard spoken in her profession. "And we have reason to believe it was done deliberately. Currently we aren't sure why, or if it's the same person or persons responsible for the kidnappings. But we suspect the actions are all connected."

She nodded again, professional enough to pretend she hadn't noticed Pennington's stumble over the word *sperm.* Or even his use of the word *sperm,* which was even more admirable on her part, if she did say so herself.

Pennington went on. "As a result of all these incidents—and this is something else you may not know, the FBI has become involved in a criminal investigation, the focus of which is Children's Connection."

"No, sir, I didn't know that," Bridget said, surprised by the revelation. "No one has mentioned it to me. Are my parents and Jillian aware of it? Are they part of it?" Surely neither of them could be suspected of any wrongdoing, she thought.

"They're aware of it now. We tried to keep a lid on it for as long as we could. And, no, although we've questioned both of them, it was only routine. None of them has ever been suspected of being a part of this. But a nurse who works for the hospital affiliated with Children's Connection—a Nancy Allen—went to the police back in January with her suspicions that a black-market baby ring might be operating somewhere within the organization," Pennington said.

"A black-market baby ring?" Bridget echoed dubiously. "Sounds like a bad movie of the week."

"I wish it was," Pennington told her, smiling a little uncomfortably.

Poor guy, Bridget thought. First, he'd had to say the word *sperm* in the line of duty, and now the words *black-*

market baby ring. Not the best day, she suspected, for Agent Pennington.

"At first," he continued on valiantly, "the local authorities were less than convinced of the woman's story."

They were probably even less convinced of the woman's sanity, Bridget thought.

"But the woman was insistent, so they pursued the charge, if for no other reason than to be able to prove to her that nothing was amiss. Unfortunately, their investigation led them to conclude that there could indeed be criminal activity occurring at Children's Connection. The police notified the FBI when they realized there were potential interstate and even international violations."

"The attempted kidnapping in Russia," Bridget guessed.

Pennington nodded. "We think there may actually be a Russian pipeline of sorts. Perhaps pipelines from several countries. Someone who's providing infants to a contact at Children's Connection. That person then offers the children up for sale to couples who are on the Connection's waiting list. Or perhaps to people who were turned down as prospective parents. And we fear those foreign infants may be being acquired illegally. At this point, we still don't know a lot. But there have been more developments since that first report that have convinced us there is indeed criminal activity going on within the organization. There's even evidence that someone stole some fertilized eggs and has been selling them illegally on the Internet."

Bridget marveled at the deeds some people would commit, all for money, no doubt, she guessed.

"We suspect that all of these crimes are related," Pennington continued, "and we're reasonably certain that there's more than one person involved. We just don't know who the people are, or what division of the organization they work in. Realistically, they could be anywhere."

"And that's why I'm here," Bridget guessed. "A combination of my FBI training and my connection to Children's Connection, however superficial."

"That connection is about to become less superficial," Pennington told her. "We need you to go undercover with another agent, posing as a married couple who are looking to adopt a child. But because you're not exactly a stranger to anyone at Children's Connection—or, at least, your family isn't—you'll essentially be posing as yourself. Bridget Logan. Daughter of Terrence and Leslie Logan. But you *won't* be an agent for the FBI. Your parents have assured us that no one at the organization knows you work for the Bureau."

"That's true, as far as I know," Bridget said. "I've never been active in my parents' avocation, and I don't really know anyone who works there, except my sister. I don't think I've even visited the place for more than a decade, probably. Still, I don't know for certain that no one in my family has ever mentioned my job to anyone there."

"They all assure us they've never discussed you with anyone. Which means you'll be completely credible as someone seeking to adopt through the organization. Up to this point, the investigation hasn't been a secret, and the agent assigned to it has questioned a number of people who work at Children's Connection in one capacity or another. So far, we don't have any suspects, in spite of our evidence to suggest criminal activity."

It really did sound like a bad movie of the week, Bridget couldn't help thinking. She couldn't believe anyone involved in her parents' pet project would be involved in things like black-market babies and sperm-swapping and stolen eggs. But the FBI didn't go around investigating crimes because it was fun and they had nothing better to do with their time, and they sure as hell didn't make up stuff like this. If they were looking into the matter, it was because they had solid evidence to suggest wrongdoing.

"At any rate," Pennington continued, "whoever it is working illegally at Children's Connection almost certainly knows about the investigation. In spite of that, we've already got two of our Portland agents undercover there, posing as prospective adoptive parents in the hope that our baby seller might approach them with an infant for sale."

Bridget nodded. That made sense. Even with the investigation no secret, there was a good chance two agents might still be credible as an anxious couple looking to adopt, and they might still lure the bad guy. That didn't explain her own presence back in town, though.

"So why am I here?" she asked Pennington.

"As I said, Logan, you're going to be posing with an agent, too, in the same capacity—as prospective adoptive parents. But we're hoping that you and he will simply be able to move about Children's Connection and uncover more information about what's going on. Since you're a Logan, we're hoping people might speak more freely around you, and that you won't look suspicious in areas of Children's Connection that our other agents might not be able to infiltrate. You'll be working in concert with them, alongside them, but you won't have contact with them. And you'll be working for a different reason. Where they're trying to draw out our suspect, you and your 'husband' will be trying to learn more about who that suspect might be."

Now Bridget understood. Four heads were better than two. Especially if one of those heads—hers—had a familial tie to the organization under investigation. While the first bogus parents-to-be tried to make themselves a temptation to the bad guy, Bridget and her phony husband would infiltrate Children's Connection more deeply as the daughter and son-in-law of its most illustrious patron.

"We're betting Bridget Logan won't look suspicious hanging around Children's Connection," Pennington continued, "since her family is such a big part of the organization. You'll be able to move about freely, ask questions and even linger in places our other couple won't have credible access to. With luck no one will suspect you of being anything other than Leslie and Terrence Logan's daughter, who's recently returned to town with her new husband and wants to adopt a baby."

It was worth a shot, Bridget thought. Before she could ask more about her duties and cover, though, Pennington began to talk again.

"Your 'husband' is familiar with all the particulars of the case," he said, "but hasn't been active in the investigation so far, so he won't be known to anyone at Children's Connection. We've created a cover for him as wealthy businessman who's just moved to town with his new wife—local girl Bridget Logan, with whom he recently eloped. Since you've been living in D.C. for so long, we've made him a wealthy corporate type from Tyson's Corner, Virginia. The two of you met while you were working as the manager of an art gallery in Capitol Hill, but you've been homesick for Portland for some time, so his wedding gift to his new wife is to relocate closer to her family, where he'll be opening new corporate offices. We've secured a house for you in your parents' neighborhood, and you and your new husband can move in immediately."

"Sounds like you've covered the big things," Bridget said. "Just one question."

"Only one?" Pennington asked, smiling.

"Okay, one big question," Bridget amended. The smaller ones could come later. She smiled, too. "Who's the lucky groom?"

Pennington's expression did change then, turning confused. He looked at Agent Jones, then back at Bridget, and she hated to think why. "I thought you already knew," Pennington said.

Bridget shook her head, and in doing so, caught a glimpse of Agent Jones from the corner of her eye. He was squirming. And she *really* hated to think why.

"Special Agent Bridget Logan," Pennington said, "meet your new husband. Special Agent Samuel Jones." He tugged open the top drawer of his desk and reached into it, then pulled out a box, which he also opened and reached into, extracting two gold wedding bands. "By the authority vested in me by the Federal Bureau of Investigation," he said, "I now pronounce you man and wife." He reached across his desk to drop one ring into Bridget's hand, the other into Sam's. "I hope you two will be very happy together," he added as he leaned back in his chair. "Go forth now, and multiply."

Two

As Sam Jones surveyed what was to be his new home—at least, for a little while—one word, and one word alone, spiraled through his mind: *unbefreakinlievable.* When it came to living in the Logans' neighborhood, he thought, a man's home really was his castle. Because that was what the exuberant, three-story Tudor reminded him of—a palace. With its perfectly manicured grounds outside and what to even his untrained eye looked to be pretty primo antiques inside, it was fit for only the most discriminating potentate. Four thousand square feet of polished hardwood floors, jewel-toned walls, mahogany trim, intricate wainscoting, plush Oriental rugs and English country manor furnishings. Having grown up in a two-bedroom brick bungalow on the other side of town—the side of town where people got their hands dirty to earn an honest living—Sam felt about as comfortable in the place as he would feel wearing a pink lacy garter belt and push-up bra.

But it was the kind of place where Bridget Logan would feel right at home, because her family lived in this very neighborhood. In fact, the Logan home was even larger than this one, Sam knew, because she'd pointed it out to him as they'd driven past. So she must feel as comfortable here as she would—

Well. He tried not to think about the pink lacy garter belt and push-up bra comparison again. Unfortunately, he had a whole lotta trouble never-minding that, because the minute the image of her wearing such a getup exploded in his brain, he just couldn't quite get it to dislodge itself again.

Great. This was just what he needed. On top of being assigned to a case he had absolutely no desire to be assigned to—black-market babies and mixed-up sperm, what the hell was up with that?—he was going to have to battle a physical attraction to a woman he couldn't stand. Because the minute he'd seen Bridget Logan standing at the baggage carousel at the airport, before he'd realized who she was, his gaze had been drawn to her and stayed there. Well, what else was he supposed to do? She was a damned beautiful woman, and he always noticed damned beautiful women. And even though she'd been tired-looking and travel-worn, she'd carried herself like someone who simply would not be messed with. There'd been a combination about her of fierceness and vulnerability that Sam had found very intriguing. And then, when she'd looked up and started to approach him, when her gaze had connected with his…

He wanted to kick himself in the ass when he remembered. For one brief, delirious moment, he'd actually thought the beautiful woman he'd been ogling was approaching him because she'd been ogling him, too, and wanted to get to know him better. And in that brief, delirious moment, Sam had planned out their entire day—and night—together. And boy, had it been good. Then, when she'd identified herself as Special Agent Bridget Logan…

He bit back a growl of frustration. Man, sometimes life just really smacked the hell out of you when you weren't looking. Then it kicked you over and over again in the ribs while you were down.

He told himself his dislike of Bridget Logan was totally irrational, reminded himself that, until two hours ago, he'd never even met the woman before. Normally he was as fair-minded as they came, and always reserved judgment on an individual until that individual had shown, through actions and words, what kind of human being he or she was. For some reason, though, he'd had a real knee-jerk reaction to Princess Bridget. She stood for everything he held profane: too much money, too much privilege, too much power, too much beauty, too much…

Well, she was just too much, that was all. She was a member of the wealthy elite, that five percent of the nation's population that controlled ninety-five percent of its resources. She'd grown up sheltered from everything that was ugly and harsh and unjust, she'd had everything handed to her before she even had to ask for it, and she couldn't possibly appreciate what the real world—hell, what real *life*—was like. Yeah, she claimed to have fought for what she'd earned, but Sam knew better. People like her never had to fight much for anything, because others were always willing, even eager, to bend over backward for them. What she considered a fight, most folks would consider a favor. He just couldn't believe she'd ever had to work hard for anything. Not the way he had.

Sam glanced around at his surroundings again, his gaze halting when it fell on Bridget Logan. Too much beauty, he thought again. He would have thought such a thing wasn't possible. But with that thick mane of dark-red hair that even her braid couldn't contain, and with those huge green eyes and that lush mouth and a body so full of curves… Well, suffice it to say she was just so damned dazzling, it almost hurt to look at her. Looking at her made him remember all the dreams and hopes and desires he'd embraced as a younger man, things he knew now that he'd never have.

And the hell of it was, she wasn't even at her best. Even travel-rumpled and exhausted, she'd managed to take his breath away when she'd walked up to him in the airport. So much so, that he'd forgotten himself for a moment, had introduced himself simply as Sam Jones, instead of Special Agent Samuel Jones.

And there was a big difference between the two men. Sam Jones was the guy who spent his weekends in blue jeans and sweatshirts, hiking in the Cascades and kayaking on the Willamette, and coaching Little League for the Boys and Girls Club downtown. Sam Jones liked reading Raymond Chandler and watching sports on TV and tipping a few with his friends at Foley's Bar and Grill in the blue-collar neighborhood where he'd grown up and still lived.

Special Agent Samuel Jones, on the other hand, was the man who put on nondescript suits Monday through Friday and investigated interstate crimes and helped put scumbags in cages, where they belonged. Agent Jones was focused, driven, no-nonsense and effective. He always concentrated on the job, and he got the job done right.

It was important that he keep Sam Jones and Special Agent Samuel Jones separate. And it was essential that he be the former when he was relaxing and the latter when he was working. That was the only way he could keep himself sane in the face of the viciousness and violence of some of the crimes he investigated.

And even if this case wasn't especially violent, he still had to keep those two men separate. Because Samuel was suddenly feeling a lot like Sam, looking at the woman with him not as a special agent who also had a job to do, but as a beautiful, desirable woman he might want to get to know better. And he couldn't allow himself to think about Agent Logan in any terms other than the professional. Not just because he didn't care for her personally—and he was having a hell of a problem warming up to her professionally, too, truth be told—but because that just wasn't the way he operated. Not as an agent. And not as a man. He and Logan had a job to do. Period. And they would do it. Period. And they would be cool and focused when they did it. Period. And then they'd go their separate ways and never see each other again.

Period.

"Wow, this place is unbelievable," she said now as she turned to look at him, surprising him both because she'd just echoed his own initial thoughts about the place and because she was impressed by what he would have thought was an unremarkable environment to her.

She stood in the middle of the big living room, bathed in the warm golden glow of a lamp that had already been on when they'd entered. Pennington had told them that someone from the Bureau had been in earlier to prepare the house for their residence, supplying some basic groceries and turning on the heat and such. They'd obviously remembered lights, too, knowing it would be dark—or nearly so—by the time they arrived. The soft light brought out flecks of amber amid the red in Logan's hair, and made her complexion seem almost radiant. He wondered if her eyes would be as luminous and was tempted to draw closer to her to find out.

And just what the hell was he doing, thinking words like *warm* and *amber* and *radiant* and *luminous* in relation to her? he berated himself. He and Logan were *working*, for God's sake. That was the only word he needed to be thinking about right now.

"You think so?" he asked, feigning blandness. But he did allow himself to stride farther into the room, halting when only a couple of feet of space lay between them. Wow. In this light, her eyes really were kind of lumi— "I would have thought it was a lot like the place where you grew up," he hurried to add. "I mean, the house you showed me as being your parents' looked even bigger than this one."

She seemed to give his comment some thought before replying, but then she nodded. "Yeah, our house was a little bigger, maybe, but my parents were more minimalist when it came to furnishings. I mean, our house didn't have nearly this much color or this much…" She threw her arms open wide, and he tried not to notice how the gesture caused her breasts to strain against her white shirt enough that he could see the outline of her bra beneath, and how it looked sort of pink and lacy. "…*stuff*," she concluded. "Everything in this house is just so…so extravagant. How did the Bureau find this place, anyway?"

Sam wondered that himself. "I don't know," he said honestly. "It might be a house the federal government owns that they keep for visiting dignitaries. Or they might have made arrangements with a homeowner who isn't using it right now because they're working overseas or taking an extended vacation. It might have even been confiscated for tax evasion. Ours is not to question why," he told her.

"Yeah, and we never do, do we?" she asked.

And Sam wasn't sure, but he thought he detected just a hint of sarcasm in the question. Well, my, my, my. Maybe Golden Girl Logan wasn't such a perfect little agent, after all.

"Can we go over this thing one more time?" she asked. "I'm sorry. Usually once is enough for me, but I haven't slept in over twenty-four hours, and my brain is just having some trouble processing everything Pennington told me. We're a just-married couple, right?" she began without even waiting for his okay.

"Right," Sam told her. "We're newlyweds. We met in the fall, then eloped to Vegas a month ago because we were so wildly in love. We just recently surprised your family with the news, and that's why there was no talk of our marriage around town before now. At the time we married, we were living in the Washington, D.C., area, but I put my house up for sale and you listed your condo right after the wedding because we knew we'd be moving to Portland after we married. I'm bringing my business headquarters out here so we can be closer to your family—that's my wedding present to you."

"Well, aren't you the generous spouse, relocating

your entire business on your trophy wife's behalf?" Logan asked with a smile. Strangely, she seemed to be teasing him when she did. Sam told himself he was just imagining it. It was *not* wishful thinking.

"Well, I am a wealthy steel baron, after all," he told her. "I can afford to be generous. Besides, from what I hear, I just dote on my trophy wife and would do anything to indulge her." And where the prospect of playing that role had made him feel like a complete sucker a few days ago, suddenly, for some reason, it didn't seem nearly as distasteful now.

"So that's how you made your reeking piles of filthy lucre," she said, still smiling. Still seeming to be teasing him. And Sam still told himself he was only imagining it and not thinking wishfully. "You're a steel baron." She tilted her head to the side and studied him. "That's going to make this role even more interesting to play, not to mention more challenging, since I've never really been a woman who went for the big-business-mogul type."

No, what was interesting, never mind challenging, Sam thought, was how badly he wanted to ask her just what type she *did* go for. Especially since she came from a family full of big-business-mogul types and seemed to be the kind of woman who had been groomed to marry just such a man. Then again, maybe that was precisely why she didn't go for them. Tamping down his curiosity, he kept his question to himself. That was none of his business. And it wouldn't be in any way helpful for working the case.

In spite of his self-admonition, however—and much to his own horror—he heard himself ask her, "Are you saying you don't think anyone will buy the idea of your being attracted to me, Logan?"

Her eyes widened at that, and her smile fell. She didn't seem to be teasing at all now, when she said, "Of course not. My God, any woman would be—" But she cut herself off before finishing whatever she had intended to say, her cheeks burning bright pink at whatever had inspired her to say it.

And damned if Sam didn't find himself wanting to move closer to her and demand to know exactly what she was thinking at that moment. Though it wasn't necessarily his desire to know what she was thinking that made him want to move closer to her. No, unfortunately he was pretty sure it was his desire to do something else entirely that inspired that. Realizing it only made him feel even more rancorous. The last thing he wanted or needed was to get any closer to Logan than he already had. And why he understood that on one level but not another made him feel like a fool.

"What?" he heard himself asking her in response to her stumble, not even sure when he'd made the decision to speak and knowing it was a mistake to do so. "Any woman would what?"

Her eyes went wide again, in clear panic, and she opened her mouth, as if she were about to finish whatever she had been about to say automatically. But then she quickly closed her mouth again, clearly reconsidering and thinking better of it. Eventually, though, she did continue. "And we met in D.C., right? Which is totally credible since that's where I went to college."

Although there was a part of him—a-none-too-small part, dammit—that didn't want to change the subject, Sam reluctantly let it be. "Right," he said. "You were living in the city, in Dupont Circle, and I was in the Virginia suburbs."

"But I was managing an art gallery at the time," she recalled correctly, "which is going to be a little tough to fake, because, quite frankly, I couldn't tell you the difference between Jackson Pollack and Jackson, Mississippi."

"Hey, at least you know Jackson Pollack's name and that he was an artist," Sam said helpfully.

"Only because I saw the movie," she said by way of an explanation. "And that's about the full extent of my art history education."

"Ah."

She shook her head ruefully and crossed her arms over her chest, and Sam tried not to be too heartbroken about that. He also tried to tell himself it wasn't a defensive gesture. But it did seem defensive. What she said next, though, told him the gesture wasn't meant for him.

"Boy, my parents would be so thrilled if this were all really true," she said, her voice tinged not with teasing now but with a hint of melancholy.

"They didn't want you to go into law enforcement?" he asked.

"Well, they always *told* me they wanted me to be whatever I wanted to be, and to pursue a career that would make me happy, because that was all that was important," she hedged.

"But?" Sam asked, because he heard the word coming.

She expelled a soft sound of resignation. "But I think they always hoped that what would make me happy would be to marry a wealthy local businessman, preferably the son of one of my father's colleagues, then buy a house up the street from them like this one and be a full-time mom to a houseful of kids, preferably with names like Ashley and Emily and Brandon and Biff."

Sam couldn't quite help but smile himself at that.

"And instead, you go for names like Destiny and Zenith and Aurora, is that it?"

Now Logan smiled, too, and where she had been merely dazzling before, suddenly she was downright beatific. And those, too, were words Sam knew he shouldn't be using in relation to her. So what if they were totally appropriate?

"Actually, it's not so much the names I object to as the actual children. Don't get me wrong," she hurried on to say before he could comment one way or another, "I think raising kids is probably the most important job out there, for a woman *or* a man. But it's not for me. I wouldn't be good at it. Which is another reason why this assignment is going to be so difficult."

It was going to be difficult for Sam, too, but for different reasons. Because there had been a time when he *did* want a houseful of kids, and they could have been named John Jacob Jingleheimer-Schmidt and Pippi Longstocking for all he cared. But just when he'd thought that family would become a reality, it had been stripped away from him, brutally and treacherously, and it had left him wary of ever wanting one again.

"It's funny, actually," Logan went on, bringing Sam's thoughts back to the present, "because I always told my family I wanted to be a cop or investigator of some kind. My Christmas list was always filled with things like chemistry sets and Trixie Belden books and weapons of destruction and handcuffs. But what I always found under the tree was Barbies and stuffed cats and Little House books and an Easy-Bake Oven. All the stuff I wanted ended up on David's side of the living room instead." She smiled. "So I just ignored my stuff and played with his."

Sam found himself wishing she would talk more about herself, about her past, about her dreams and hopes, about her… Well, just about *her,* but he stopped himself. None of that was any of his business, he told himself again. None of it was germane to the case at all. Besides, once you got a woman like Logan talking about herself, she probably wouldn't shut up. He had other things to think about right now. And any minute, he'd remember what they were, too, by God.

Thankfully, Logan also seemed to remember the case, because she suddenly stopped smiling and looking all dreamy-eyed, and clipped herself into a sturdier posture. "Anyway, getting back to the matter at hand, our first order of business as newlyweds moving closer to my family is to consult my family's pet project, Children's Connection. Because we're anxious to start a family right away and can't. Is that correct?"

"That's correct," Sam said.

"And the reason we already know we can't have kids the old-fashioned way is because…?"

She didn't know the answer to that question, Sam knew, because they hadn't gone over it at the field office. And the reason they hadn't gone over it at the field office was because Sam had hustled Logan out of there before Pennington had had a chance to give her the rest of the particulars. Sam didn't much care for the rest of the particulars, even if they were part of a bogus history designed to snare a crook. Still, he knew she was going to have to be filled in on them. They did have to keep their stories straight if they were going to pull this thing off. Nevertheless, he wished someone had consulted *him* before working up their phony backgrounds.

"We can't have kids because…" He sighed, resigned

himself to it, and just plunged in. "Our cover story goes that you're actually my second wife, and I tried to have kids with my first, but couldn't. When wife number one and I looked into the matter, it was discovered that I'm…infertile," he said, trying not to stumble over that last word. Then, when he realized what he had said, he hurried on to clarify, "Because *the guy I'm pretending to be* is infertile. Me, personally, I have absolutely no problem in that regard. None whatsoever. That's a negatory on that. Nada. Nil. Zilch. Zero. No worries at all on that score."

He wasn't sure, but he thought Logan smiled at that. And okay, maybe, just maybe, he'd gone a little overboard on the reassurances. But a guy really couldn't be too adamant about making something like that totally, completely, profoundly clear.

"Really," she said. "You've fathered a number of little Joneses, have you?"

He hooked his hands into the pockets of his trousers and rocked back on his heels. "Well, none that I'm aware of," he said, hoping he didn't sound too smug.

"Ah…yeah," she replied, not sounding too impressed.

He dropped his hands back to his sides. "It was just a joke, Logan," he told her.

"A small one, huh?" she asked.

He opened his mouth to tell her that no, as a matter of fact, it wasn't a small one at all, and that he had absolutely no problem in that regard, either—none whatsoever, that's a negatory on that, nada, nil, zilch, zero, no worries at all on that score—then realized she was talking about the joke, and not his— Well, that she was talking about the joke. In fact, she was the one joking now. At least, Sam thought she was joking. He hoped so.

Because he really didn't have any problem in that regard. None whatsoever. That was a negatory on that. Honest.

"According to our cover story," he said, returning to the case and wondering why they kept veering off it, "the fact that I—the guy I'm pretending to be, I mean—was diagnosed as infertile was part of what led to the dissolution of my first marriage. My first wife decided to find a guy who could provide her with the children she so badly wanted," he added, trying not to choke on the words because they were so laughable when compared to the developments in his own marriage. His own *former* marriage, he hastily corrected himself. And the words were only laughable to a casual observer, he further amended. Unfortunately, he hadn't been casually observing when his then-wife told him she was pregnant by another man. No, laughter had been about the last reaction Sam had had to that particular news.

"So I have no trouble getting pregnant," Logan deduced from his explanation. "Or, at least, the woman I'm pretending to be has no trouble getting pregnant," she clarified. And then her smile returned. "Not that I, myself, have any problem in that regard, mind you," she said. "None whatsoever. That's a negatory on that. Nada. Nil. Zilch. Zero. No worries at all on that score."

"Mothered a number of little Logans, have you?" Sam quipped, smiling in spite of himself.

This time Logan was the one to tuck her hands into her pockets and rock back on her heels smugly. "Well, none that I'm aware of," she said.

Yeah, yeah, yeah.

"Look, Logan," Sam began.

"You're going to have to stop calling me that," she interjected before he could go any further.

"What?" he asked, not sure what she meant.

"You can't keep calling me Logan," she told him. "You're supposed to be my husband."

Oh, yeah, he thought. "So then…I should call you, what? Babe?"

She cringed noticeably. "Okay, granted, that's what a lot of older husbands might call their trophy wives—"

"I'm not *that* much older than you, Logan," Sam interjected this time. Because he wasn't that much older than she was. Dammit.

Her response was another one of those teasing little smiles that he was beginning to kind of like. Until he remembered that he shouldn't like them, because he was Special Agent Samuel Jones working a case. Period.

Then she ignored his interjection by finishing, "I just don't think I could respond to being called Babe in any way other than by throwing my drink into your face. So we'll just have to settle for Bridget."

Fine, Sam thought. He could call Logan that.

"And I'll call you…?" she asked.

Hmm, he thought. Lord and Master had a certain ring to it. Or maybe Master and Commander. Or The Good Master. Or—

"Sam," he finally said. "Sam is fine."

"Sam it is, then."

Until she said it aloud like that. Then he remembered he'd needed to be Special Agent Samuel Jones for this job. He should have asked her to call him Samuel. Because when she called him Sam, it made him feel like Sam. In fact, it made him feel better than Sam. It made him feel…

No, he probably shouldn't think about how it made him feel. So instead, he thought about the case. The case where he had to be an indulgent, infertile millionaire who wanted to impregnate his beautiful, bodacious wife but couldn't, so they'd be trying to adopt through her family's pet project, the Children's Connection.

Oh, man, he really wished they'd assigned someone else to this case.

"I need to call my parents," Logan—or rather, Bridget—said, interrupting his thoughts, for which he was extremely grateful. "I'm going to get an earful from my mom for not calling or stopping by the house before now."

"Tell her we'll see her tomorrow," Sam said.

"We?" Logan—he meant, Bridget—echoed.

"Yeah, *we,*" he said emphatically. "You and me both. Your mother is the one who set up our meeting with the adoption counselor at Children's Connection. Pennington thought it would give us that much more credibility. I thought you knew."

Logan—or, rather Bridget—sighed heavily and lifted a hand to her forehead, pushing her hair back from her face in what was clearly a gesture of exasperation. "I don't know anything," she said, sounding more tired than ever. "I haven't spoken to my mom for a week. This whole thing just came about so quickly and out of nowhere. A few days ago, I thought I was going to be working in Vienna on a matter of national security. Now, suddenly, I'm back in Portland pretending to be a stay-at-home wife whose greatest desire is to become a mother. And my mom and dad are going to want to see me tonight. And, really, I want to see them, too." She lifted her other hand, too, cupped it over her forehead and sighed again. "Even if I do feel like my brain is about to explode."

For one brief, fleeting moment, Sam actually felt sorry for her. She looked so exhausted, so confused, so…human. Delicate, even. Like someone who had been carrying around a heavy load for way too long and was desperate to put it down someplace safe for a while so she could rest. And he found himself wanting to offer to take it off her hands for a while, so that she could get the rest she needed, preferably by lying down next to him. What was really odd was that, in that moment, that was all Sam wanted to do. Just lie beside her. Just be close to her. For as long as she needed him to be there.

Then she dropped her hands back to her sides, squared her shoulders and lifted her head. And he remembered that she was a federal agent, just like him, and she knew she couldn't afford delicacy any more than he could. She didn't need him, he thought. She didn't need anyone. Just like Sam didn't need anyone, either.

"Keep it brief at your parents' house," he gently advised her. "Tell them you'll see more of them tomorrow. Then come back here and get some sleep. You'll need to be at your best tomorrow if we're going to pull this thing off. We need to be convincing as newlyweds and prospective parents. We'll have to go over this with your mother before our appointment, anyway. She's going to go with us to Children's Connection and introduce us to the woman who'll be handling our case. Laurel Reiss is her name. She's actually currently on leave because of a family situation, but she's doing your mother a favor, being our case worker. Your mother thought she would be best for the job."

"Does Laurel Reiss know about the investigation?" Bridget asked.

"I'd wager she knows there's an investigation ongoing," Sam said. "Considering how workplace grapevines operate, there probably isn't anyone at

Children's Connection who doesn't know about the investigation, and we've questioned quite a few people there. Laurel Reiss may very well be someone the agent assigned to the case has talked to, but she doesn't know that you and I specifically are a part of it.

"As far as everyone at Children's Connection is concerned, nobody, and I mean *nobody,* knows you or I work for the FBI, except for your mother and sister— everyone's being given our history according to our cover story. And your mother, father and sister are under strict orders not to reveal our true identity to anyone, orders they'll follow, because they know it could endanger you if the information got out. So when we go to Children's Connection tomorrow, it's as Mr. and Mrs. Samuel Jones, wealthy, upscale newlyweds who have recently relocated to Portland and who are anxious to start a family, but can't, so they want to adopt."

Bridget nodded. "Mrs. Samuel Jones," she repeated. She lifted her left hand and surveyed the heavy golden ring on the third finger. It matched the larger one Sam wore, both of them, Pennington had joked, a wedding present from the Bureau. "I never, ever, thought I'd give up my name for anyone," she said.

And Sam had never, ever, planned on asking anyone else to take his name again. But he *had* asked someone to do that once upon a time. And the woman he'd asked had agreed to do it. Then she'd made a mockery of his name. And him. He wasn't likely to let something like that happen again.

"It's only for show," he reminded her. "I doubt it's even real gold." He lifted his own left hand and wiggled his fingers against the strange weight. It had been a while since he'd worn one of these. And the one he'd owned before had only been a cheap bit of gold-plated metal that had turned his finger green. Appropriate, really, all things considered.

"Oh, it's real gold," Bridget said, turning the ring first one way, then another. Even in the dim illumination from the lamp, it caught the light and threw it back in a bright twinkle.

And, of course, she'd know real gold, Sam thought. She was, after all, a Logan. Well, for now, she was a Jones. Somehow, the realization made a funny knot form in his belly.

"But I know the marriage is only for show," she replied quite pointedly, dropping her hand back down to her side. "There's no way I'll ever get married for real," she hastened to add.

Not that Sam disagreed—he didn't plan on marrying again, either. But he knew his reasons for that, and he'd made his decision based on personal experience. Bridget Logan, he knew for a fact, had never been married. From what he'd heard, she'd never even been that seriously involved with anyone. And she was still young. For all her insistence that she was a seasoned agent and a mature adult, she was only twenty-five, an age when many people were still trying to figure out exactly who they were and what the hell they wanted to do with the rest of their lives. Not that Sam was an ancient sage, by any stretch of the imagination. But he wondered how she could make such a certain, sweeping statement at her age.

That was her business, he immediately answered himself. Not his. All he had to know about Special Agent Bridget Logan was that she was as dedicated to wrapping up this case as he was. He looked at her again, at the way the soft light filmed her hair in amber and made her skin glow and her eyes luminous. He noted the soft curves of her breasts and hips that even her baggy clothing couldn't hide. In her sleep-deprived state—and hell, probably out of it, too, Sam thought—she looked soft and tempting and vulnerable.

Yeah, he thought. They *both* needed to dedicate themselves to wrapping up this case.

The sooner the better.

Three

The meeting with Laurel Reiss, the social worker at Children's Connection with whom Bridget's mother had made their appointments, went as well as could be expected, all things considered. Those things being that Bridget and Sam barely knew each other, never mind even *liked* each other, so playing the part of loving newlyweds whose fondest wish was to start a family together hadn't exactly been easy. All Bridget could hope at this point was that it had been convincing. Unfortunately, though, she couldn't even be certain of that.

It was strange, because she had never felt uncomfortable or unconvincing playing a role in the field before. She'd worked undercover as everything from a call girl to a drug dealer to a Mafia princess, and she had always been able to play the parts persuasively, often in situations where her very life depended on her performance.

Yet today, she had been performing in an environment that was completely safe, and had been trying to pass herself off as something that required very little effort on her part. Yet she'd felt as nervous and jittery as a preteen at a dance.

It didn't bode well for the rest of the assignment.

The social worker had been friendly and outgoing, and had walked Bridget and Sam through the adoption process. It sounded like a long and arduous procedure to Bridget, one for which there seemed a million opportunities for disappointment. But Children's Connection, Laurel had assured them, was by far the best organization for them to use, something Bridget didn't doubt for a moment, having witnessed for herself the success of her parents' pet project. Still, she was glad she wasn't going through this for real. Between the ninety-day waiting period, and the notices to—and appearances in—the court, and the home study, not to mention the sheer cost of adoption, a person would have to want a family awfully badly to be so patient, so understanding and so generous.

But then, Bridget thought, that was probably what parenting was all about anyway. Still, she was happy she'd made the decision long ago to remain single. She didn't ever want to be responsible for anyone but herself.

In the end, Laurel had told them that their names would be added to a waiting list that included other couples waiting to adopt. That, alas, just because Bridget was a Logan, Children's Connection couldn't make any special allowances for her, but that she was hopeful it wouldn't be more than a year or two before an infant became available for her and Sam to adopt. Bridget had assured the social worker that she didn't expect any preferential treatment because of her family ties, and that that was one of the reasons she and Sam had sought to start the adoption procedure so soon after marrying, because they had realized it might be a while before they actually brought their new baby home.

And, indeed, being put on the waiting list was in keeping with what Bridget and Sam wanted for this investigation. It would give them both time and opportunity to snoop around and fish for information. Though Bridget would doubtless be doing most of that herself, using the excuse of her mother's and sister's presence at Children's Connection to drop in for impromptu visits...and impromptu snooping.

Still, Bridget was beginning to understand that there was going to be a lot more to this case than she had originally anticipated. If she and Sam were going to play the part of wanna-be parents convincingly, they were going to have to go through all the proper steps, and that realistically the investigation could span months.

They might have to fool a lot more people than just the bad guy. And she might just be here in Portland for a lot longer than the few weeks she'd originally anticipated. After the nervousness and discomfort she had felt simply speaking with the social worker today—nervousness and discomfort she'd sensed from Sam, too—she just hoped they'd be able to pull it off.

And she hoped it wouldn't take months to do it.

After the meeting concluded, Sam cited a need to go into the Portland field office to catch up on some work, so Bridget sought out her mother, whom she knew would be spending much of the day at Children's Connection, and offered to treat her to a late lunch. Leslie suggested inviting Jillian along, too. So, feeling celebratory in the face of Bridget's return home, the three Logan women bypassed the hospital cafeteria and headed off to a nearby bistro instead.

As always, Leslie Logan looked wonderful. Bridget was close to her mother and secretly delighted that she resembled her so much. She'd gotten her auburn hair from her mother, whose own reddish-gold tresses were swept back today with a gray velvet headband, in contrast to Bridget's loosely plaited locks. She'd also inherited her mother's mouth and the shape of her eyes, but Leslie Logan's were brown instead of green, like Bridget's. Their clothing preferences, too, were similar—both stuck to understated, classic styles and forsook fashion trends. Today, Leslie had opted for gray wool pants and a shell-pink sweater set, where Bridget had dressed in brown tweed trousers and a cream-colored turtleneck.

At sixty years of age, Leslie could easily have been mistaken for someone much younger. A native midwesterner, she had always been plainspoken and down-to-earth. She'd met Terrence Logan in college, and, as family lore held, it had been love at first sight for both of them. Leslie had earned her degree in social work and had worked in the field for some time before giving birth to Robbie. His kidnapping had been understandably difficult on both elder Logans—it had even put their marriage in jeopardy for a while—but Leslie, Bridget knew, had been hit hardest. Although it had all happened before Bridget was born, she knew her mother still grieved for her stolen and murdered child and always would.

And although Leslie had ultimately found happiness in her other children, Bridget felt confident that much of her mother's work at Children's Connection stemmed from her still-unresolved feelings about Robbie's death. Leslie herself had been aided by Children's Connection in adopting Bridget's brothers Peter and David and David's twin sister, Jillian. And those successful adoptions, too, had contributed to Leslie's desire to volunteer so much of her time for the organization. But it was Robbie's death that had started it all, and that, Bridget felt certain, still colored much of what her mother felt and did today.

At thirty, Jillian was five years older than Bridget. And although she and David had been adopted after Bridget was born, it had been when Bridget was only a year old, so she couldn't remember a time when Jillian *hadn't* been her sister. Still, Bridget knew, as everyone else in the family did, that Jillian and David had come from a situation that was as far removed from the Logans' lifestyle as it could possibly be. The children of a drug-addicted mother, they'd spent the first six years of their lives with an infirm grandmother who'd had difficulty caring for them. As a result, they'd required a lot of tender loving care during those early years following the old woman's death, when the Logans had taken them in. Eventually, though, through love and attention and therapy, they'd blossomed. To this day, the twins enjoyed a unique closeness and intimacy precisely because of those early experiences. And Bridget had often wondered if it was Jillian's loving treatment during that time that had led her to become a therapist herself. She did wonderful work at Children's Connection.

But where the rest of the Logans were outgoing, Jillian was something of an introvert. She was shy and quiet, and embraced only a small circle of friends. Girl-

friends, anyway, since Jillian dated only very sporadi-
cally, and never one man for very long. Her clothing
today was in keeping with her quiet nature, a full skirt
patterned in pale blue flowers and an even paler blue
sweater that hung loose on her curvy frame.

They had no trouble getting a table at the bistro,
since it was well past the lunch hour by the time they
arrived. Although a few brave souls had thumbed their
noses at the chilly afternoon by opting to dine alfresco,
the Logan women compromised by taking a booth
inside near a window. That way, they could watch the
bustling activity of downtown Portland but still stay
warm and dry. After giving the waiter their orders and
getting drinks, Leslie looked at Bridget and smiled.

"So, how's married life treating you?" she asked, her
eyes fairly twinkling with mischief.

Bridget smiled back. "I'm afraid the honeymoon's
over," she said with a sigh of feigned melancholy.

"So soon?" Jillian asked, playing along. "Gee, and
here I've been working under the impression that
marriage was supposed to be bliss. You and Sam just
seem so perfect for each other."

Oh, sure, Bridget thought. Sam Jones was everything
she was looking for in a life mate: arrogant, surly,
uncommunicative and coarse. What wasn't there to love?

She sipped her coffee and tucked a stray strand of hair
behind one ear. "Yeah, well, marriage probably *is* bliss
under other circumstances. Circumstances like…oh, I
don't know. Like, say, when you're in love with your
husband. Or when you even *know* him, for that matter."

Leslie's smile grew broader as she said, "Well, I
certainly wouldn't kick Agent Jones out of bed for
eating crackers."

Bridget and Jillian both gaped at the comment. But it was Bridget who offered the exclamation, "Mother!"

"Well, he's very good-looking," Leslie said.

Oh, sure, Bridget thought, recalling Sam's thick brown hair that just begged a woman to run her fingers through it, and those blue, blue eyes that made a woman want to wade so deeply into them that she never found her way out again, and that sexy mouth that she was sure could wreak havoc on a woman's body, and those sturdy, broad shoulders that seemed capable of holding the entire world at bay, and those strong arms that promised limitless shelter and infinite embraces, and—

Well, she just agreed with her mother, that was all. But just because Sam was easy on the eye didn't make him husband material, phony *or* real.

"Oh, I'm teasing you, sweetie," Leslie said as she lifted her own cup to her mouth for an idle sip, scattering Bridget's errant thoughts. "Honestly, are you so wrapped up in your work these days that you don't even recognize a joke when you hear one?"

"Not when it's a sexual innuendo coming from my mother, no," Bridget said.

Leslie laughed. "Then you've been away from home for too long."

Bridget opened her mouth to deny it, then remembered that since leaving Portland to go to college, she could count on one hand the number of times she'd been home to visit for any length of time. How could it be that she spent so little time here? she wondered. She was just too busy to manage any more visits home than the occasional Christmas trip. Her life was so full. Full of work, she thought. Full of work and…and more work. And also…work. But she took time off from work, she reminded herself. And when she did, it was always to…work. Because even when she managed to get away for a weekend here or there, she always took her laptop with her and checked into HQ regularly.

But that was because she was so dedicated, she reminded herself. She *liked* her work. And she was good at it. She didn't work so hard because she didn't have anything else to occupy her life. Work *was* her life. And she liked it that way.

"I'm sorry," she told her mother in spite of her little pep talk with herself. "You're right—I should come home more often. But you guys all get to D.C. fairly regularly, especially David and Dad."

"Mm," her mother replied noncommittally.

"And there's always the phone," Bridget added.

"Mm," her mother said.

"And e-mail."

"Mm."

Bridget narrowed her eyes at her mother. "Why do I feel a lecture coming on?" she asked.

"No lecture," her mother told her. "Just…concern."

"About what?" Bridget asked.

Leslie expelled a soft sigh as she settled her cup back into its saucer, then she braced both forearms on the table. It was a posture that belied her words, because it was her lecture posture. Bridget recognized it well. After all, she'd probably received more of Leslie's lectures over the years than any of the other Logan offspring had, thanks to her having traveled an alternate route than the rest of them when it came to things like, oh…life in general.

"About the fact that you're only twenty-five years old," Leslie said, "and if it hadn't been for this case, you'd be someplace in Europe right now completely out of touch with the family and mingling with terrorists. How could I not be concerned about that? A part of me is almost grateful for the problems that have been plaguing Children's Connection. At least they've brought my daughter home to me and kept her out of danger."

Yep. It was going to be a lecture, all right. And Bridget really should have seen it coming. Last night, when she had visited briefly with her family, the focus of the conversation had simply been getting caught up with what everyone had been doing in their individual lives. Now that they'd finished with that, the next order of business was, as it always was, Bridget's needing to explain why she had strayed so far from home and the loving bosom of her family. She just wished she *could* explain that to her mother. But she scarcely understood it herself. She'd just never felt complete in Portland, had always felt as if she was missing out on something. Felt as if there was something missing from herself. There was a big, wide world out there, brimming with all sorts of sights and experiences, and she wanted to be a part of it. There were just so many things to do out there. And she wouldn't feel satisfied until she'd done every last one of them. Then, maybe, she wouldn't feel that strange emptiness inside herself that she'd felt for most of her life.

"Mom, that's my job," she said gently. "And I'm perfectly well trained for what I was supposed to be doing. They wouldn't have assigned me to the counterterrorist task force if they hadn't thought I could handle it. More importantly, I know I can handle things like that. You don't have to worry about me."

"I'm your mother," Leslie said unnecessarily. "It's my job to worry about you. I worry about all of you. It's what mothers do."

And it was especially what mothers did when they'd lost a child, Bridget thought. She shouldn't be so hard on her mom, she told herself. Leslie, more than most mothers, knew how endangered a child could become, even in the most benign circumstances. Robbie had been snatched from the front yard of his best friend Danny Crosby's house, while Danny's mother Sheila was inside. And Leslie had never forgiven Sheila for allowing her son to be stolen.

Of course, even before Robbie's kidnapping, there had been little love lost between Leslie and Sheila. Leslie had never made it a secret that she'd considered the other woman to be a shallow, greedy, materialistic social climber, everything Leslie was not. Her midwestern upbringing had given her solid values, and she'd never aspired to an affluent lifestyle or marriage to a dynamic corporate leader. Ultimately, she'd welcomed the opportunity, though, because being the wife of a wealthy businessman had enabled Leslie to stay home with her son, to whom she became utterly devoted the second he was born. Sheila, however, had been neglectful when it came to her own children, had often left them in the care of others when she could have been spending time with them herself. She'd preferred spending her husband's money and lunching with her girlfriends instead. Her mother, Bridget knew, had never been able to understand that.

And, truth be told, her mother had felt sorry for Sheila, at least back then—that had never been a secret, either. Leslie had always said she thought Sheila's behavior must have stemmed from her unhappiness, trapped in a life that held no purpose for her, no direction. Jack Crosby, rumor had held, hadn't been an easy man to live with, and Bridget knew for a fact that the man had enjoyed numerous affairs quite openly before he and Sheila divorced. That had to have taken a toll on her.

But Sheila had been unfaithful to Jack, too, something else Bridget knew for a fact, and that behavior had dropped her in Leslie's estimation even more. Bridget even recalled her mother saying that, on the day Robbie was taken from the Crosbys' front yard, Sheila had been talking to one of her lovers on the phone, too distracted to keep an eye on the boys playing in the yard. Robbie had been easy pickings for the kidnapper, thanks to Sheila's neglect. And Leslie had never forgiven her for that.

So all in all, Bridget knew she shouldn't come down hard on her mother for being overly protective and overly concerned about her. Being worried for Bridget's welfare and safety was, after all, just another way her mother showed how much she loved her.

So instead of feeling irritated, Bridget smiled and covered one of her mother's hands with her own. "You don't need to worry about me," she said. "I promise I'll be fine." *Translation,* she thought, *I promise I won't be snatched away from you the way Robbie was.*

Leslie smiled back sadly, something that told Bridget her mother had picked up on her unspoken assurances. Nevertheless, she turned her own hand to weave her fingers with Bridget's. "You might be fine," she said, "but I'll still be worried about you."

The waiter returned with their appetizer then, relieving the tension that had threatened to descend on the trio. Bridget used the opportunity to change the subject, turning it to one of her mother's favorite topics. "So what else can you tell me about everything that's been going on at Children's Connection?" she asked.

Leslie sighed heavily as she reached for a cracker to scoop up some of the hot artichoke dip. "You're probably privy to more information than I have been," she said. "The FBI won't tell us much of anything that they've learned from the investigation so far. I should probably be asking you the same question."

"I wish I could tell you more, Mom," Bridget said, "but there are certain things the Bureau wants to keep quiet for now, for reasons of security. And although I've been informed of the particulars about the illegal activities and such, I don't know what kind of toll it's taking on the people involved, since I haven't actually interviewed anyone and won't, thanks to being undercover. So how's the mood at Children's Connection right now?"

Leslie's expression grew melancholy. "Not good, I'm afraid," she said. "It's been hard on everyone, from the housekeeping staff to the board of directors. Whoever's doing this could be working in any department, in any capacity. No one wants to believe that. It's terrible to think that someone we've all come to trust and like could be doing something so heinous as stealing and selling babies, and deliberately sabotaging people's desires to create a family. But the FBI tells us they're convinced the ringleader must be someone who works inside, and that all the things that have happened are related."

"You don't think so, though?" Bridget asked.

She herself was trying to keep an open mind, though from what she'd gleaned so far from the investigation, it appeared the FBI was right. There had been enough breaches of security to warrant a close look at the employees, and maybe even some of the clients.

"I don't *want* to think it could be someone inside," Leslie hedged. "It just doesn't seem possible. We strive so hard to hire good people. And the organization does so much good. I just can't believe so much…" She paused, obviously struggling to find the right word. What she finally settled on, though, was, "so much… badness has come about lately. It just doesn't seem fair."

Bridget nodded. "Well, whoever's behind it, Mom, we'll find them. And then Children's Connection can go back to doing good work again."

"I just hope we'll be able to. The terrible press we've received over the last several months has really hurt the organization. And after all we've done over the years, creating so many families, finding homes for so many children. I'd hate to think something like this would put an end to all that good work."

Jillian added, "Mom's right—it's affected everyone, and not in a good way at all. You'd like to think something like this would bind people together, but a lot of the employees are looking over their shoulders, wondering if the person working next to them is involved in illegal activities. Some people have already quit to look for work elsewhere, because they're sure this is the end of Children's Connection, and they want to get out while the getting's good.

"And some of the families who've been coming to us for counseling have stopped making appointments," she added. "A handful of couples who started adoption procedures have pulled out and gone elsewhere, sometimes to places that aren't entirely legitimate."

"And there have been financial repercussions," Leslie said. "I hope the organization doesn't go bankrupt as a result of all this."

Bridget wasn't sure what to say in response to their concerns. So she gave her mother's hand another gentle squeeze and smiled at her sister. "Sam and I and the other agents involved will do our best to find out who's behind it all. And then you can both help Children's Connection rebuild."

Jillian smiled back, but the smile didn't quite ring true. "I just hope whoever's doing this to Children's Connection leaves something for us to start rebuilding with."

Four

When Sam came home from work that evening, he didn't come home from work. Not to his usual home, the brick bungalow in the Portland suburbs he'd bought from his parents when they'd decided to move to the sunnier, drier climate of San Diego. That home would have welcomed him, with its broad cement front porch and its worn-out wooden swing swaying at one end, and its creaky hardwood floors that still bore the scars from the beating they had taken from the two growing, rambunctious Jones boys. He would have done what he always did when going home at night—shed his suit and tie and loafers in favor of battered blue jeans and a flannel shirt and heavy socks. Then he would have made himself a simple dinner and taken it and a longneck into the living room to watch the news while he ate.

After that, he would have spend the rest of the night

either watching a game or reading some vintage mystery, probably one of the greats like Raymond Chandler or Dashiell Hammett. Or maybe, if he were feeling socially inclined, he would have headed down to Foley's to shoot some pool and tip another longneck with guys he'd known since childhood. Or, if he were feeling *really* socially inclined, he might have picked up the phone to call Denise. Or Donna. Or Francine. Or Lynette. Or one of the other neighborhood girls who viewed life the same way he did.

Because that was what he did when he went home at night. He left Special Agent Samuel Jones at the office, and then let Sam Jones kick back and relax. Usually alone, but sometimes with friends. Sometimes with friends who were more intimate than others. But none of his friends were *that* intimate. None were more than just friends. His was a quiet life. A solitary life. An uneventful life. It was exactly the kind of life he'd always figured he would lead—except that there had once been a time when he'd figured he'd lead it with someone else, too. Sam liked where he came from, and that was where he always wanted to stay. He'd never been able to understand these people who felt driven to move hundreds, even thousands of miles from home, just to feel like they belonged somewhere. Portland was where Sam belonged—right in the neighborhood where he had always lived. Everything he wanted, everything he needed, was all right here at home.

And if maybe, sometimes, he felt like there was still something missing, well… That was only because no one was ever allowed to be entirely content. Which was just as well, because in Sam's opinion, contentment led to complacency. And complacency led to carelessness.

And when people stopped caring, well, what was the point of going on? So it was good that Sam didn't feel entirely satisfied with his life, right? It was good that there were some nights when he lay awake wondering if maybe he should be doing something differently, right? And it was good that there was still a part of himself that wasn't entirely happy, right?

Damn right.

Because nobody ever got everything they wanted. Sam, at least, had everything he needed. And he had it all right at home.

But tonight, he wasn't at home. Not his, anyway, he thought as he closed the front door of the big, extravagant Tudor manor behind himself and bolted it. Tonight, he'd come home to another man's house. Another man's "wife." There was absolutely nothing of his own to welcome him here. Nothing he wanted. Nothing he needed. Nothing personal. Nothing familiar. Nothing comfortable. Nothing to make him feel warm or easy or safe.

"Hi. Welcome home."

At the softly uttered words, he glanced in the direction from which they'd come, and saw Bridget Logan stretched out on the couch in the living room, a longneck bottle of beer, half-empty, sitting on the coffee table beside her. She was dressed in softly faded blue jeans, a baggy flannel shirt and heavy socks. Her back was supported at one end of the sofa by the fat, fringed throw pillows that had been so carefully arranged at opposite ends that morning, her legs stretched out toward the other end. Small black-framed glasses were perched on her nose, and she lowered a book into her lap as she returned his gaze. She looked relaxed and intimate and warm, and in that moment, she made him feel warm and easy and safe.

Until he reminded himself that this wasn't his house, and she wasn't his wife. All of this was a put-on, a masquerade manufactured to catch a criminal. None of it was real, and it damned sure wasn't cozy. So whatever those strange feelings were that began to wind through him when he saw her sitting there, those couldn't be real or cozy, either.

"Hi, yourself," he said, forcing himself to sound genial even as he felt himself go tense.

"You always work this late?" she asked.

He lifted his arm to check his watch. It was nearly eight o'clock. "Actually, I usually work later," he said.

She nodded, then smiled. But the gesture didn't seem any more genuine than their situation was. "Me, too," she told him. And before he could comment, she added, "Have you had dinner?"

He took a few steps forward, propelling himself out of the foyer and into the living room proper. "Yeah, a couple of the guys who are working a pretty high-profile case are going to be working all night, so somebody sent out for sandwiches and got me one, too. You?"

"I had dinner at my parents' house."

This time Sam nodded. And had no idea what else to say.

Bridget seemed to be suffering from the same problem, because she only gazed back at him in silence. Then again, he supposed it was his turn to say something, though she hadn't exactly provided him with any kind of decent volley, had she?

"Beer?" she asked, reaching for the one on the coffee table. "There's a six-pack in the fridge. Well, a five-pack now," she amended as she lifted the bottle to her lips.

Now *that* was a much better volley, he thought. In

spite of that, he told himself to decline the offer, that if he was having this much trouble coming up with something to say after a simple exchange of greetings, it would only get worse if they tried to prolong it. Strangely, though, he found himself wanting to take her up on the offer. He told himself it was only because it had been a bitch of a day, and a cold beer sounded like a very good punctuation mark to put on it. It wasn't because he wanted to visit any longer with Bridget Logan.

"Sounds good," he said. He really wanted to go change his clothes first, to make himself more comfortable, but something made him hesitate before excusing himself and turning toward the stairs behind him. Changing into something more comfortable just seemed like an oddly intimate thing to do at the moment. And intimate wasn't how he wanted to be with Bridget. He didn't care if they were supposed to be man and wife. Behind closed doors, he wanted to keep things formal.

So he only loosened his necktie and unbuttoned the top two buttons on his white dress shirt. Then he made his way to the kitchen and opened the refrigerator door.

She'd gone to the grocery, he saw. Although there had been some meager supplies in there the day before, courtesy of someone at the Bureau who had seen fit to supply the basics before they arrived, now there were other things alongside the requisite milk and orange juice and sodas and sandwich fixings. Now there was the aforementioned beer—Sam's favorite brand, incidentally—plus a bottle of white wine, assorted fruits and vegetables, yogurt, cheese and—oh, gross—soy milk. Girly-girl food, he couldn't help thinking. Then he opened the freezer and saw a couple of fat steaks and some decent-sized pork chops, along with some frozen

dinners—a few low-fat and low-cal, but others adver-
tised as being made expressly for manly men—plus a
pint of Häagen-Dazs raspberry sorbet and a gallon of
chocolate ice cream.

He closed the freezer and reopened the fridge, then
grabbed one of the beers and headed for the pantry,
opening it to see what had changed there. Alongside the
cans of soup and boxes of pasta the Bureau had provided,
and mingled with the health-conscious snacks she clearly
preferred for herself, were potato and tortilla chips, a jar
of extra-hot salsa, some cheese puffs, a big can of roasted
peanuts and an industrial-sized bag of Oreos.

Okay, so either Bridget Logan was very familiar with
the diet of the typical single male, or else her eating
habits were identical to his own. And considering the
presence of the yogurt and soy milk and raspberry sorbet
in the fridge and freezer, it sure the hell wasn't the latter.
So it must have been the former. She knew how to feed
the typical single male. Which meant she was probably
more than a little familiar with a typical single male.
And since she wasn't living around her brothers, that
meant she was involved with some other man. Well
enough to know what he liked to eat.

So maybe Sam shouldn't be too concerned about his
attraction to Bridget, however superficial and based on
physical chemistry it was. Because chances were
looking very good that she wasn't interested in him, or
any other man, save the one whose pantry she knew so
intimately. Oh, she might be attracted to Sam—and
judging by the way he'd caught her looking at him at
times, he was reasonably confident she was—but her attraction was obviously as superficial and as based on
physical chemistry as his own was, right? So it

shouldn't be that difficult for either of them to keep their hands to themselves, right?

Damn right.

"Thanks for picking up groceries," he said when he returned to the living room with his open—and already a quarter empty—beer.

She looked up in surprise, but whether she was surprised because he was thanking her, or because he'd even noticed, he couldn't tell. Nor could he bring himself to call her on it. Let her think he was one of those Neanderthals who took women for granted and naturally expected them to handle all the domestic chores. It would serve as a reminder to him just how poorly she knew him, how little they had in common— longnecks and flannel shirts and superficial physical chemistry aside—and how important it was to make sure they kept their distance from each other.

"You're welcome," she said. "I wasn't sure what you liked, so I got a little of everything."

"You hit it right on the mark," he told her.

"So then, it was okay to get the soy milk," she said. "I wasn't sure. A lot of guys turn their noses up at it."

He narrowed his eyes at her, and was about to object, but halted when she smiled. Not just because he realized she was joking, but because of the way her face changed with the gesture. He'd thought she was beautiful when he first saw her, but had altered that to breathtakingly gorgeous over the course of the last two days. When she smiled the way she was now, however... Well, even the word *gorgeous* didn't seem to suit. *Exquisite* and *ravishing* came to mind, but what Sam finally settled on was *mouth-wateringly magnificent*. Because sitting on the sofa that way, with her hair spilling loose around her shoulders and those little black glasses perched on her nose, and that radiant smile lighting up the room...

Suddenly Sam wanted to get very physical and chemical with her indeed. And there was nothing at all superficial about what he wanted to do with her next.

With no small effort, he pushed the uncharacteristically graphic thought aside and made himself focus on the matter at hand. Which was... Damn. What was the matter at hand again? Oh, yeah. The case.

"So what happened at Children's Connection after I left today?" he asked.

Her smile fell, and she sighed, settling her book on her lap, spine up. Sam moved closer and tilted his head to see if he could make out the title, but couldn't quite manage. When he looked up, Bridget was watching him, obviously having discerned his interest.

"It's Agatha Christie," she said. "I love old mysteries."

Sam nodded but said nothing.

So she backpedaled to what he had asked before. "Well, gee, I wish I could tell you some guy came up to me and gave me his name and address and offered to sell me an infant he'd stolen from its mother in Moscow, but..."

"But what *really* happened?" he asked.

"What really happened was that after you left, I took my mother and my sister to lunch," she told him.

"And what did you find out?"

"Nothing much more than we already know," she said. "Except that everything that's been going on there over the past several months is really starting to affect the place as a whole. Mom's worried the organization is going to go bankrupt, and Jillian's worried that some of their clients are going to wind up dealing with other agencies who are in no way legitimate. And evidently everyone's working under a lot of stress, wondering if the person behind it all is someone they all know and like."

"That's not surprising," Sam said. "By now, everyone's got to be forming theories and becoming suspicious of people they'd otherwise trust implicitly. It could actually end up negatively affecting the investigation if everyone starts getting paranoid."

"We need to get to the bottom of this as soon as possible," Bridget told him, her voice edged with something akin to sorrow. "I hate seeing people I care about going through something like this."

"We'll find the guy, Bridget," Sam said, a thrill of something warm and electric washing through his midsection when her name rolled off his tongue the way it did. He liked calling her that. He knew he shouldn't, but there it was all the same.

Her gaze connected with his and held it. "How long do you think it will take for our guy to make contact with the other agents?" she asked. "I mean, between the waiting list and all the stuff that goes into this adoption process... How do we know this isn't going to take months?"

"I don't know how long it will take," he told her honestly. "I guess it just depends."

"On what?"

Sam strode farther into the living room and folded his big frame into one of the plump velvet chairs that flanked the sofa. "On how spooked our guy has become by the investigation and how badly he needs money."

"So what do we do?" Bridget asked.

He shrugged. "It's been a while since we've had any indication our baby seller is still operating. The investigation of Children's Connection has to have slowed down his activity significantly, and he's got to be feeling the heat. If he's got clients waiting, or babies he's keeping an eye on, he's going to have to come out of the woodwork soon. So I guess all we can do is wait for him to hopefully approach our colleagues soon. And *we* do our best to dig discreetly for more info that might lead us to him sooner."

Bridget nodded, but looked thoughtful. "So then we'll wait. And we'll dig. And we'll hope our guy is starting to get desperate."

Everett Baker was starting to get desperate. As he sat in his office in the accounting department of Children's Connection, staring at the pile of papers on his desk but seeing none of them, his head swam with regrets and what-ifs. His life seemed to have become a massive boulder rolling down a mountainside at breakneck speed, and he had no idea how to stop it. In the past year and a half, everything had seemed to go wrong. And that was saying something, since his life had never really been "right" to begin with.

What had started off several months ago as a surefire way to make easy money was blowing up in his face, and he didn't know what to do to stop it. And the man he'd thought was his friend was turning out to be anything but. He and Charlie Prescott had seemed to have so much in common when Everett first met him at the bar that night. But now Charlie was acting like a common criminal.

No, an uncommon criminal, he thought further. Because only the lowest of the low tried to murder someone.

Murder. The word circled around in Everett's head like a bad dream. He'd nearly been involved in someone's murder. And not just anyone—but Nancy Allen. Nurse Nancy, he thought with an affectionate smile, who'd started off as an easy mark and a way to get information to feed his and Charlie's schemes, but who over the months had become so much more. When had he fallen in love with her? Everett asked himself. But try as he might, he couldn't pinpoint the moment when that had happened. Probably, it had been gradual, growing a little more every day. He only knew he cared for Nancy more than he'd ever cared for anyone, and miracle of miracles, she seemed to care for him, too.

He still couldn't believe Charlie had broken into Nancy's apartment and tried to kill her. But hadn't Charlie told Everett he was going to do just that? Thank God Everett had been there to stop him. But he hadn't stopped things with Nancy. Not that he'd wanted to stop that—it had felt so good to hold her and kiss her, even though he'd been totally unprepared for the romantic developments. He'd been even less prepared for the realization of how much he had come to care for her and how much he wanted things to work out for the two of them. But there was little chance now that he would find happiness with Nancy. Or anyone else, for that matter.

Oh, what a mess. Where had everything gone wrong?

That night he'd met Charlie in the bar, they'd hit it off so quickly, and so well. Charlie was the first friend Everett had made in a long, long time. Now, though, Charlie was just one more bad thing to happen, and that meeting had been the genesis of everything that was spiraling out of control. Though really, if Everett was going to be honest with himself, he had to admit that even before Charlie had entered the picture, his life had been ripe for something to go wrong. In many ways, his entire existence had been nothing *but* wrong, thanks to Lester and Joleen Baker. His parents, such as they were.

Or, at least, the only parents he could ever remember having. Everett had been flummoxed when Joleen told him on her deathbed in St. Louis that he wasn't her biological son, that her husband Lester—who'd abandoned both of them years before, when Everett was still in high school—had kidnapped him from the front yard of a home in the suburbs of Portland, Oregon, half a continent away. His real name was Robbie Logan. He'd been stolen from his biological parents more than two decades ago.

Her revelation had helped Everett make sense of some things—the fact that he didn't resemble either of the Bakers, and the deep-seated bitterness he'd always harbored for them. Of course, they'd been emotionally and verbally abusive the whole time he was growing up, and that was how he had always explained his anger and resentment toward them. But after he'd learned the truth, it had made even more sense.

More than anything, though, hearing Joleen reveal his origins had made Everett understand better the fleeting, nebulous memories that had plagued him since childhood. There had been times when he was able to remember a smiling woman who sang to him at bedtime, and a tall, laughing man who used to lift him high into the air. But he'd always assumed those memories were actually fantasies, because the people in them bore no resemblance to Lester or Joleen. He'd figured he must have made them up in an effort to dispel the pain of his reality. They were perfect parents he'd created in his mind to replace the damaged ones he had in his life.

Now, though, he realized those fantasies had indeed been memories, and that what he'd thought were made-up people were actually his parents—Leslie and Terrence Logan. He'd known that the moment he'd laid eyes on them, days after his arrival in Portland. They were the people from his fantasies. And they weren't a fantasy at all.

After Joleen's death, Everett had been drawn to Portland, the place from which he'd been stolen, as if a homing device had been activated in his brain. He couldn't have stayed away from here if he'd tried. And he *had* tried. After learning the truth of his identity, he'd done everything he could to uncover the circumstances of his abduction and to learn about his real family. And what he'd learned had made him realize he could never return to them. Because he would never be one of them.

He'd been taken from them when he was six, old enough that he should have had more memories of them than he did. All he could conclude was that he had been so traumatized by the kidnapping, and so brainwashed by the Bakers afterward, that he'd buried his memories deeply enough in his mind that they only came out in dreams and fantasies. Once he'd learned his real name, though, Everett had done his best to learn even more. Joleen had kept a scrapbook about the kidnapping that she'd given him to look at. But he'd also gone on the Internet to see what else he could discover about Robbie Logan.

And he'd discovered a lot.

He'd read story after story about the missing Logan boy, in Portland and other Oregon newspapers, as well as in newspapers as far away as New York and Miami. He'd discovered photos of his parents, distraught and ag-grieved, archived news stories on dozens of different sites about his disappearance. For months, Terrence and Leslie Logan had kept the investigation front and center of the Portland Police Department. They'd remained convinced that their son was alive and had sent out periodic pleas to the kidnappers to release him and return him to the two people who loved him more than anything else in the world. They'd offered millions of dollars of reward money for his recovery. Then, a year later, the police discovered the remains of a young boy erroneously identified as Robbie, and the Logans' quest had ended.

But even at that, their hopes hadn't been completely extinguished. Because Everett had found one newspaper interview with Leslie Logan that had occurred on the tenth anniversary of Robbie's kidnapping. In it, she had said that she still dreamed sometimes that he was alive, that she would be able to hold him in her arms, and tell him how much she loved him.

But that would never happen, Everett knew. Because yes, Robbie Logan was alive, but if Leslie found out the truth about him, she'd never want to hold him in her arms. And she certainly wouldn't be able to love him. Because Everett Baker wasn't Robbie Logan. Not by a long shot. Oh, they might share the same DNA, but they weren't the same person. According to everything he'd read, Robbie Logan had been a beautiful, bright, vivacious little boy, full of spirit and playfulness and good humor. He'd been precocious and creative and utterly fearless. A champion Little Leaguer, popular at school and well-liked by the other kids. A "golden boy." That was how the newspapers had referred to him again and again.

Everett Baker, on the other hand, had been nothing but a disappointment to the Bakers. He'd been timid and insecure, withdrawn and insignificant. He'd been so stupid, he'd often failed in school and had to take summer classes. He'd been awkward at sports, and the kids at school—those who'd noticed him—had called him everything from a freak to a psycho to a queer.

Robbie Logan could have been anything he wanted in life. Hell, he could have been president of the United States. Everett Baker, though...

Well, Everett was a criminal, plain and simple. And according to Charlie Prescott, he couldn't even do that right.

After learning more about the Logans of Portland and their missing son Robbie, Everett had told himself he could never go home again. His parents—his *real* parents—and the family they'd created after his disappearance were everything he wasn't—good, decent, likable people who deserved children like they had. Not a pathetic loser who hadn't even tried to escape his captors or uncover the truth of his own identity. It didn't matter to Everett that he'd been a terrified boy of six when he was stolen. If he'd been a real Logan, the kind of person his parents and siblings obviously were, he would have succeeded in finding his way home. Instead, he'd given up, hadn't even tried to put up a fight and had spent his life cowering in fear.

But even knowing he could never be a part of the Logan family, Everett had been drawn to Portland. After Joleen's death, he'd sold what few meager belongings they had left, had withdrawn his scant savings from the bank, and he'd driven thousands of miles to the city of his birth. And he'd heard about the Logans almost immediately, read an article in the newspaper within days of his arrival describing a star-studded, black-tie fundraiser Leslie Logan had hosted for a local organization called Children's Connection, where she volunteered much of her time and much of her husband's money. Everett had read on the Internet about how Children's Connection had helped the Logans rebuild their family after they'd lost their son Robbie, so reading about the event had been eerily in keeping with everything else that had brought him west.

And after reading about Children's Connection again, Everett had found himself wanting to see this magic place that created families. He supposed, in hindsight, there had been a part of him that wanted to reconnect with the Logans on whatever level he could. And as he'd sat there reading the newspaper, trying to figure out a way that might bring him closer to them, destiny had moved its holy hand upon his. Because Everett had opened the classified ads of the same newspaper to look for an accounting job, and had seen a listing that seemed perfect for him—at Children's Connection.

Once again, fate had stepped in and lurched his life into a new direction. And Everett, too dazed and befuddled by all his newfound knowledge, had been too stupid to remember that he was fate's whipping boy.

Because when he'd answered that ad, he'd been hired on the spot, asked if he could start work the next day, because they were in something of a bind at the agency. Naturally, Everett had said he could. And in less than a week, he'd both glimpsed his biological mother for the first time in nearly thirty years, and he'd stumbled upon a way to make potentially millions of dollars by misusing Children's Connection contacts. The first event had been body-numbing, the second had been mind-blowing. And both had given Charlie Prescott everything he needed to hatch the unholiest of plans.

Everett never should have responded to that ad in the paper. And he never should have listened to Charlie. He should have just done what he had come to Portland to do—see his real family, if only from a distance, and wonder what his life might have been like if the capricious hand of fate hadn't swooped down and smacked him when he was too young, too confused and too terrified to hit back.

No, he shouldn't even have done that, he told himself now as he gazed through his office window at the gray, drizzly day that seemed almost a manifestation of his current mood. In coming to Portland, he'd made a stupid mistake. The only way Everett Baker had been able to survive was to live his life by never looking back. Never looking back, and never looking forward. One day at a time—that was how he had lived since he was a little boy. That had been the only way he was able to stay sane and coherent during all the years of abuse and neglect at the Bakers' hands.

But coming to Portland had been the ultimate look back. And it had been the supreme mistake. Because now Everett was involved in things he had no business being involved in. He just wished he could remember when it had gone from bad to worse. And he couldn't help thinking that, like everything else in his life, worse would eventually—inevitably—go to worst.

And as he gazed out at the gray, ugly day, he got a very bad feeling that it would happen soon.

Five

The first two weeks of Bridget's involvement in investigation went by without even the tiniest new development, something that frustrated her to no end. Even though she and Sam had played their parts well over several orchestrated visits to Children's Connection for every contrived reason they could, they'd learned little more than the FBI already knew. Even when Bridget had stepped up her own solo visits, ostensibly to visit with her mother or take her sister to lunch, there wasn't a peep out of anyone that might be construed as suspicious in any way.

And that made her crazy.

What made her crazier was spending her days pretending to be Mrs. Samuel Jones, millionaire's trophy wife. Sam, at least, had ongoing cases he could work, and most days he went to work at the field office as he normally would. If anyone followed him—and Bridget sincerely doubted anyone would—they'd see him enter the Crown Plaza Building, which housed not only the FBI field office, but a fictional business created by the FBI called SBJ Steel International, Inc., whose CEO was none other than Mr. Samuel Jones, recently married millionaire who'd just relocated his business offices from Washington, D.C. But Bridget wasn't a local FBI agent, and she had no cases to keep her occupied. So she spent her days at her phony house, mostly being bored out of her gourd.

Because if there was one thing Bridget Logan was *not*, it was idle. A type-A personality from the moment she'd emerged from the womb, kicking and squalling and demanding, she just couldn't take things easy. Even her hobbies—what few she had—tended to be those that kept her active: tennis and horseback riding, cycling, boating, being outdoors. And although she did call a few of her old friends to engage once or twice in such activities during those first two weeks, by the end of them, she was growing impatient for work. Because when all was said and done, work was life to Bridget. Without it, she just didn't feel whole. And although she spent a good bit of her time familiarizing herself with the particulars of the case thus far, it wasn't enough to keep her occupied the way she needed to be. More involvement, that was what she needed. That and movement. Of the case. Forward.

So, by the end of that second week, when nothing seemed to be happening to move the case forward, Bridget decided it was time for her to get it moving herself.

She and Sam had, naturally, taken separate bedrooms in the house—in entirely different areas of the house, in fact, so that they'd be far enough removed from each other to maintain some semblance of personal privacy. It *wasn't* because there continued to be a certain level of animosity between them, in spite of the almost friendly way they had interacted that first night at the house. That first night had obviously been an anomaly, the result, she was sure, of her own fatigue and Sam's effort to make the best of a bad situation. Since then, they'd barely been able to be in the same room together without sounding and acting—and feeling and being—uncomfortable.

Bridget ascribed that to a simple chemical reaction—there was just something in each of them that rubbed the other the wrong way. Maybe they were too much alike, she'd reasoned, something that had caused both of them to want to be in charge of a situation where neither could be in charge. Or maybe they were too different, she'd reckoned, something that had caused both of them to want to approach the case in ways that clashed. Or maybe it was just that they simply didn't like each other, for whatever reason. In any event, over those two weeks, they'd done their best to stay away from each other when they could, and during those times when they'd been forced into each other's company, they'd done their best to at least look like they belonged together.

In spite of their efforts to avoid each other, though, there had been a handful of inescapable evenings when they both happened to be home at the same time. And those evenings had only reinforced how much they didn't *want* to be home at the same time. Whenever they were, an odd sort of tension suddenly erupted out of nowhere, and Bridget was confident they both felt it. Fortunately, those evenings had been few. Sam, she had noticed right away, was a lot like her in that he seemed to work late frequently. And although she hadn't had a job to go to herself, she *had* done her best to stay out of the house in an effort to maintain her sanity.

So by the end of that first two weeks, there were no new developments in a lot more than just the case. There were also no new developments in the way she and Sam interacted. Or, more accurately, in the way she and Sam avoided interacting.

Therefore, that Friday morning, when she woke at her usual 6:00 a.m. without even having set her alarm, Bridget forsook her trophy-wife clothes and instead donned her rat-race clothes—in this case, a crisp white shirt coupled with soft gray trousers and matching suit jacket—and wove her hair into the fat braid she preferred for working. Then she hustled herself downstairs, hoping to catch Sam before he left for the office.

Because she intended to go with him.

The scent of strong, black coffee and the sound of movement in the kitchen wafted up the stairs to greet her as she descended, letting her know that Sam hadn't yet left. So Bridget squared her shoulders and prepared herself for the eruption of tension that would undoubtedly arise the moment she entered the room. And then she did her best to saunter confidently into the kitchen, making her way straight to the coffeemaker to pour herself a cup of hot bravado.

Sam was standing at the counter with a cup of coffee in his hand, the morning paper open in front of him, but he glanced up when she entered, his expression one of clear surprise. He, too, wore a white dress shirt and suit, though his was navy blue and had the added accessory of a wine-colored necktie. His dark hair, she noticed, was still damp from his shower, curling softly around his ears and at the top of his collar in back. But there wasn't a hint of sleepiness or fatigue about him. He looked alert and sharp and ready for whatever the day might have in store for him. Clearly he was a morning person, too.

"You're up early," he said as he watched Bridget pour herself a generous mug of coffee.

"Not really," she told him as she returned the carafe to the warmer. "I always wake up at six. I've just tried to stay upstairs every morning until after you leave, to keep out of your way."

She wasn't sure, but she thought he arched his eyebrows just the tiniest bit at that.

"So what brings you down today?" he asked.

She enjoyed a sip of the fragrant black brew, then lowered her cup and met his gaze levelly. "I'm going to work with you."

Now his eyebrows definitely shot up. "Oh?"

She nodded, hoping the action looked more self-assured than it felt. "This case is going nowhere, Sam. Nothing's happening with the other agents *or* us. We need to do something to nudge things along."

"Not that I'm arguing with you," he said, "since I agree that things don't seem to be happening as quickly as we'd hoped, but how do expect to change it? We knew going into this that it might take a while."

"I know, but I'm going nuts," she said frankly. "I can't just be passive here. I thought I could be patient, but I've discovered that I can't. So I have an idea. I want to pass it by Pennington first, to make sure I don't step on any toes, but I think you and I need to start socializing more."

Sam narrowed his eyes in confusion. "What do you mean?"

"I mean that since our job is to try and learn more about the goings-on at Children's Connection through the people who work there, then we need to start spending more time with the people who work there."

He leaned back against the counter, giving her his full attention. "We're already making regular visits to Children's Connection," he reminded her. "More than are necessary, really, when you consider what the usual couple experiences there. If we go any more often, we're going to raise suspicions. If we haven't already."

"I'm not talking about hanging out at the agency," Bridget said. "I'm talking about hanging out with the people who work there, someplace other than Children's Connection. Where they might be more amenable to chatting. Where they might have a drink or two to loosen their tongues."

"I'm not sure I follow you," Sam said.

"Look, if the investigation is no secret, then whoever's behind all this has to be majorly on his guard right now. Not only is he going to be careful about who he approaches with a baby for sale, but he's going to be careful about what he says and does around his co-workers."

"Right," Sam agreed. "Which is why the Bureau thought Bridget Logan, returning prodigal daughter, might have a chance of gleaning information that another agent—or other agents—wouldn't."

"But even if I'm chatting up the people who work at the Connection while in the persona of my mother's daughter, I'm still in an atmosphere of professionalism that inhibits conversation. Do you know what I mean?"

Sam nodded. "People don't like to indulge in office gossip. Or they're afraid they might get caught indulging in office gossip and get into trouble."

"Right," Bridget said. "So if we can arrange some occasions where the employees of Children's Connection might mingle on a more social level, it might be easier to get people to impart more information."

"So what do you propose?"

She shrugged, but the gesture was more one of restlessness than it was one of not knowing the answer. She'd lain in bed wide awake last night mulling over her idea, and she had more than a few suggestions. "If I were really Mrs. Samuel Jones, I'd be doing a lot of socializing," she said. "And I'd make sure my husband was with me. Hey, you've just arrived in my hometown, after all. And you've just opened new offices. People like us would be going out of our way to get our faces out there to meet people and make connections. At the very least, I'd be doing some entertaining here at my home, to extend a welcome to my husband's new colleagues. And I'd invite a lot of people he didn't know so that he could expand his social and professional horizons. And since I haven't been home for a while, I'd rely on my parents to help me with the guest list. Especially my mother. And *a lot* of my mother's acquaintances and connections are through—"

"Children's Connection," Sam supplied for her.

"Bingo," Bridget said with a smile. "And speaking of my mother," she continued, "if I *were* actually her newly returned, newlywed daughter, my mother would be doing a lot to introduce me and my new husband around town. She'd make sure we got to know all of her friends from her pet project, where she volunteers so much of her time."

"Children's Connection," Sam said again.

Bridget nodded. "Yep. Between me and my mom, I

think we can probably find a number of opportunities that will offer Mr. and Mrs. Samuel Jones the chance to mingle freely with quite a few employees from Children's Connection, in settings that will lend themselves to a much freer exchange of dialogue. And that, in turn, might make it just a little easier for Special Agents Logan and Jones to do the job they've been assigned to do."

Sam said nothing for a moment, clearly giving much thought to Bridget's proposal. Judging by his initial expression, though, he didn't seem to much care for the idea of the two of them being more social as a couple. Probably, she thought, because it would necessitate them spending more time together. And although she was no more enthusiastic about that than he obviously was, she knew it was necessary if they wanted to uncover the information Pennington had indicated he wanted them to uncover.

"But I thought we were newlyweds," Sam finally said halfheartedly, clearly struggling with whether it was more important to catch the bad guy or keep his distance from Bridget.

And oh, wasn't *that* just an incredibly flattering thing to realize? she thought. How difficult a call that that would be for him to make. Not that she hadn't been struggling with the same call herself since making the decision to become proactive in the case, because she wasn't exactly thrilled at the prospect of spending more time with him, either. But it didn't make it any easier to stomach his own obvious unwillingness to be anywhere near her.

How they felt about each other was in no way significant, she reminded herself. All that mattered was catching the bad guy, so what was the big deal anyway?

"And newlyweds are supposed to keep a low profile, aren't they?" he asked, bringing her thoughts back to the matter at hand.

Nevertheless, his remark stumped her. "A low profile?" she echoed. "What for?"

In response to her question, his gaze skittered away from hers. He turned his body away from her, too, to place his cup on the counter. Then he shifted his weight from one foot to the other and ran the pad of his finger nervously around the rim of his cup. He was fidgeting, Bridget realized. He was uncomfortable about something. Something other than the usual just being in the same room together. But what else could he be uncomfortable about?

"Because," he said softly, "newlyweds are supposed to be, you know, preoccupied."

She still wasn't following him. "Preoccupied? By what?"

When he lifted his gaze to hers again, it was only long enough to have it bounce away. Then it ricocheted over everything else in the room that wasn't Bridget. "By, you know, other things."

"What other things? What are you talking about?"

He emitted a low growl of clear frustration. "I'm talking about *other things*," he repeated. "You know. *Newlywed* things. *Wedding-night* things. *Honeymoon* things."

"Ohh," she said aloud. "*Those* things. Sex things."

"Yeah, *those* things," he echoed. But that was all he echoed. His gaze met hers again, and if she hadn't known better, Bridget would have sworn he was blushing. But men like Sam Jones didn't blush. Certainly not over something like what traditionally kept newlyweds preoccupied. He seemed less embarrassed, though, than he did irritated. And if he was irritated, it could only be because he thought Bridget was such a blockhead about *those* things.

But how was she supposed to know what he was talking about? It wasn't as if he'd been specific about it. And she'd never been a newlywed, so how was she supposed to know how newlyweds acted? She'd certainly never given any thought to wedding-night or honeymoon behavior, having decided early on that there wouldn't *be* a wedding night or honeymoon in her future. Not that she was any stranger to the activity that newlyweds generally engaged in—well, not *too* big a stranger to it—but she wasn't preoccupied by thoughts of sex, either. Not just because she hadn't been intimately involved with anyone for a long time, but because she just didn't have time to think about sex. Even when she was sexually involved with someone, she didn't spend that much time thinking about it. She had work to do. Sex had just never been all that preoccupying for her, that was all.

The few men with whom she had been romantically involved had no more been the forever-after type than she was. Oh, she'd liked them well enough. And they'd liked her well enough, too. One or two she'd liked more than the others, enough to become more intimately involved, but she'd never intended anything to go too far, even with the intimate ones. She hadn't wanted anything to interfere with the job she had to do.

"Okay, yeah," she conceded now, "I guess newlyweds do keep a low profile for *that*. But that's not *all* they do."

She met Sam's gaze levelly, and when she saw the way his pupils had expanded, nearly eclipsing the blue of his irises, she began to feel…something. Something weird. Something she'd never felt before. She told herself it must be doubt, a reaction with which she was in no way familiar. Funny, though, she'd never figured doubt would generate a fire in her midsection that way...

"Is it?" she added in a very small voice.

For a minute he said nothing, and she got the impression it was because he was thinking about something very, very hard. Finally, though, he said, "Where I come from, newlyweds tend to disappear for a few weeks after the wedding. And not because they're on their honeymoon in Hawaii, either. Where I come from, people can't afford honeymoons in Hawaii. So they honeymoon at home. But they still disappear for a while because they want to...enjoy each other in private. Get to know each other intimately. Discover all the things about each other that they never knew before."

His expression hardened as he added, "But in your world, I guess I can see where newlyweds might forgo what you call 'the sex thing' to get out and about, since they obviously have other more important things to do than become intimately acquainted."

Bridget narrowed her eyes at him. "What are you talking about? What do you mean, in *my* world?"

He lifted one shoulder and let it drop in what she supposed was meant to be a shrug. But there was nothing casual in the gesture. There was nothing casual in him at the moment. On the contrary, he suddenly seemed very, very menacing. His lip fairly curled with contempt as he said, "Just that in the upper-crusty, blue-blooded, rarefied atmosphere where you grew up, I guess people tend to marry for reasons other than love and devotion and passion. So maybe once the honeymoon is over, it's really, really over."

Bridget gaped at him. "Oh, is that a fact?" she said coolly, her back going up at the antagonism he didn't even bother to hide. Where was all this animosity coming from? she wondered. A few minutes ago they'd been speaking to each other like the professionals they were. Now, suddenly, everything had shifted, and they were snapping at each other like toddlers on a playground. "Like what kind of reasons?" she asked. "Can you give me a for instance?"

He employed another one of those fake shrugs, then he said, "Sure, I can give you lots of for instances. There are real estate holdings to consider, for example. Got to get some of those to add to the family coffers whenever you marry off a daughter. Or business mergers. Cheaper to marry into a new business than to buy it outright. And then there's the need to further the family line with the proper mix of DNA. Make sure the blood stays blue."

"Hel-looo?" Bridget interjected. "What century did you just arrive from, Charlemagne? That real-estate stuff sort of went out with the feudal system. Not that you'd realize it, since you seem to still embrace that whole droit du seigneur thing."

"That whole what?" Sam said crisply. "You'll have to excuse me. I went to public school, and we didn't learn all those fancy French phrases you private schoolies got. We focused mostly on *Où est Pierre?* And *Mon crayon est jaune.*"

Bridget rolled her eyes at him. "Forget it. It's not important."

"I think it is."

She expelled an exasperated sigh. "Fine. Droit du seigneur was the feudal lord's right to deflower all the virgins who worked his land on their wedding nights, before their husbands had the chance to do it."

Sam glared at her. "And you think that would appeal to me, do you?"

"Yeah, I do," she said, "if you're over there assuming that just because my family is wealthy I'd prefer to marry for financial gain instead of love. You're obviously living in the Middle Ages, pal."

"And you'd rather marry for love than financial gain, is that what you expect me to believe?" he asked.

"I'd rather not marry at all," she retorted. "Not that it's any of *your* business. And why the hell are we arguing?" she further demanded, her voice raising another decibel.

"Because we're newlyweds!" he cried.

"I thought we were supposed to be too preoccupied with *other things* to be arguing!" she shouted back.

He opened his mouth to reply, doubtless with something caustic and loud, then seemed to realize how stupidly they were behaving. Bridget had to admit she had no idea how they'd degenerated to this point herself. She, too, quieted, forcing herself to calm down.

It was the stress of the case, she told herself. She and Sam both were just frustrated by the appalling lack of success they'd had so far with this thing. That was why they were going at it this way. That was why they were fighting over something as stupid as why people married and what they did on their wedding night. This was nuts. And it just emphasized more completely the reason why they should become proactive and *do* something to get things rolling.

"As I was saying," she began again, keeping her words soft and even and sane. She decided to pretend that the last few minutes had never happened and hoped Sam would, too. "We need to get out more," she said. "We need to interact with the employees of Children's Connection on a level other than professional."

Sam studied her in silence for another minute, and she wondered what he was thinking about. Was it the case? Or was he wondering, too, what the hell had come over them for those few minutes they'd been locked in combat?

He nodded again. "I guess it wouldn't hurt to try. We'll need to clear it with Pennington, like you said, but I certainly don't have a problem with it, if it will help us learn something new that might shed light on the case and move things along."

"Move things along?" she echoed to herself. Sure, with the case, maybe. With her and Sam, things seemed to be hurtling down the tracks like an out-of-control train with squealing brakes. She just wished she knew what it was speeding toward. Other than death and dismemberment, she meant.

But the sooner they got things moving with the case, Bridget thought, the sooner they could wrap the case up. And the sooner they wrapped the case up, the sooner she could be on her way. Off this case, and out of Portland, and back to doing the sort of work she really enjoyed in a place that was fascinating and fast-paced. She didn't kid herself that the position in Vienna would be waiting for her once she'd completed this assignment. They'd needed someone there right away, and when she'd been pulled from duty, they'd sent someone else in to take her place. But she still wanted to be part of a counterterrorism task force somewhere—preferably somewhere interesting and exotic. And there was a very good chance that something else would open up that might be almost as good as the position she'd lost. She hoped so, anyway.

However, she couldn't even think about that yet. Right now, she needed to focus on this case and work it to the best of her abilities. She'd never thought her up-bringing as a Logan of Portland would benefit her in law enforcement. But she would ask her mother to tap every last person she knew at Children's Connection for whatever social occasions they could conjure up. And she would do her best to milk every last person for whatever information she could. Whatever it took to bring this assignment to a successful conclusion.

Whatever it took to conclude things with Sam Jones.

Sam listened with grudging admiration as Bridget outlined her plan to Pennington an hour later, noting that she was quick, articulate, savvy and efficient as she did so. He had no choice but to admit that she was doing a better job with this case than he was. She'd recognized what wasn't working and she'd realized some possible ways to improve their chances. And she was eager to do it. She was enthusiastic about what was ahead. She was ambitious. Smart. In other words, she was exactly the kind of agent he'd normally like to be partnered with. So why was he still so irritated at their having been thrown together on this case the way they had been?

And what the hell had that argument in the kitchen earlier been about?

He still couldn't understand what had come over the two of them to go after each other the way they had that morning. He'd replayed the incident over and over in his mind during the drive to the field office—hell, what else was he supposed to do, since the two of them hadn't spoken a word to each other?—but he still couldn't pinpoint where things had gone sour. Ultimately, he'd concluded that it wasn't that things had *gone* sour—it was that things had *been* sour all along, from the moment Bridget Logan had approached him at the airport.

They just rubbed each other the wrong way, that was all. Sometimes that happened—two people simply didn't like each other, for whatever reason. Usually, the problem was remedied by avoiding the person you didn't like. This time, though, the two people were partnered together, and there was no way to ask for a reassignment. Worse, the partnering required a level of intimacy that Sam, for one, normally didn't share with another person. Certainly not publicly. He suspected that Bridget Logan was much like him in that regard—she didn't seem the touchy-feely, let's-talk-about-our-feelings-and-then-hug type, either. He was just going to have to make the best of it. And so was she.

He only hoped her idea about trying to glean information for the investigation via more social networking worked, because Sam wanted something to happen with this case *now*. He wanted to wrap it up, move on to something else. And he wanted to be rid of Bridget Logan.

Then he could get his life back and start living it again. With all its peace and quiet and solitude. And all its work and solitude. And all its relaxation and solitude. And all its solitude and solitude. Which was exactly how Sam liked it.

"Well, it certainly couldn't hurt to try," Pennington said after Bridget finished describing all the things she wanted to do, not the least of which was throwing a party at the house the two of them were occupying as faux man and wife. "How soon can you put it all into action?"

"I'll organize the party at the house as soon as I get home," Bridget said. "It'll be small, since it's short notice, but it'll get the ball rolling. And I'll make sure I include as many people from Children's Connection on the guest list as I can. And I'll have my mother organize a larger party at their country club to introduce us to all their friends, again being sure to include a good number of people from Children's Connection.

"Really, that's something she would have done for us as soon as we arrived in Portland," Bridget continued, "had Sam and I actually been married. I should have thought about it as soon as I learned of the assignment. There's also a fund-raiser for the agency later this month that we can attend. And tomorrow night there's a group from the Connection attending the symphony. Jillian and I had planned to go with my parents, but Jillian won't mind letting Sam take her ticket." She grinned. "Jillian really isn't all that crazy about Dvorak anyway."

"Neither am I," Sam muttered, even though he wasn't even familiar with Dvorak, to the point where he didn't know if that was the name of a composer, a musician, the conductor, an instrument or a piece of music. If it wasn't blues or R&B played on electric guitar, Sam wanted no part of it. He did have standards, after all.

He glanced up to find Pennington glaring at him. "You'll like Antonin Dvorak tomorrow night," his boss told him. "Or you'll find another job elsewhere."

Sam gritted his teeth. "Oh, *that* Dvorak," he said. "Gosh, I just love him. I thought you guys were talking about Bernie Dvorak, who sat behind me in third grade. That guy was a schmuck."

He wasn't sure, but he thought Bridget expelled an exasperated breath at that. Probably, he thought, she was concluding that he was an ill-bred clodhopper who didn't have any appreciation for the finer things in life and had no idea how to behave in polite, refined society. But that wasn't true at all. For one thing, he'd been bred for speed and agility—not to mention good looks and smarts. For another thing, he had a very deep appreciation for the finer things in life—especially things like girls named Bambi and Mitzi wearing string bikinis, and the rumble of a V-8 engine in a cherry-red '64 Mustang convertible, and an ice-cold bottle of Rolling Rock on a hot summer afternoon. For yet another thing, he knew exactly how to behave in polite, refined society: like a stiff. So take that, Princess Bridget.

Hell, he couldn't wait for tomorrow night.

Six

Although they did hear a few potentially helpful things while mingling with the Children's Connection contingent at the symphony the following night, the main thing Sam learned was that he'd been right without even realizing it—he didn't like Antonin Dvorak the composer any more than he'd liked Bernie Dvorak the schmuck. But, as had been the case in third grade, he hadn't been allowed to change his seat tonight, either. Of course, his seat at the symphony was considerably better than his seat in Mrs. Doolittle's class had been. Because back then, his third-grade crush, Melissa Gordon, had sat clear on the other side of the room from him. But tonight, Bridget Logan sat right at his side, in the privacy of the elder Logans' box at the symphony.

Not that he had a crush on Bridget Logan, he was quick to remind himself. He was just a little preoccupied by her tonight, that was all. But, hell, how could he not be preoccupied by her when she was wearing a dress like *that?* He still wasn't sure what was keeping the black strapless number aloft, since it completely exposed her shoulders and a good portion of her back. Especially with her auburn hair swept up in that fancy 'do. And what shoulders. He hadn't been able to help noticing them as he'd contemplated the dilemma of the gravitational pull on her attire. What a back. He hadn't been able to help noticing that, either.

Especially after he, at one point, in an effort to help her steer her way through the crowd, inadvertently opened his hand over the small of her back, only to discover too late that the gesture left his bare flesh pressing against hers. She'd jerked forward upon the contact, making him realize she must have felt the same jolt of heat he had. Either that, or his hands were a lot colder than he realized. After that, he'd been careful to keep his hands to himself. His fingers twitched every time he recalled the episode, though. And he'd recalled the episode whenever his mind had strayed from the symphony performance. Which was often.

Like, for instance, now.

He closed his eyes in an effort to banish the skin-on-skin memory, but that only brought it into sharper focus. So he opened his eyes again, but that left him gazing at a stage full of black-clad musicians who cared a lot more about the music they were playing than he did. So Sam let his gaze wander along with his mind. Unfortunately, with the lights low, he could see little in the cavernous auditorium. Until his gaze roved to his right, where Bridget sat in her black dress and naked shoulders, her only adornment a simple pearl choker encircling her throat.

And then, out of nowhere, a very vivid, very graphic scene exploded in Sam's brain, one that featured Bridget Logan wearing that pearl choker and nothing else. Unless you counted the way Sam's naked body was wrapped around hers, in which case she was fully dressed. Because in his vision, his body pressed into hers from head to toe…and then some.

And, good God, where had that indecent image come from? he asked himself as he snatched his gaze away from her and focused on the darkness again. Man, show him a little flesh, and suddenly he was ready to make a meal out of the woman who owned it. He'd obviously gone way too long without satisfying his baser instincts if he was thinking about Bridget Logan in such a way. Hell, just how long had it been, anyway, since he last…?

His eyes widened when he tallied the number of months. Oh, surely not, he thought. No man could go *that* long without a sexual encounter of some kind. But another quick calculation only confirmed the number. Jeez, no wonder he was having these thoughts. He had to start thinking about something other than work. Like going out immediately and getting—

"I love this part," Bridget said then, interrupting his thoughts, not so much because she spoke, but because she leaned close to him to murmur the words softly into his ear so that no one else would be disturbed by them.

But Sam sure was disturbed. When she leaned over the way she did just then, he was surrounded by the scent of her, something soft and sweet and seductive, and the whispered words were made even more poignant as a result. Also made poignant was the way her bare shoulder brushed against his upper arm. Even through the double layers of his suit jacket and dress shirt, he fancied he could feel the heat radiating from her skin and seeping into his own. And then, just like that, those graphic images of the two of them naked and wrapped around each other kicked in again, and Sam was once more overcome by the need to go out immediately and get—

"The way the music swells here is so thrilling," Bridget whispered, pressing her body even closer into his.

This time Sam couldn't help glancing over at her. And when he did, his gaze fell to the creamy shoulder pressing against him, then lower still, to the curve of her breast where it bloomed from the front of her dress. It rose higher as he watched her, because she sighed heavily at something, the soft, pale flesh pressing tighter against the black fabric of her dress. And suddenly, Sam felt his own flesh press tighter against the fabric of one of his own garments.

"The sheer magnitude of it is just staggering," Bridget murmured, this time reaching across herself to curl her fingers over Sam's upper arm. She was wearing elbow-length, black satin gloves with her dress, and where Sam had initially thought them a bit excessive, even for formal attire, suddenly he considered them to be profoundly erotic. Especially when her fingers curled even tighter into his arm. And especially when she whispered excitedly, "It fills you so full, until you think you just can't take anymore, and then it just steals your breath away from you."

Sam closed his eyes tight and wished she had phrased her musical critique a little differently than she had. Because words like *swells* and *thrilling* and *fills you so full* and *can't take anymore*—and, hell, all modesty aside, even *magnitude*—sounded way too sexual in his current frame of mind, and they only served to remind him of just how much he needed to go out immediately and get—

"And then everything inside you begins to rush so deliciously," she added, sounding a little short of breath.

Oh, it certainly does, Sam agreed.

"Pulsing and thrashing."

Yep. That, too.

"And then it explodes into a crescendo that leaves you feeling so exhausted and satisfied by the experience."

Not to mention badly in need of a cigarette.

Gee, maybe classical music did have one or two things to recommend it, Sam thought as Bridget leaned even more eagerly into him. Maybe he should look into subscribing next season.

The impression was only heightened after the symphony and the conductor took their final bows and the lights in the auditorium went up, because then Sam could see Bridget clearly. And judging by the stain of pink on her cheeks and the bright shine in her eyes, he suspected she'd been...*moved* by the music in much the same way he had been. Maybe it had been a while since she'd enjoyed a sexual encounter of some kind, too, he thought then. In fact, maybe he wasn't the only one who was thinking about how he needed to go out immediately and get—

"—laid tonight," he heard Bridget saying, bringing him back to the matter at hand. Sort of.

"Uh, what?" he asked, certain he must have misheard her, thanks to the din of the departing crowd below their box. And also thanks to his own wishful thinking.

She gave him a funny look, and he wondered if the bright auditorium lights revealed too much in his expression, too. "I said, 'I can't believe how beautifully they played tonight.'"

"Oh," he said, realizing he had indeed misheard. Dammit. "Yeah. Yeah, they did. Play beautifully, I mean. Tonight, I mean."

She sighed with much disappointment. "You weren't even listening, were you?"

He shook his head guiltily. "I guess I, um, sort of had my mind on something else."

She eyed him thoughtfully for a moment, and for that moment, he feared she could see right through him, straight into his brain at the very thoughts he'd been having all evening about her naked shoulders and back and how great they'd be if they were paired with nothing but her black gloves and his own naked body.

Aloud, though, she only said, "The case?"

He nodded, even more guiltily. "Uh, yeah. Yeah, the case." Because he had been thinking about the case. In a roundabout, naked shoulders, not-really sort of way.

She nodded, too, as if she understood, something he sincerely doubted. "I know. It's been on my mind tonight, too."

Not the way it had been on his, he'd bet.

"But we're doing everything we can," she reminded him.

Well, not quite *every*thing, he thought.

"In the meantime, we might as well try to enjoy ourselves."

Oh, he had been.

"Mom and Dad have invited us to the house for a drink on our way home," she added.

Which meant they wouldn't be enjoying themselves

the way he'd envisioned earlier. Ah, well. Couldn't have everything, he supposed.

"But I told them we'd probably just go on home," she added. And for some reason, the way she said *home* made it sound, well, homey. And, strangely, the thought of returning to the big Tudor mansion that didn't belong to them actually kind of *felt* like going home to Sam.

"We can visit with your parents for a while, if you want," he told her. "Sounds good to me." And he was surprised to discover he was telling the truth. It did sound good. Anything that involved Bridget and her naked shoulders and black gloves sounded good. Hell, even without the naked shoulders and black gloves, it sounded good. Though, mind you, he liked the naked shoulders and black gloves part, too. Especially the naked shoulders. A lot.

"No, I'd rather go home," Bridget told him.

And, of course, so would Sam. Anything to be alone with her. Not that he should be, he reminded himself. Not with all the naked thoughts he'd been having tonight.

"I'm kind of tired," she added.

And he told himself he should be relieved. Because if Bridget was tired, it was a sure bet she'd be taking herself and her shoulders right to bed. Without Sam.

So why didn't he feel relieved at all?

They chatted with her parents as they waited for the crowd below to thin out some, and Sam discovered to his surprise that he liked Terrence and Leslie Logan. Leslie reminded him a lot of Bridget, in looks, if not in personality. Leslie was more outgoing than her daughter, more engaging. She was clearly more people-oriented than Bridget, and had honed her social skills to a fine point, though her sociability was clearly natural and not manufactured. Terrence, too, was gregarious, though where his wife spoke more about their friends and local goings-on, he tended to focus more on business. It was from him that Bridget had gotten her no-nonsense approach to work, Sam could see.

When the crowd had dispersed, they all stood, and as Terrence Logan helped his wife into her evening jacket, Sam held Bridget's gold velvet wrap for her. The shawl didn't seem like it would be enough to keep her warm in the chilly April evening, but what did he know about fashion and practicality? And as he settled the shawl on her shoulders, he tried not to notice the puff of sweet perfume that greeted him. Though, truth be told, he couldn't help but notice it. It was more intoxicating even than a nightcap at her folks' house might be.

At the beginning of the evening, Sam had driven himself and Bridget the three blocks to the Logan estate and had left their borrowed Mercedes there, so that the foursome could drive to the symphony together in Terrence's car. So now Terrence drove them all home in his roomy black Jaguar, which left Sam and Bridget sharing the back seat, something Sam hadn't done since he was in high school. Back then, he hadn't minded taking the back seat, because it had offered its hormonally enthusiastic adolescent occupants the perfect opportunity to make out. As a grown man, however…

Oh, who was he kidding? Spending his evening rubbing elbows—and more—with Bridget in a dress that defied gravity left him feeling much the same way as he had back then. Hormonal and enthusiastic. Good thing her old man was sitting in the front seat instead of one of Sam's high-school buddies. Otherwise, he would have been putting the moves on her like nobody's business. And remembering the way she'd looked after the lights came up, he halfway thought she wouldn't have discouraged him.

And, man, this case was getting weird.

Somehow, Sam managed to keep his hands to himself during the drive home, and after saying their farewells to the elder Logans, he and Bridget drove the short distance home…or, rather, back to the house that belonged to someone else where they happened to be cohabiting for their job and felt in no way comfortable.

And they spoke scarcely a word to each other the entire way.

The tension between them was back. Somehow, though, he knew it was there for a different reason this time. At least it was for him. He could only take so much of Bridget in a strapless gown before he started to notice things about her. Like how great she looked in a strapless gown. And like how much he wanted to see the rest of her out of the strapless gown.

Damn, he hoped this plan of hers worked, and that they flushed out their perp soon. Because the last thing he could handle was an attraction to a woman he neither needed nor wanted, a woman who wouldn't even have been in town if she hadn't been assigned to duty here.

Sam wheeled the borrowed Mercedes into the big three-car garage, then flipped on the security system after they entered the house. He still couldn't believe there were people who lived this way every day. Who spent more money on their cars than some people spent on their homes, and who had to purchase sophisticated alarm systems to protect their expensive possessions. If anyone broke into Sam's house, the only thing they'd find of any value would be his collection of beer bottle caps from around the world. Here in this house, though…

He turned from the back door to see Bridget walking through the kitchen, her bare back smooth and pale in the soft light, her long, long legs encased in smoky stockings, her slender arms wrapped in those black silk gloves. Here in this house, he thought as he watched her move fluidly and elegantly across the room, there was much to value and protect.

As if she'd heard him speak the thought aloud, she spun quickly around, naturally catching him in the act of ogling her. Sam didn't apologize, however, nor did he offer any excuses. Why should he? She'd dressed to be admired, and by God, he was admiring her. See? He really did have a deep appreciation for the finer things in life.

And that was when it hit him, why the two of them rubbed each other the wrong way. Or, at least, why she rubbed him the wrong way. Because he wanted her. In the most basic, most primitive, most intimate way a man could want a woman. And there was no way, he knew, that he could ever have her. She was just too far out of his league.

"So you enjoyed the performance tonight?" he asked her, even though he already knew the answer to the question.

She smiled, seeming relieved that he'd asked something so benign. "Yes, I enjoyed it very much."

"You like the symphony, huh?" he asked further, even though he knew the answer to that one, too. Unable to help himself, he took a few steps forward, his shoes making a soft scraping sound on the linoleum as he approached her. But not another sound joined it, something that made the echo of it seem even louder, and somehow more ominous, than it should have.

She gave him a quizzical look, but nodded. "I love going to hear the symphony play. I've been going ever since I was a little girl. My parents took all of us when we were young. We had family subscriptions to all the arts."

Sam nodded, too, and kept striding forward. Her parents had taken her to the symphony when she was a child. Presumably the ballet and opera, too. No doubt, they'd enjoyed art museums and such, as well. Sam's parents, on the other hand, had taken him and his brother Jeff to the movies. Or to ball games and church picnics. Those kinds of thing.

Of course Bridget Logan had always loved the symphony, he told himself. He'd wager she'd loved the ballet, too. Maybe even the opera. She probably still enjoyed spending time in places like art galleries, and attending garden parties, too. And he was the kind of guy who'd much rather watch a bunch of sweaty guys chase a small round object around, be it on a football or baseball field, a basketball court or a hockey rink. She looked completely at ease all dolled up in a dress that had probably cost more than his weekly paycheck, while he was more comfortable in jeans and flannel from the discount store. She came from a very long line of very blue blood, a family that had come by their money the old-fashioned way: by inheriting it. Sam's blood was a soup of ethnicity from every corner of the globe where backbreaking labor was the norm.

She couldn't have been more different from him. So why, in that moment, did he want her so much?

Too long without sex, he told himself. It was nothing more than that. At this point, he'd find any woman desirable. Bridget Logan could be dressed like a giant duck, but as long as she had two X chromosomes, he'd want her.

And he really did want her.

"I don't think I told you how beautiful you look tonight," he said as he came to a halt in front of her with only a few scant inches separating their bodies. And he surprised himself when he heard the comment. He'd been thinking it all evening, but he hadn't planned on saying it aloud. Why had it popped out now? Still, once the remark was out in the open, he didn't much want to call it back. It was the truth, after all.

Bridget was obviously surprised to hear it, too, because her eyes went wide, and her lips parted softly in astonishment. "I… No, you didn't tell… Thank you for…" She stumbled over the words as if she couldn't quite hold on to one response long enough to make sense of it or speak it in its entirety.

Sam instructed himself to tell her good-night and then hie himself off to bed before he said—or did something else that got him into trouble. But he couldn't quite bring himself to leave. He knew the reason—he wanted to prolong their time together in whatever way he could. In spite of not much caring for the symphony, he'd had a surprisingly good time this evening. And that could only be because of the company he'd kept. Besides, he was too keyed up to go to bed just yet. Her parents had had the right idea, wanting a nightcap before calling an end to the night. Maybe having a drink with Bridget would calm him down some, he told himself.

Oh, sure it would, he thought wryly. And maybe the next WWE Heavyweight Champ would be named Stone Cold Sheldon Abernathy.

"How about a nightcap?" he heard himself offer.

She wanted to say no. He could see that by her expression. But she didn't want to say no because she didn't want to have a drink with him. He could see that by her expression, too. She wanted to say no for the same reason he wanted her to say no: because it wouldn't be a good idea. Not with both of them looking at each other the way they were at the moment.

In spite of that, Bridget smiled a little tentatively and said, "Sure. A nightcap would be great."

Sam extended his hand to their left, toward the hallway that led from the kitchen to the den, where there was a wet bar tucked into one corner of the room. Bridget preceded him, knowing that was where he wanted them to go, and he followed her the short distance to the den. She tugged off her gloves as she walked, and all the while, she felt his gaze on her back as surely as if he were brushing his warm fingers over her bare flesh. And she wondered what he was thinking.

God, she wondered what *she* was thinking, to even think that. What did she care what Sam Jones thought about her or her back? Then again, what had she been thinking earlier, to have donned this dress in the first place? It was much too revealing, and normally she wouldn't have purchased anything like it. But she'd needed something to wear to the symphony, since she hadn't brought any appropriate clothing home with her. And she'd told herself she needed to dress like a good little trophy wife should, so that she would make her cover more authentic. This dress certainly did that.

And, dammit—she made herself admit it—she'd wanted to look nice for Sam, too.

She told herself it was only feminine vanity that had made her feel that way, that she'd wanted to be at her best simply because that was what she always strove to be. But she *had* been thinking about Sam in particular when she'd first pulled the revealing little dress from the rack at the boutique, she had to confess. And she'd been thinking about him again when she put it on tonight. She just didn't know *why* she had been thinking about him.

Because he was so handsome, she told herself. Any man who looked like him, whether he was a corporate big shot or a construction worker, would take his pick among women. She'd wanted to make sure anyone who might be observing them would believe she had been the type of woman he would pick.

But would he really? she asked herself. Had they not been playing a part for a sting operation, would Sam still find her attractive? As attractive as she found him?

And why did the answer to that question matter so much to her?

It was silly to indulge in such uncharacteristic wondering, she told herself. It didn't matter if Sam found her attractive or not. And the fact that she found him attractive was totally immaterial. Because the two of them *were* just playing a part for a sting operation. And once that operation was over and they'd caught the bad guy and sent him to jail, she'd be leaving Portland—and Sam—and would probably never see him again. The last thing she needed to do was to develop feelings for him or to engender feelings in him.

So why was she trying so hard to attract him? And why couldn't she ignore the reaction she had toward him?

She pushed the questions out of her head without answering them. None of it mattered. Because Sam was too professional to let anything happen between them. And Bridget was, too, she reminded herself belatedly. Besides, at their very first meeting, he'd made it clear that he didn't approve of her. Yes, they'd been getting along fairly well since then, but first impressions were lasting ones. Deep down, Sam probably still didn't approve of her. He might not even like her. She was just asking for trouble—on a number of different levels— to give in to her fascination with him.

Oh, she really should have just told him she was going to bed.

The den, like the rest of the house, was sumptuously decorated, its forest-green walls hung with oil-on-canvas paintings of hunt scenes, its furniture big, ornate mahogany pieces that had obviously been designed for a man. Built-in bookcases were full of books on topics that ranged from fly fishing to big business, and a couch pushed against one wall was covered in fine oxblood leather and was as large and arrogant as the rest of the furnishings. The room was a man's retreat, plain and simple, and Bridget felt small and vulnerable standing in the middle of it.

Especially when Sam followed her in. He was enormous and overbearing and masculine, too. The dark suit he'd worn to the symphony made him seem big and potent. It was cut in such a way that his shoulders looked even broader, and the dark color made him seem even taller. And where she had noticed that he usually began to dismember his suits the minute he walked through the door after work, tonight, for some reason, his attire was still flawless.

He crossed to the bar in the corner and, without even asking her what she preferred to drink, pulled down two cut-crystal old-fashioned glasses from a shelf. Then he bent to open a lower cabinet—and Bridget tried very hard not to notice how the back flaps of his jacket opened enough for her to glimpse the taut derriere beneath—to pull out a bottle from among the varied assortment contained within. She recognized it immediately as a lovely old mellow Scotch.

He held it up for her approval. "Okay?" he asked.

She nodded. "But I'd like it on the rocks with a splash of water. Please," she added in a belated attempt to be polite.

He dipped his head forward in what she thought might be approval, then turned to fix their drinks. He, she noticed, preferred his straight up, but he poured only a couple of fingers instead of filling half the glass as most men might have.

"There aren't many women who like Scotch," he said as he turned around to hand her her drink.

She didn't bother mentioning that that was the very reason she'd cultivated a taste for the spirit. In the man's world where Bridget worked, she wanted to be respected as one of them. Then she remembered that, for Sam, at least, she'd wanted to play up her feminine side, too.

So which is it, Bridget? she asked herself. *Do you want Sam to respect you as a co-worker or view you as a desirable woman? You can't have it both ways, you know.*

And why not? she asked herself in reply.

But herself didn't seem to have an answer for that one.

When Bridget took her drink from him, his hand accidentally—at least, she thought it was an accident—got tangled with hers for a moment, and the brush of his fingers felt warm and affectionate against her own. Ultimately, she had to bring up her other hand to take the glass so that it didn't spill, muttering a nervous, "Thank you," as she did. In spite of the fact that it was only an unintentional, quick caress, her heart began to pound rapid-fire in response to it. And her pulse rate doubled when she brought her gaze up to meet Sam's, because his eyes seemed darker than they had a moment ago.

He lifted his own drink to his lips as he watched her, and after inhaling a deep breath that she hoped might slow her heart rate, Bridget tasted her drink, too. But the fine smokiness of the spirit was lost on her; it could have tasted like ashes for all she knew, because all she could focus on in that moment was the way Sam Jones was looking at her.

Just what was he thinking? she wondered.

She received an answer to that question as quickly as she would have had she spoken it aloud, but it wasn't quite the answer she expected. Because after Sam swallowed his Scotch, he looked her right in the eye, parted those sexy lips of his, and said, very quietly, "So you think this socializing thing will work?"

And just like that, all the strange little fluttering inside Bridget fizzled right out. Yep, he was professional, all right. Damn him.

She stalled by enjoying another, larger, taste of her drink, letting the liquor warm her mouth and throat on its way down. And then, just for good measure, she sucked down another swallow, too. And then one more for even better measure. And, okay, one more, for the best measure of all.

"I hope so," she said. Then, when she realized how nervous she sounded, she enjoyed yet another swallow of her drink. Oh, yeah. That was definitely helping. "I wouldn't have suggested it if I didn't think it had a chance."

Sam nodded at that, but his eyes were still fixed on her face, and he still seemed to be thinking about something else. Bridget decided, though, that she was mistaken about that when he continued, "Of all the departments at Children's Connection, where do you think our baby seller is most likely to be working? Where's he most likely to be effective?"

She, too, focused her gaze on Sam's face, mostly his eyes—his gorgeous, sexy, blue, blue eyes—but asked, "Are we certain it's a he? Because I'm not so sure."

And really, in that moment, with Sam looking at her the way he was, Bridget wasn't sure of anything. Except that a slow ribbon of heat was gradually uncurling inside her, starting in the pit of her stomach and easing its way upward, toward her heart. From there, she supposed, it could go anywhere, potentially overtaking her entire body. So she tried to think about something else instead. The case. Her drink. The symphony's performance this evening. The average annual rainfall in Albuquerque. Anything. Unfortunately, she discovered that all she could think about was Sam. And his blue, blue eyes. And his full, delicious-looking mouth. And his broad shoulders. And the way he was lifting his hand toward her face…

He took a step closer to her then, even though he had only been standing a few inches away, so that his big body was nearly flush with hers. He really was tall, she noted a little breathlessly. Tall and broad and solid. And still his hand was rising, until his fingertips brushed lightly over the line of her jaw, and—

Oh, boy.

Without uttering a word, he dipped his head to hers, his thumb curving along her cheekbone as his lips made contact with her own. So surprised was she by his kiss that Bridget gasped, sucking in the musky Scotch taste of him before his tongue even made contact with hers. The fingers on her cheek moved again, toward her hairline, then over the back of her head. Vaguely, she registered him setting his drink down on a bookshelf near her head, then plucking her own from her fingers and setting it beside his own. That left him with both hands free to touch her, and touch her he did.

The hand on her hair swept over the crown of her head, then down to where she had cinched her hair into an elegant French twist. With a few quick flicks, he freed the silky tresses, spilling them down over his hand and her shoulders. Bridget gasped again at the gesture, and Sam deepened their kiss, opening his mouth wide over hers, thrusting his tongue to the back of her mouth. And all she could do was cling to his shoulders and kiss him back, and marvel at the fire that had exploded in her belly on first contact.

His kiss took her breath away. Literally, figuratively, in every way possible. All Bridget could do was kiss him back. The fingers she had curled into his shoulders moved lower, down over his arms, her fingertips registering every subtle rise and fall of muscle beneath the fabric of his clothes. He pulled her closer then, wrapping one strong arm around her waist, tangling his other hand in her hair, giving it a gentle tug to tip her head back farther. Bridget opened one hand over his chest, tucking her fingers beneath the lapel of his jacket, then dragged the other back up over his arm and shoulder, to cup it around his warm nape. And then she held on to him tightly, waiting to see where he would take her next.

And where he took her was paradise.

Never in her life had Bridget been kissed with such exquisite care, or such generous attention. Sam's mouth was first insistent, then tender, then a delicious mixture of both. His tongue played lightly with hers, then he brushed his lips over her own once, twice, three times, four, before bringing his tongue back into play, tracing it along the plump, sensitive curve of her lower lip. Bridget wanted to melt right there on the spot, and she was helpless to stop the soft sigh of delight that escaped her.

Sam responded to that sigh by moving the hand at her waist higher, skimming it up over her back, then across her bare shoulders, then down again, to the top of her zipper. But he only thumbed the metal tongue a few times without taking hold of it, hesitating as if he were silently asking her permission to continue. Bridget told herself to deny it, to pull away from him now and flee from the room with her dignity, if not her professionalism, still intact. But she couldn't quite bring herself to tell him to stop. Instead, she only continued to kiss him, loving the feel of his mouth on hers, becoming more and more intoxicated with every brush of his lips over her own.

He must have interpreted her silence to be her agreement with whatever he wanted to do, because he did take hold of her zipper then and slowly…oh, so slowly…began to drag it downward. Millimeter by millimeter the zipper hissed, and with every new whisper, Bridget felt the fabric of her dress parting, felt the kiss of cool air on her bare skin. She remembered then that she wasn't wearing a bra, that the cut of the dress was such—and, alas, her endowment was so meager—that the additional garment was unnecessary. The hand that had been tangled in her hair moved to her back, too, then, gripping one side of her dress to pull it wider, then splaying open over the sensitive skin between her shoulder blades.

For one brief, delirious moment, Bridget allowed him the liberty of opening his hand over her naked back, mostly because she wanted to allow herself that liberty, too. Just one minute, she told herself. That was all she'd allow either of them. Just long enough to enjoy the feel of a man's hand on her bare flesh, because it had been so long—too long—since she had enjoyed even that simple pleasure. And in that stolen moment, she registered the rough-callused pads of his fingertips skimming lightly over her sensitive flesh, and the way his kiss grew more impassioned, the way he tasted her so deeply, as he pressed his hand intimately against her. He pushed his big body more urgently into hers, too, and as she rubbed instinctively against him, she felt him ripen and grow hard against her belly.

And that was when Bridget realized things were getting out of hand, and that she'd gone too far. But still, she couldn't make herself stop kissing him, couldn't make herself pull away, couldn't push him away from herself, either. It just felt so good to kiss him. And he was only touching her back…

But then, without warning, he urged her dress lower, tugging the top half down until it fell away from her breasts. And before Bridget could say a word to stop him— maybe, she had to confess, because she really didn't want to stop him, not yet—he moved one hand between their bodies and cupped it gently over her bare breast.

And that, finally, gave Bridget the strength to pull away from him. Because that, finally, made her want to surrender to him completely. Spinning away from him, she jerked her dress back up over her breasts, then reached behind herself to zip it. But her entire body was trembling from the intensity of their embrace, and her hands shook too badly for her to do the zipper. She fumbled with it for several frustrating moments, managing only to drag it up a few inches. And she wanted to cry at being so ineffective in succeeding at that simple task. She wanted to cry for a lot of reasons, she realized. But she'd be damned if she would allow a single tear to fall.

Then, Sam's fingers were there with her own, brushing them gently away. Reluctantly, Bridget stopped battling with the zipper, pulling both arms in front of herself to hold up her dress. Without a word, Sam tugged the zipper easily back up into place, pausing a moment with his fingers still holding on to it before releasing it. And then, again without speaking a word, he stepped away from her.

Bridget couldn't make herself turn around to look at him. So many emotions were swirling around inside her that she didn't know how to act. The embrace she'd shared with Sam had shaken her to her core, had made her feel happy and excited and needy and hungry. But there was shame and guilt and embarrassment and regret in the mix, too. Shame that she had behaved so unprofessionally. Guilt that she had capitulated so easily. Embarrassment that he didn't seem to have been nearly as affected by what had happened as she. And regret that it wouldn't happen again.

Because it wouldn't happen again. This was a complication neither of them needed. There was no reason for them to get involved, and every reason for them to avoid it. But now there would be this between them, this intimacy neither had expected or wanted. This intimacy that she, for one, would never forget. As much as she wished she could.

And still she didn't know what to say or do.

Sam, however, spared her having to say or do anything by simply mumbling softly, "Good night, Bridget."

She heard, rather than saw him collect their glasses from the shelf where he had set them. Then he carried them out of the room with him, presumably heading for the kitchen. She turned enough so that she could see the door of the den, then listened to the sound of water running in the kitchen as Sam rinsed the glasses out. Then she saw the light in the hallway suddenly go dim, as if he had turned off the light in the kitchen. And then she heard his footsteps as he walked out the other way, followed by his heavy tread on the stairs as he went up to bed.

And even after all that, Bridget still didn't know what to say or do.

She was still wide awake an hour after Sam had held her, kissed her, fondled her good-night, lying in her bed and staring up into the darkness. She was also brushing her fingertips lightly across her mouth and cheek and jaw, everywhere his lips had touched her. Her skin felt overly warm and unusually sensitive, though whether that was because of the friction of her fingers, or because she was blushing at the memory of what had happened, or because Sam's kisses had left her overstimulated everywhere, she honestly couldn't have said. Nor could she have said what exactly had happened in the den tonight, why he had kissed her and touched her so intimately, or why she had welcomed his kisses and touches so enthusiastically.

She told herself it was bound to have happened sooner or later, that they'd been dancing around a strange electricity that had been arcing between the two of them since their first encounter at the airport. She understood now that the animosity that had blown up so suddenly and thoroughly that day, and the tension that had plagued them since, was a result of their own unwanted attraction to each other and nothing more. It made sense. He was a handsome man and, all modesty aside, she wasn't a bad-looking woman. They'd been thrown together in unusually intimate surroundings, expected to act like two people who were wildly in love. Of course they eventually would have reacted to each other the way they had tonight.

Of course they would.

They'd been out for a festive night, and both had been dressed to the nines. They'd shared a drink in intimate surroundings. They'd acted on impulse. Maybe not wisely, but it was too late for second thoughts and recriminations now. What was done was done. In a way, maybe it was good. They'd gotten the inevitable physical contact out of the way, and now they could move forward. Right?

Right.

It was just a kiss, she told herself. A deep, open-mouthed kiss, yeah, but a kiss nonetheless. And okay, maybe a little groping, too. And some fondling. So it had been openmouthed kissing, and naked flesh on naked flesh groping and fondling. Big deal. She'd done that before with other guys and lived to tell the tale. She'd done more than that with other guys and lived to tell the tale. She'd even gone on to maintain fairly good relationships with some of them. She had to put this into perspective.

There was no need to dwell on it any further, she told herself. Besides, she'd bet good money Sam wasn't lying in bed right now, replaying the whole thing in *his* head and trying to make sense of it. Men didn't do that the way women did. Sam had probably thought, *Whoa, that was fun,* and then rolled over and fallen right to sleep. When he woke up in the morning, he probably wouldn't give it a second thought. For him, it would just be business as usual. So she should make sure that was what it was for her, too.

This was nuts, she thought, rolling restlessly onto her side. She punched her pillow a few times to fluff it— *not* because she was so frustrated she needed to hit something—then laid her head on it and closed her eyes. *Sleep,* she commanded herself. *You need to sleep.* That was why she was so fixated on what had happened with Sam tonight. That was why it had probably happened in the first place. Because she was tired. Because this case was making her crazy with its lack of activity and progress. Thinking about anything—even kissing Sam—would be preferable to thinking about that.

Especially the way his mouth had been so hot and hungry against hers, and the way he had smelled, so spicy and clean and masculine. His fingertips brushing over her bare skin had been as gentle as his mouth was demanding, a delicious dichotomy of sensation for her to enjoy. She wondered what it would be like to have him touching her elsewhere, wondered what would have happened if she'd let him pull her dress lower, down over her hips and thighs. She wished now that she'd had the opportunity to touch him, too, maybe splay her own hands over his naked chest and broad back. Even if she'd only skimmed her fingers along his jaw and down the strong column of his throat, she'd have experienced a bit more of him than she had. His skin would have been rough beneath a day's growth of beard, she thought, but it would have been hot and alive, too. And his hair, she recalled, when she'd threaded her fingers through it, had felt like silk. His bare skin, she some-how knew, would be silky, too, warm and smooth and salty to taste…

Sighing softly to herself, Bridget finally tumbled into a shallow slumber. And her dreams that night were the sweetest she'd had in a long, long time….

Seven

"Are we going to talk about what happened last night?"

It was Sam, not Bridget, who posed the question during their drive to the field office the following morning. He'd promised himself when he awoke that morning that he would follow her cue, that if she pretended nothing happened, then he would, too. But if she wanted to talk about it, then, by God, he'd steel himself for the inevitable discussion. But she'd breezed into the kitchen with a bright smile and a cheery, "Good morning," and hadn't offered one indication that today was any different from those that had preceded it.

At first Sam had told himself to be grateful, that the last thing he wanted to do was revisit what had happened last night. He still didn't know what had come over him to try and consume Bridget the way he had. Well, okay, maybe he knew what had come over him—pure, unmitigated lust—but he couldn't imagine what he'd been thinking to let himself give in to it. Then again, he *hadn't* been thinking, he reminded himself. He'd been reacting. Reacting to the realization that he was alone with a beautiful woman who was a consenting adult, just like him, and that the beautiful woman was looking at him as if she wouldn't mind consenting to just about anything he proposed, nor would she mind doing a little consuming of him in the process.

She'd been sweet as hell, though, he recalled. The way her body had melted into him, and the way she'd opened her mouth under his…

"No, we're not going to talk about it," she said.

He nodded. Okay. That was fine with him. Wasn't it? Hell, men never wanted to talk about that crap. He'd be doing a disservice to his entire gender if he pursued this. So he'd just shut up now.

"It's just," he heard himself say, and he cursed himself for it, "I think we should talk about it."

He glanced over from the driver's seat long enough to see Bridget staring straight ahead, then turned his attention back to the road. Although they were headed into the field office, she was dressed to play the part of Mrs. Samuel Jones today, wearing a lightweight pants-and-shirt outfit the color of a dark emerald. She'd cinched the man-style shirt with a woven belt, but she'd left her hair loose, for which Sam was profoundly grateful. He still remembered the way the silky mass had felt falling over his hand the night before, and nothing would have made him happier at the moment than burying his fingers in the thick tresses again, preferably while he opened his mouth over hers and tasted her as deeply as he had the night before.

But then, they weren't going to talk about that, were they?

"What's there to talk about?" she said.

Or maybe they were. Still, Sam clamped his teeth together at the question. *Well, hell, honey,* he thought, *if it didn't move you enough even to remember it, then I'll just have to try harder next time.*

Oh, yeah. That would be a great way to respond. Not only did it make him sound like a petulant teenager, it indicated there would be a second time. And he, for one, was going to make damned certain that didn't happen. As amazing as it had been to hold and touch and kiss Bridget the night before, he'd been grateful that she, at least, had had the sense to put an end to it. The last thing they needed was to let this thing between them turn sexual. Yes, it would have been incredible between them, had they succumbed to what they had both so clearly wanted to do last night. But it also would have been pointless. And it would have made things unbelievably awkward with the case they still had to solve. So Sam had resolved upon going to bed that he'd keep a lid on his urges and impulses from here on out. Hell, he still didn't know what had possessed him to reach out to her the way he had. And then to kiss her. And undress her. And fill his hand with her warm, sweet, luscious breast.

Oh, man, he really didn't want to talk about this right now. Because talking about it made him think about it. And thinking about it made him want to do it again. Only this time, he didn't want to stop right when they were getting to the good part.

"Look, Sam," Bridget said before he had a chance to say anything more, "last night we had wine at the symphony and then a nightcap when we got home. Obviously we overindulged."

Yeah, sure, he thought. Except that he'd been stone-cold sober when they arrived at the house, and had barely consumed two sips of his drink when they had come together. And Bridget had been as clearheaded as he was. Yeah, she'd sucked down the first few sips of her drink, but no way had she had time to become inebriated from it. She'd been as clearheaded as he when things had gotten out of hand. Into hand. Well, into *his* hand.

Dammit.

"We kissed," she said. But her voice sounded a little thready when she said it. "Big deal. It didn't mean anything."

"We did more than kiss," he told her, remembering the way her breast had fitted so perfectly in his hand. If he'd just had another minute, he would have had her dress completely down over her waist and hips, and she would have been half-naked in his arms, and it would have taken him no time at all to get himself half-naked, too, and then there would have been no turning back for either of them.

"Maybe," she conceded. But her voice was even softer, even less certain when she spoke this time.

Sam couldn't stand it. Maybe it was his masculine pride that piqued his irritation, or maybe he just didn't like hearing that he'd had such a lack of effect on a woman who'd affected him profoundly. In any event, before he could stop himself, he said, "I held your naked breast in my bare hand, Bridget."

He glanced over at her again and saw her close her eyes as a bright circle of pink blossomed on her cheek.

Turning back to look at the road again, he added, "And if you hadn't pulled away from me when you did, I would have had it in my mouth, too."

"Sam, don't—"

"And then I would have had other parts of you in my hand. And my mouth."

"Sam, please—"

"I wanted you so bad last night," he told her, all pretense gone now. Why the hell should he keep his thoughts tame when he and Bridget had been so wild the night before? "I wanted to peel that dress completely off your body and take you right there on the sofa."

"Sam—"

"And then again on the floor."

"Sam—"

"And then I would have carried you up to my bed and had you there, too."

"Sam, stop it."

"If you hadn't put a stop to things when you did, I would have. You know I would."

"You're skirting a sexual harassment charge here," she warned him.

"The hell I am," he countered. "There were two people being sexual last night. And there was no harassment involved."

She said nothing in response to that. Hell, what could she say? It was true. So Sam continued, "Where I come from, honey, if a man holds a woman's naked breast in his bare hand, it means something."

At first, he didn't think she was going to say anything in response to that, either. But when he turned again to glance at her, he saw that she was looking at him full on, and she didn't look away when he caught her eye.

"You know, that's the second time you've said something like that."

He turned to look back at the road, not sure what she meant. "What are you talking about?"

"That's the second time you've used the phrase, 'Where I come from.' You said the same thing when we were talking about the behavior of newlyweds."

"So?"

"So the first time you said it, I thought you did it because you wanted to put me in my place. Because you have some kind of hang-up about where I'm from, and the kind of life I've led."

"That's not true," Sam said.

"No, I realize that now," she agreed. "Because now that you've used it a second time, I realize you're speaking more about yourself than you are about me."

"Meaning?" he asked crisply, not sure he was liking where she was going with this.

"Meaning that maybe it's *you* who has some kind of hang-up about where you come from and the kind of life you've led."

Sam gritted his teeth. She was as wrong about that as she'd been when she'd thought he was trying to put her in her place. He loved where he came from. And he was proud of his background.

"I don't have any hang-ups about where I come from," he said adamantly. "In fact, I'm so proud to call my old neighborhood home that I still live in the house where I grew up. I bought it from my folks after my dad retired and they moved south." He threw her a meaningful look before returning his attention to the road ahead. "I didn't run thousands of miles away to escape where I come from, like some people do. And I didn't have to be dragged back to my roots against my will because my family was in trouble."

"Okay, point taken," Bridget said stiffly.

But Sam wasn't finished yet. "The place where I grew up is full of warm, wonderful people. Real people. People who understand what life is truly all about."

"Meaning the place where I grew up is full of phonies," she translated coolly.

"Not phonies," Sam corrected her. "But not real, either. I don't mean that as an insult," he hastily added, surprised to realize he was speaking the truth. "I just mean that the lifestyle you knew growing up wasn't anything like what the average person experiences. You never had to do without anything, Bridget. You had every opportunity, every advantage, every privilege. Dispute it all you want, but you know it's true. You didn't have to fight for anything when you were a kid, and you weren't denied anything. So you learned early on to believe you could always have things your way. And that just isn't true. For anyone."

"You're changing the subject," she said.

"I thought that was what you wanted," he told her. "And besides," he added before she had a chance to comment, "I want to make it clear to you how wrong you are about me." *In a lot of ways,* he couldn't help thinking. But for now, he'd focus on this one. "I love where I come from. I love Portland. I love the working-class neighborhood where I grew up. I'm proud that my father and mother raised two kids on the meager salaries earned by a mail carrier and a school secretary, and sent them to the colleges of their choices. I like going home at night to a snug, two-bedroom bungalow that could use a few improvements I'll get around to making someday.

I like going to Foley's Pub, three blocks away from my house, with friends on the weekends. I like watching the Blazers and the Hawks and the Beavers on TV, or from the cheap seats if I can get tickets. I like hiking in Bonnie Lure Park and kayaking the Willamette. If I never set foot outside of this city again for the rest of my life, I'll still die with a smile on my face. Working-class Portland is my home, Bridget. It's where I'm from, and where I live. It's in my blood. It's me. And I wouldn't have it any other way."

She said nothing for a moment, and when Sam stole another glance at her, he saw that she had turned her head to look out the passenger-side window at the swiftly passing scenery. He didn't think she was going to say any more, so he returned his attention to the driving.

She'd missed the whole point of his spiel, he thought. She probably hadn't heard a word of it. And why would she care, anyway? he asked himself further. She wasn't going to hang around his town any longer than she had to.

They drove in silence for a few minutes, and then, very softly, Sam heard Bridget say, "I don't believe I can always have things my way."

Something in her voice told him she knew that was true. Nevertheless, he said quietly, "Don't you?"

"No. I don't."

He nodded, but kept his gaze fixed on the road.

"And I wish I had roots as deep as yours," she added, her voice still quiet. "I wish I belonged somewhere the way you do."

Sam opened his mouth to ask her what she meant— hell, she belonged right where she was, living the life she'd made clear was what she'd mapped out for herself—but she halted his question by speaking again.

"Anyway, we're not going to talk about what happened last night," she said again. "Because it *won't* be happening again."

"Bridget—"

"No, Sam," she said more forcefully now. "What happened last night happened because we're both a little overwrought these days, feeling frustrated about this case."

"Bridget—"

"And okay, speaking for myself, anyway," she continued relentlessly, picking up steam, "it's been a while since I've…you know…been with anyone."

"Bridget—" he tried again.

"And I admit I find you attractive. But that doesn't mean—"

"Bridget!"

"What?"

He turned to look at her again, and he tried to smile, even though happy was the last thing he felt. He didn't want to hear such confessions from her. Probably because they sounded a lot like confessions he should be making himself. And Sam just wasn't the confessional type. "I think we just talked about it," he told her.

She blew out a long, exasperated breath, then chuckled a little nervously. "Yeah, I guess we did," she said, sounding surprised by the realization. "And now, please, let's be finished with it, okay?"

He nodded reluctantly, but couldn't let it go just yet. "I just need to add one last thing, though," he said.

She sighed heavily again. "What?"

"I agree with you about it not happening again," he said. Even though he wasn't sure he agreed with that at all. It wasn't that he didn't want it to happen again. On the contrary, it was going to be a while before the memory of her tongue tangling with his and her naked breast in his bare hand left him.

Hell, who was he kidding? He'd remember those things for the rest of his life. And he'd probably get hard every time. But he would do his best not to think about it. And he would make damned sure it didn't happen again.

"Let's just try to give each other a lot of space when we're at home alone, okay?" she said.

Sam nodded. A lot of space. Sure. They could do that. He just hoped removing themselves to different parts of the big house would be enough. Because, speaking for himself, it would take moving Bridget to the South Pole and himself to the North before he could even think about not wanting her.

He hoped like hell that their guy at Children's Connection showed himself soon.

When all was said and done, Charlie Prescott was a pretty weasely, mean-looking character. Everett didn't know why he hadn't noticed that before. Probably because he'd been sitting in a dark bar having a drink on his way home from work, and Charlie had made a point of seeing to it that Everett had had another drink. Then another. And another. By the end of that first evening with him, Everett could have been told that Charlie looked like Marilyn Monroe, and he would have believed it.

Of course, his willingness to trust and like Charlie was probably as much a result of his lifelong loneliness as it was his temporary inebriation. Everett hadn't had many friends growing up—or any, really—and he'd been so grateful for Charlie's fellowship that he'd let himself believe it had only come about because he genuinely liked Everett. He should have known better. Because now he understood that what he'd thought was Charlie being his friend was only Charlie manipulating him. Using him. It wasn't because Charlie liked him. No one had ever liked Everett. Well, until Nancy. But if she found out about all the things he had done, she'd want no part of him, either.

And now it was too late for Everett to undo all the things he'd done. He'd even done things that, if discovered, could send him to jail. Despite his realization that Charlie had only befriended Everett because he wanted something he couldn't get by himself, Everett was powerless to sever his ties to the man. He was in way too deep. And even though he now knew Charlie to be someone capable of murder, Everett still couldn't break free of the man, because Charlie was blackmailing him now, reminding him that if Charlie—otherwise known as the Stork—got caught, he'd take Everett down with him. And if Everett tried to leave town, Charlie had promised to frame him for everything that had happened, including the attempt on Nancy's life. He'd sworn he would pin all the crimes on Everett alone. And Everett didn't doubt for a moment that Charlie would—and could—do it.

Everett's only hope now was to try and bargain his way out of his relationship with Charlie in whatever way he could. Then he'd try to do the right thing from here on out, live a decent life and hope like hell no one ever found out about his involvement in the black-market baby ring and everything else.

He only hoped Charlie *would* let him bargain his way out of the relationship. Because Everett didn't want to be part of this anymore.

He would do anything to be able to turn back the clock to that first night at the bar when, too drunk to know any better, he'd told Charlie about the realization he'd made while working in the accounting office at Children's Connection. About how the clients the Connection had turned away might potentially be gold mines, desperate to start families in whatever way they could. There were so many babies out there being born to women who couldn't afford them or didn't want them, he'd mentioned casually, and it would be so easy to match them up with people who had enough money— and desperation—to pay top dollar for them, no questions asked. And it would be a piece of cake to make those bartered babies look like legitimate adoptions, too, Everett had told Charlie that night. If someone had the right connections…

Little had Everett realized then that Charlie had had those connections. And he'd wasted no time in urging Everett to join him in such an enterprise. At first, Everett had naturally balked, had known it was unethical, illegal and immoral. But Charlie had sweet-talked him into believing it was a noble thing to do, matching up unwanted children with people who would love them and care for them. Those bartered babies would have much better lives as a result of Charlie's and Everett's efforts. They'd be with people who wanted them, not mothers and fathers who would, at best, neglect them and, at worst, hurt them.

And Charlie, like Everett, knew what it was to be neglected and hurt by his parents. He'd told Everett about his own past, about how he himself had been an adopted child, united with his parents by none other than Children's Connection. But Charlie's parents, like

Lester and Joleen Baker, hadn't been good people. And like Lester and Joleen, they'd mistreated their son. Charlie's parents had been even worse than the Bakers, Everett knew.

Of course, now that Everett could look back on the conversation where Charlie had revealed all that, he understood that much of Charlie's motivation had come about because he wanted revenge. Revenge on Children's Connection for allowing him to be adopted as an infant by such unfit parents. It was Charlie who had maliciously switched the sperm vials so that two innocent women—maybe more, who knew?—became pregnant by men they hadn't approved as fathers. And it was Charlie who'd stolen the fertilized eggs and sold them on the Internet. Everett hadn't known about those acts until it was too late to do anything about them. But now that he understood the full extent of Charlie's viciousness, he knew he needed to get away from the man.

It didn't matter that Charlie's childhood had been as bad as, or even worse than, Everett's. That didn't excuse him for doing all the terrible things he had done. And it didn't excuse him for luring Everett—stupid, unwitting Everett—into his schemes.

Still, it had been Charlie's sob story about his past, and his assurances that he and Everett could prevent any more children from experiencing such hurt themselves, that had ultimately swayed Everett. He knew what it was like to be unwanted by one's parents, understood neglect better than anyone. In his inebriated state, he'd told himself that the end justified the means. And that if he and Charlie didn't undertake such an enterprise, someone else would. And that someone else might not be as caring as Everett and

Charlie were. Their intentions might not be as good. Even when he'd sobered up the next day, Everett had convinced himself that no one would be hurt by what Charlie had proposed.

But people had been hurt. And Everett had discovered, too late, that some of the babies Charlie had "acquired" for parents here in the U.S. had been taken from mothers in Russia and other countries who didn't want to give them up. What Everett had told himself was a noble enterprise was actually nothing more than a way for greedy men to line their pockets. Charlie *was* someone who didn't care, someone whose intentions weren't good. And now Everett was someone like Charlie.

But even more stupid than discussing with Charlie how money could be made through Children's Connection, in an effort to show off that first night, to make Charlie like him even more, Everett had told Charlie who he really was—Robbie Logan. And now Charlie used that, too, to keep Everett in line. He'd threatened to tell Leslie and Terrence about Everett's true identity, and what kind of criminal he'd become. And Everett couldn't have the Logans finding that out. They would have been so disappointed in him. They'd already had their hearts broken once, and it was all his fault. No way did he want them to be hurt all over again.

Oh, why hadn't he just kept his mouth shut that night? he asked himself as he waited in the same bar for Charlie, who had called him at the office earlier and demanded they meet. Being an accountant suited Everett well. It was quiet, solitary work that kept his mind occupied and off matters he'd rather not think about. Being a criminal did not suit Everett at all. But then, he hadn't set out to be a criminal. No, he'd only wanted to make a friend. Which was ironic, because these days, he felt more alone than ever.

"So you showed up after all."

Everett turned on his bar stool to see Charlie standing behind him, the pale yellow light of the bar making him look even more menacing than usual. Which was odd, because Charlie wasn't a big man. Even though he and Everett stood eye to eye at five-ten, the other man seemed much smaller, because he was so was scrawny and slope-shouldered. His features, too, were small, his eyes dark and beady, his lips thin and drawn. He dyed what little hair he had a shade of brown that looked anything but natural, and topped it with a cheap toupee that looked worse than no hair at all would.

Still, Everett knew the Stork considered himself to be quite a looker. Evil, he supposed, was as blind as love.

"Why did you want to see me?" Everett asked without preamble.

Charlie smiled unctuously. "What? Aren't you going to buy a drink for your old friend?"

"You're not my friend," Everett said, a splash of heat washing his belly at his own defiance.

Charlie pouted like a debutant. "Why, Everett, don't you realize it by now? I'm the only friend you do have." He sat down on the stool next to Everett's and dragged it close. Too close. Everett had to tamp down the urge to lean away from the other man. "And that," Charlie said in a low, dangerous voice, "is why you'll do exactly as I tell you to do."

Everett's heart hammered hard in his chest. He really hated Charlie. "That's not why I do what you tell me to do."

Now Charlie grinned his greasy grin again. "Then it

must be because you realize that your life as you know it will be over if you don't."

Everett said nothing. What, after all, was there to say?

Charlie ordered a drink and told the bartender to put it on Everett's tab. When the bartender glanced at Everett for his okay, he nodded reluctantly, then heard Charlie chuckle with much satisfaction. The two men sat in silence until the bartender returned with the bourbon straight up, and after Charlie had enjoyed his first sip, he turned to Everett.

"Have you taken care of Nurse Nancy?" he asked.

Everett wanted to slug the other man for using his own endearment for Nancy, especially since when Charlie said it, it sounded like an insult. After he'd chased Charlie from Nancy's apartment that night he'd tried to kill her, Everett had managed to convince him that it wouldn't be necessary to return for Nancy, that Everett would be able to discredit anything she might say that would incriminate him or Charlie. He'd had to say something to keep Charlie from going after Nancy again. And so far, Charlie had left her alone.

"I told you I'd take care of it," Everett said levelly.

"Just see to it that you do." Charlie said. Lowering his voice, he added, "And in the meantime, I've got another job for you."

"I don't want any more of your jobs," Everett muttered, surprising himself with his defiance. He'd just had enough, that was all. Enough of Charlie and his vengefulness and his viciousness. "I don't want to do this anymore, Charlie," he said. "I want out."

"Out?" Charlie echoed incredulously. "You can't get out of this, Everett. You're in too deep, you're over your head and suffocating."

Not yet, he wasn't, Everett countered to himself. Yes, he'd done things he shouldn't have, but he hadn't sunk as low as Charlie had. Everett hadn't hurt anyone, or worse, tried to kill anyone. There was still a chance, if he got himself out of Charlie's clutches, that he might be able to start anew. He could forget about what had happened, what he'd done, and go in a new direction. With Nancy. There was still a chance he could make things work with her. If he washed his hands of Charlie once and for all.

"I want out," he said again. "Just leave me alone, Charlie. Find another patsy to do your dirty work. I won't say a word to anyone about you or your baby-selling operation. If you'll just let me be, I'll pretend I never saw you."

At first Charlie said nothing in reply to Everett's petition, and Everett thought—hoped—the other man would just slink away, and that would be the end of it. But then Charlie started to chuckle, an evil menacing sound. And then he began to laugh, a sound that was even worse.

"You'll pretend you never saw me?" he repeated through his laughter. "Oh, that's rich. Like I believe that."

"It's true," Everett said. But his assurance sounded anything but reassuring, even to his own ears.

"Forget it," Charlie said. "Even if I did believe you, you've become too important to this operation for me to let you leave it."

"You'll find someone else," Everett said.

"The hell I will," Charlie retorted. "And why should I try, when I have you all trained just the way I need?"

"I want out, Charlie," Everett said again. ·

"Well, that's too damned bad. You're not going

anywhere. You know too much, and you're too important. And I have a job that needs doing *now*."

Everett swallowed hard and squared his shoulders, sitting up as straight as he could on the bar stool. With all the courage he could muster, he said, "What if I refuse to do it?"

There was an eerie silence from Charlie again, but it wasn't followed by laughter this time. No, this time it was followed by a very softly, very scarily uttered, "Then I might have to do something you wouldn't like."

Heat splashed through Everett's belly, and his shaky bravado evaporated. "What do you mean?"

Charlie's smile was nothing short of malevolent. "Well, for instance, it would be a shame if anything happened to your long-lost sister, wouldn't it?"

Everett felt himself pale. "I don't have a long-lost sister," he said, even though he knew exactly who Charlie was talking about.

"Sure you do," Charlie countered. "Bridget Logan Jones. She married herself a man who's even richer than her family is. Why, he can give her anything she wants. Except a baby. So they're on the waiting list to adopt one from Children's Connection. I've been watching her since she showed up. She's a pretty little thing, isn't she? Maybe I could give her that baby she wants. And not by selling it to her, either."

With every new word Charlie spoke, Everett's stomach burned hotter. Bridget Logan Jones. Robbie Logan's sister. *His* sister. By blood if nothing else. Everett had glimpsed her a few times at the Connection since her return to Portland, but he hadn't had the nerve to approach her. She resembled Leslie Logan in many ways, was graceful and elegant like her mother. She seemed as nice as Leslie, too, and had the same smile. Like everyone else at the Connection, he'd heard about her recent elopement and the newlyweds' desire to start a family. From what Everett knew about her, he liked Bridget. And he hated it that Charlie had taken such a sick, twisted interest in her.

"You wouldn't dare hurt her," Everett said, even though he was confident of no such thing. There was no telling what Charlie would do.

"Oh, wouldn't I?" Charlie replied. "Forget about making a baby with her. It might even be kind of fun to take Bridget Logan out of the picture altogether. Hurt the Logans the way they hurt me by letting their precious Children's Connection place me with the god-awful parents I had."

Take Bridget Logan out of the picture, Everett repeated to himself, nausea rolling in his belly now. Surely Charlie didn't mean he would kill her? But then, hadn't he tried to kill Nancy? He was totally capable of murder.

"Yeah, it's exactly what you're thinking." Charlie said as the revolting thoughts unrolled in Everett's head. "If you try to weasel your way out of this operation, Everett, you'll read about your sister's death in papers." He leaned forward, his mouth close to Everett's ear now, his breath hot and sour as he added in a malicious whisper, "But I promise I won't kill her until after I've had a little fun with her."

Everett squeezed his eyes shut tight at the other man's repugnant promise. Oh, God, Charlie would do it, too. He'd hurt Bridget Logan in the worst possible way, and then he'd dump her body someplace for the authorities to find, the way they'd discovered what they thought was Robbie Logan's body nearly thirty years ago. The Logans would have to relive the horror of losing a child all over again. And just like before, it would be all Everett's fault.

No, he decided then, his eyes snapping open. No more. Not again. This ended now. It had to. Whatever Charlie asked him to do, Everett would do it. But he'd make sure it was the last job Charlie ever assigned to him. And he'd make sure it was the job that took Charlie Prescott *down.*

"All right," Everett said. "Tell me what you want me to do."

"You'll do what you always do," Charlie told him. "The way we always do it. But this time we're offering a group discount. We're going to approach more than one couple with our usual spiel. There's been so much heat at the Connection since this investigation started that we've got sniveling little brats backed up in the pipeline. And since we haven't been able to move 'em, we're running out of money. So tomorrow you'll go into that social worker Reiss's office, and you'll pull some files that look promising, and you'll copy 'em. And then, when we get all our ducks in a row, you'll contact some of those poor schmucks who want to start a family and tell them you have just the kid they're looking for. Though God knows why they'd want to ruin their lives that way. Ask me, families don't bring nothin' but trouble and misery."

As much as Everett wanted to argue with that, he kept his mouth shut. Not every family was damaged, he knew. In spite of his own experiences—and Charlie's— there were plenty of families out there that were happy and well-adjusted. Like the Logans, he couldn't help thinking. And he, for one, wanted to make sure they stayed that way. So he'd do what Charlie instructed him to do, the way he always did. This time, though, Charlie wouldn't dictate the outcome.

Because this time Everett had something else entirely in mind....

Eight

The week following Bridget and Sam's first attempt at being newlyweds about town, they widened their net, inviting guests to their home and visiting local restaurants and events that were magnets for Children's Connection employees. Everywhere they went they did their best to pick up any new information that might aid in the investigation. And although they did learn things here and there that broadened the investigation, they still had nothing solid to point directly to any one individual.

What was almost worse, though, for Bridget, was that the more time she spent with Sam, pretending to be his wife, the more she found herself enjoying his company. Despite the antagonism of their initial meeting and the ensuing days, and despite the brief awkwardness that had followed their embrace the night of the symphony, she discovered that she really did like Sam very much.

Not just as an agent, but as a person. And, regrettably, as a man. He was smart and focused and hard-working, never mind extremely easy on the eye, and with each new day she spent in his presence, she found herself looking forward to the next with happy anticipation.

And she called herself every kind of fool for doing it.

Although they tried to keep their distance from each other when they were home together, they found themselves gravitating toward each other anyway. Bridget had discovered while trying to find ways to kill time that she enjoyed cooking, and she was often in the kitchen when Sam came home from work. That always led, naturally, to her extending an invitation to him to join her for dinner—hey, it was the polite thing to do, right?—because she seemed incapable of cooking enough for only one. After all, who wanted to cook for only one person when you'd just discovered you enjoyed cooking? And Sam, too hungry to decline the invitations, invariably accepted. And then the next night, he'd insist on cooking for her to return the favor. Then she'd want to return his favor, and the cycle continued.

And there were evenings, too, when Bridget strode into the living room with a book in one hand and a beer in the other, only to find Sam already parked on the couch with a book and a beer of his own. And although she always excused herself to find another place to read, he told her not to be silly, that they could certainly both sit in the same room. It wasn't as if one of them was composed of matter and the other of antimatter, so they wouldn't spontaneously combust. What harm could come of it?

Lots, Bridget would discover when she went to bed that night and dreamed about other things the two of them could do, sharing that couch together.

And every morning, upon waking from such dreams, she had to remind herself that, in spite of the way they had turned to each other on the night of the symphony, Sam didn't feel about her the way she found herself feeling about him. He was too cool, too casual, too collected—too professional—for him to still be entertaining memories or fantasies about that night. To him, it had been a physical exchange and nothing more, brought on by the anxiety and concern he felt for the case. And although Bridget tried to tell herself it hadn't been anything more than that for her, either, deep down she had to admit that the reason she had allowed things to go so far that night was because she had, even then, begun to care for Sam in a way she really shouldn't.

And that feeling only grew with each new day.

She noted thankfully that Sam evidently didn't reciprocate her feelings. She told herself this was actually a good thing, because even if the two of them started something here, they'd have to finish it here, too. Bridget wasn't going to stay in Portland any longer than it took to wrap up this case. And Sam had made it abundantly clear that he loved calling Portland home and couldn't imagine living anywhere else. Plus, she had to admit, they were too different from each other in too many ways. Yes, there was a definite physical attraction, and yes, they liked each other. But that wasn't enough to build a lifelong commitment on. And Bridget didn't want a lifelong commitment anyway. And neither, she was certain, did Sam.

Still, telling herself all those things didn't make it any easier to be with him. Because whenever she was with him, she wanted to, you know, *be with him*. And she knew that would never happen.

So it was with no small amount of trepidation that Bridget looked forward to their arrival at Tanglewood Country Club for the reception her mother had organized for the happy newlyweds and to which she had invited virtually everyone she knew from Children's Connection. Tonight, as they had done on so many occasions already, she and Sam were going to have to put on a show to convince other people that they were a loving couple who couldn't keep their hands off each other. And Bridget, for one, was beginning to feel like an even bigger fraud than she was.

Because for the people who didn't know she was part of an investigation, she was pretending to be something she wasn't—married and looking to start a family. And for the few people who *did* know she was part of the investigation, she still felt like an impostor, because lately she was interested in a lot more than just the investigation. She was interested in Sam. She was beginning to feel as if, since returning to Portland, her life had become a blend of two fantasies, neither of which felt quite right. When she put them together, though, something about them just felt…right.

It was the weirdest thing.

She told herself not to think about it as Sam rolled the big black Mercedes to a halt at valet parking at the country club, made herself remember what she used to do whenever she felt nervous those first few times when she went into the field. She reminded herself that in many ways what she was doing was just playing a game. *The Newlywed Game,* she couldn't help thinking, trying to cheer herself up. So what if the stakes were higher than they'd been on that old show from her childhood? So what if she and Sam were playing not for a bedroom suite and new carpeting, but the capture of a criminal who was bartering in human life? She was up to this task. More than up to it. She'd been trained for it. Hey, this case was lightweight compared to some of the others she'd been a part of in the past.

So why did this one make her so much more nervous? she wondered. So much more shaky? Why did it feel as if so much more than a black-market baby ring were on the line? Why were there times when it almost felt as if her very life was at stake?

Because, she immediately answered herself, it wasn't the case causing her to feel anxious and fearful.

"Ready to play?" Sam asked from the driver's seat as they waited for the valet.

Play, Bridget repeated to herself. Now there was a word that had way too many implications. "I'm ready," she told him. She just didn't tell him what she was ready for. Frankly, she didn't know.

"Then let's do it," he said.

Oh, she really wished he'd used some other phrase than "do it." Nevertheless, she inhaled a deep breath and, when the valet opened her door for her, exited the car, checking her attire as she emerged. But her black chiffon cocktail dress with its beaded straps looked fine, so she waited for Sam to hand off his car keys to the teenage attendant, then tucked her black satin evening bag into one hand and looped her other arm through the one he crooked for her when he came up alongside her. He, too, was dressed very nicely for the evening, wearing a dark suit cut expertly to showcase his broad shoulders and trim waist, along with a white dress shirt and wine-colored silk necktie.

Very yummy, was all Bridget could think when she

looped her arm through his. Oh, all right, she could think of some other things, too, but they didn't bear repeating in polite and mixed company.

The country club was elegantly decorated for the event, with twinkling white lights in all the potted trees, colorful paper lanterns strung from the ceiling of the enclosed patio, and white linen tablecloths on all the tables. A quartet was playing lively jazz when they entered, and a handful of couples had ventured out to the dance floor. Bridget recognized her parents immediately, and then her brother Eric and his fiancée, Jenny, dancing close in spite of the fast number, and also David and Elizabeth. Peter and Katie were already there, too, standing off to one side, speaking to Katie's brother Trent. It was good to see Peter and Trent speaking so comfortably—even amiably. And Katie and Peter were obviously very much in love. At last, there had been an easing in the family rivalry.

Bridget smiled when she thought again about the marriage outbreak that seemed to have hit her family recently. Then she frowned when she realized the unions only seemed to apply to the male siblings. She and Jillian were still very much singletons. Which was precisely how Bridget, at least, wanted it to be. Right? Right.

But when she looked over at Sam, saw him lift a hand in greeting to someone and smile, her heart performed a funny little flip-flop in her chest, and she didn't feel anywhere near the certainty she once had about that decision. Why him? she asked herself, not for the first time. Why, of all the men with whom she'd come into contact over the years, did it have to be Sam Jones who'd made her question her convictions? And why, after making the decision to stay single, had she had to cross paths with him?

He must have felt her eyes on him then, because as he dropped his hand back to his side, he glanced down at her. And when he saw her expression, his smile fell, his expression turning serious, sober and very interested. "Nice music," he said, the light observation belying his somber appearance.

She nodded. "Yes, it is. I love jazz."

He tilted his head toward the dance floor. "Wanna?" he asked.

She arched her eyebrows in surprise. "Dance?" she asked, certain she must have misunderstood his intentions.

"Sure. Why not?"

Why not indeed? she asked herself. She was about to echo his own words and say, "Sure, why not?" but before she could get the words out, she heard someone calling her name. When she turned around, she saw her sister Jillian striding toward her, a glass of wine the only accessory to her simple black cocktail dress. Leslie Logan was with her, looking stunning in a cap-sleeved, cream-colored dress whose very plain design only made her appear that much more beautiful.

"I'm so glad you two are here!" Jillian said as she approached them, her voice a little louder than it needed to be. Bridget was beginning to wonder if maybe her sister's hearing was okay, but then Jillian added, "Usually *newlyweds* like yourself don't want to be out in a crowd, because *newlyweds* like yourself would rather be alone! Especially if those *newlyweds* are trying to start a family!"

Somehow, Bridget managed to refrain from rolling her eyes. When her sister drew close enough, though, she bent to whisper in Jillian's ear, "It's okay, Jillian. I think we've got the cover down solid."

"Well, I was just trying to help," Jillian whispered back.

But not, evidently, quietly enough for Sam not to overhear. Because he smiled and said, "And we appreciate it, Ms….ah, Jillian," he quickly corrected himself.

Jillian smiled knowingly. "See? You two need all the help you can get. Stop acting so stiff."

Bridget's mother nodded her agreement, then gestured toward the dance floor. "Go out there and enjoy yourselves."

Sam's expression was philosophical. "Shall we?"

And just as Bridget was about to say yes, she was joined by her brothers and sister-in-law and sister-in-law-to-be, who also wanted to know how the *newlyweds* were faring, and gosh, they were just glowing like *newlyweds,* and how was *newlywed* life treating them, anyway, and obviously the honeymoon wasn't over yet for the *newlyweds*. And although Sam managed to laugh off their ribbing good-naturedly, Bridget found herself blushing like, well…a *newlywed*.

It was like that for them much of the night. Every time Sam tried to get her out on the dance floor, they were interrupted by yet another well-wisher wanting to know how they were doing. Even when dinner was served, it posed no deterrent to the current of people who wanted to extend their congratulations. By the end of the evening, in spite of the bits of valid information cleared, Bridget was actually beginning to look at the dance floor rather longingly. It would have proved a nice escape from the probing eyes and questions that she had to duck or lie in response to. Only after the majority of party-goers had left did Sam finally approach her and ask her again, "Think we could get out onto the dance floor now?"

Bridget looked first one way, then the other, but no one seemed inclined to approach them. So she smiled, nodded and extended her arms toward Sam.

Just then the saxophonist of the quartet said, "Thanks very much, everybody! You've been a great crowd! Good night!"

And then Bridget's arms fell limply to her sides, but she couldn't help the chuckles that bubbled up from inside her. Sam laughed, too, then reached for her hand, threading his fingers through hers as if it were the most natural thing in the world to do.

"Come on," he said. "Let's go home."

And there was just something in the way he said it that made Bridget's heart hum happily inside her. So she smiled, nodded and said, "Yeah, let's."

And, strangely, home felt very much like home when they arrived there. Funny, Bridget thought, how that first night they'd been here, the place had seemed so overblown and excessive. She hadn't felt comfortable at all amid the luxury and opulence of the place. Normally, she didn't go in for that conspicuous consumption look. But it must have grown on her over the past few weeks, because passing through the back door and into the kitchen felt like the most normal, most natural thing in the world for her to do.

Automatically, she reached to her right and flicked on the lights without even having to look for the switch. Then she pushed the appropriate buttons on the security system without having to even think about what she was doing. Sam joined her, his arm brushing hers as he strode past, but where a few weeks ago he might have jumped away upon contact and apologized for touching her, he barely seemed to notice. He was too busy loosening his necktie and going to the refrigerator for a beer.

"Want one?" he asked as he pulled two longnecks out of the door.

"Sure," she told him, loving how comfortable everything felt all of a sudden, almost as if they were...well, married.

"You know, we never did have that dance we were supposed to have tonight," he said.

Until he said that. And then Bridget grew decidedly *un*comfortable.

He twisted the top off of one beer and handed it to her, and a quick thrill of electricity shot up her arm when his fingers made contact with hers. Okay, comfort zone definitely breached now, she thought. Next stop, Uneasy Street. Because the way Sam started looking at her just then...

She took the beer from him and enjoyed a long swallow, thinking it wasn't what she usually drank when dressed up, but somehow finding it perfectly appropriate for the occasion. "No, you're right, we didn't have our dance," she agreed after swallowing. "We were too busy being *newlywed*ded to death."

He smiled as he screwed off the top of his own beer with a pleasant-sounding hiss. "Your family and friends from Children's Connection mean well."

"True," she said.

But they'd all been just a little *too* gleeful in their newlywed name-calling, she added to herself. As if they really wanted the moniker to fit. But then, that was what always happened to people who found themselves in love and engaged and married. They suddenly wanted everyone else in the world to be in love and engaged and married, too.

And Bridget wasn't about to let herself fall in love. Not with Sam Jones. Hey, it was nothing personal. She wouldn't fall in love with anyone. She couldn't afford to. She had places to go, people to see, a career to build. Her life was clear across the country in Washington, D.C. If she had her way, her life would even be *out* of the country, thousands and thousands of miles from Portland. Yet Portland was the only place Sam would ever be happy. And that was great. For him. But Bridget had different plans for herself. It would be pointless to fall in love with a man like him.

When she looked at him again, it was clear that he wanted to say something more. His gaze was fixed on her face, and his lips were parted, as if he'd started to speak and then reconsidered. Bridget waited to hear what he would say, if he said anything at all.

And then she was astonished when she heard him murmur softly, "We could do it now, here."

Do it? she echoed to herself. *Now? Here? Do it?* But this was so sudden... Kind of...

Then she realized he was talking about their dance.

"Dance?" she asked. Just to be clear on the matter, of course.

He nodded. "Sure, why not?"

Why not indeed? she wondered. Gosh, maybe because, considering what had happened the last time they'd found themselves in each other's arms, it could only lead to trouble? That was a pretty good reason.

"Come on, Bridget, dance with me," he cajoled. And then he smiled again. "I'll go put on some music. Meet me in the living room. There's a pretty elaborate stereo system in there. Surely there's some music appropriate for the kind of dancing we want to do."

We? she wondered.

Dancing? she wondered.

Appropriate? she wondered.

Just what kind of dancing was he talking about? she wondered.

When had the earth shifted on its axis sending everything into another dimension? It hadn't been that long ago that the two of them were both stressing how they needed to keep their distance from each other. Now Sam was inviting her close again. And she was much too eager to get close to him. Just what was going on?

Before she had a chance to ask, he spun around and headed through the kitchen door toward the living room. Bridget didn't want to follow him, though, because the look on his face when he'd asked her—no, *told* her— to meet him in the living room had been very strange. Briefly, she pondered the possibility of fleeing through the back door, but then she had to ask herself why she would want to do something like that when it was raining outside, an environmental condition that wasn't exactly suited to her current mode of dress.

It was, however, well suited to doing things indoors. Like dancing, for instance. Among other things.

As if realizing that had somehow wreaked a magic incantation, the lights overhead in the kitchen flickered and then went out. She told herself it was only the fact that she didn't like being alone in the darkness that made her tiptoe cautiously toward the kitchen door and stealthily follow the route Sam had just taken. But halfway down the hall to the living room, she heard the sound of music. Soft music. Slow music. Music with lots of saxophones and a woman singing in a low, throaty voice. The kind of music that made people dance very, *very* closely together and think about things they probably shouldn't.

Gosh, had she thought she was scared of the dark? That was nothing compared to her fear of dancing.

She told herself it was only simple curiosity that made her continue. It was, after all, very nice music. And with the electricity out, it was magic music, because that elaborate stereo system in the living room couldn't possibly be working without a jolt of the ol' ac/dc. She just wanted to know how Sam had achieved music in such conditions. And she wanted to know who the artist was. Yeah, that was it. She might want to listen to it again someday. Someday when she had no desire to dance slowly with a very handsome man who had kissed her earlier and made her entire world go haywire.

When she entered the living room, though, she couldn't see a thing. Thanks to the rain outside, not even a glimmer of moonlight filtered through the windows. Bridget was about to call out to Sam, but a tiny burst of light near the fireplace suddenly flashed then calmed, and she saw he was lighting a fire that had already been laid in the hearth. Little by little, the tinder caught, and Sam became more visible with the leap of every new flame. He stayed crouched there until he was sure the fire was burning well, then straightened and lit two candles at one end of the mantelpiece.

In the fine amber light, his hair seemed to be tipped with gold, and his profile, which she had initially thought all strong planes and angles, softened some. He looked younger in the fainter light, less distant, more carefree. Less overwhelming, more approachable.

Less unattainable. More irresistible.

She honestly wouldn't have thought it possible for him to be more attractive, but in that moment, he was. Although Bridget had done her best to fight her attraction to Sam since the beginning of their assignment together, she hadn't been able, or even willing, to lie to herself. He was very, very attractive. Handsome, smart, interesting, confident, all the things she liked in a man. But he'd plastered Keep Away signs all over himself, and any woman could have seen he simply wasn't interested in getting involved in any sort of relationship. Which was fine with Bridget—she didn't want to get involved at this point in her life, either. That hadn't stopped her from finding him attractive, however. It had only stopped her from acting on that attraction. Now, though…

Now she wasn't sure she wanted to stop herself from acting. Worse than that, at some point in the evening, Sam seemed to have removed all of his Keep Away signs. And now she couldn't help wondering what else he wanted to remove. More to the point, she found herself wanting to remove a few things, too.

Oh, what could it hurt? she asked herself. He was a grown man, and she was a grown woman, and they naturally experienced all the impulses and desires any other adult human being experienced. They'd been on their own for years and had both been successful in steering their lives in the directions they'd mapped out for themselves. Neither of them was a trembling ingenue unschooled in the ways of the world and the whole man-woman thing. They were both obviously attracted to each other. They'd both had relations with other people.

If they felt desire for each other now, and yet neither wanted a long-lasting relationship, what problems could possibly arise if they responded to their impulses?

As if she'd asked the question aloud, Sam snapped his head up to look at her. But she stood in a pool of darkness on the other side of the room, far removed from the meager illumination of the fire and candles. She told herself he couldn't possibly see her expression or know what she was thinking. Somehow, though, he seemed to know exactly what she was thinking. Because his eyes found hers, even through the darkness, and he held her gaze captive as he began to stride slowly toward her.

"Looks like we lost the power," he said softly as he approached.

Oh, I wouldn't say that, Bridget thought. She was feeling all kinds of electrical surges herself. In spite of that, she concurred, "Looks like."

"Could be out all night," he added, taking a few more leisurely steps.

She nodded slowly. "It's possible."

"Whatever will we do to pass the time?" he asked, drawing nearer still. "I mean, what can two people do alone in the dark at night when there's no electricity?"

"And just where is that music coming from, if there's no electricity?" Bridget asked, telling herself she wasn't trying to change the subject. It was a legitimate question.

"Stop trying to change the subject," he said.

"It's a legitimate question," she replied.

He grinned. And took another step forward. "Part of the elaborate stereo system is a basic, garden-variety boom box," he told her. And took another step forward. "Batteries included."

"Oh."

"So we at least have music. That'll just make it more enjoyable to do the one thing I can think of that two people can do alone in the dark at night when there's no electricity."

Bridget swallowed with some difficulty and told herself to respond to the remark with something flip and carefree to alleviate the tension that suddenly settled over the room. But no words came to her rescue. All she could do was watch Sam, and the way he moved through the darkness, and note how the air seemed to grow warmer with every step he took.

Time seemed to stand still as he made his way toward her. And even though she told herself she still had time to make some lame excuse and flee to her room, she stood rooted in place, watching him come.

He just wants to dance, she reminded herself. That was what he had said in the kitchen. That was the one thing he could think of for two people to do alone in the dark at night when there was no electricity. The minute he pulled her into his arms, though, Bridget knew.

Sam was no more interested in just dancing than she was.

Nine

She realized Sam's intentions the instant he pulled her body against his and wrapped his arms around her, splaying his hands over her back. She felt the heat of his palms sear her through the thin fabric of her dress, remembered then that the only thing holding it up was two skinny straps that could be broken by the merest tug. Somehow, knowledge of that only made her heart race faster, though. Probably because she immediately began to fantasize what would happen if Sam did just that.

And those fantasies only multiplied and became more graphic when one of his hands began slowly to creep downward from her shoulder blade to her waist to the small of her back. And then lower still. So Bridget, in an effort to make it at least look like she was only interested in dancing, reached behind herself to impede his progress, curling her fingers firmly around his wrist and replacing his hand on her waist. But Sam obviously wasn't a man to be put off so easily, because he began the journey again with his other hand. So Bridget reached behind herself again with *her* other hand, repeating her actions, too.

Too late, she realized that in placing both of her hands behind her back the way she did, she left her front arching more completely—and more arousingly— against Sam, her breasts thrusting forward to skim against his chest, her torso pressing intimately into his. And, too late, she realized how her position left her almost entirely helpless to change that. Because before she had a chance to alter it, Sam was doing it for her, expertly flipping his hands over to wrap his fingers around her wrists and hold both of her hands in place, lightly imprisoning her against him.

And then he smiled. Salaciously. Even in the darkness she could see it.

"What are you doing?" she asked, hoping he didn't notice the way her heart had begun to pound, but thinking he probably did, since it was banging so hard against his own.

"Can't you tell?" he asked. He tightened his fingers around her wrists and, with a gentle push, crowded her body even more intimately against his. Now, though, Bridget could feel his heart pounding, too, and somehow, that made her feel better.

For all of a half second.

She realized that if his heart was pounding the way hers was, then he was as affected by their current position as she was. And that meant he was probably having the same thoughts that she was, and now there really would be nothing to stop them from carrying this through to its logical conclusion. Suddenly she didn't feel nearly as cavalier about that as she had only a few moments ago.

"Ah, no," she lied. Badly. "I have no idea what you're doing. I mean, I know you said you wanted to dance, but this isn't a step I'm familiar with."

"Yeah, well, it's a dance I haven't done myself for a while," he told her. "So I guess we'll just have to improvise some."

"I, uh…I'm not much good at improvisation," Bridget told him.

"I don't have any complaints so far," he said softly, dipping his head toward hers. "Besides, I'm *very* good at improvisation myself. I'll lead, and you can just follow along, okay?"

For one brief, delirious moment, Bridget thought he was going to kiss her, but he only rested his forehead lightly against hers. Then he began to sway their bodies slowly back and forth, keeping time with the mellow, jazzy music, and she had no choice but to follow him. Funny, though, she didn't mind following this time. In fact, she was kind of looking forward to seeing where he would lead her.

That wasn't quite right, she realized as she let herself relax against him. She did have a choice in the matter. And she chose to stay here with Sam. Because she wanted to. Because she needed to. Because she—

Well. Just because, that was all. And as far as she was concerned, it was a very good reason.

For a long time, they only moved slowly back and forth in time to the music, the rain pattering softly against the windows, the flames crackling and hissing in the fireplace, their feet scuffing lightly over the hardwood floor. One tune segued into another, each one more seductive than the one before. And with every new song, Bridget found herself nestling more deeply into Sam, looping her arms possessively around his neck, pressing her body more intimately into his. And he seemed in no way bothered by the closeness. On the contrary, he only made more room for her, adjusted his body so that the two of them fitted together even better and draped his arms around her, too.

As they danced, Bridget grew more and more aware that the soft friction of their swaying bodies was increasing, generating an enticing sort of heat. It began as a soft shimmer of warmth that curled indolently through her, then gradually, it escalated, threatening to become an urgent fever that demanded satisfaction. Sam must have become aware of it at the same time she did, because his hands began to move slowly over her body at exactly the same time hers began to wander over his.

When he pressed his hand into her back and let it drift lower, she moved hers to his chest and opened it over his heart. When he skimmed his fingers down over her hip to her thigh, she countered by raking her fingers over his shoulder and down one arm. When he curled his hand intimately over her thigh, she tucked her other hand beneath the fabric of his jacket and began to push it away from his shoulder. So Sam retaliated by dipping his hand to the hem of her dress and pulling it higher.

"I want you, Bridget."

The words seemed to come at her from a silvery mist, quiet and soft and shimmering. Unreal somehow, in spite of their heavy impact. And she was helpless not to reply, "I want you, too."

Her quiet words must have been all the encouragement Sam needed, because he dipped his head then, to the sensitive place where her shoulder joined her neck, nuzzling her throat softly with his nose before skimming his mouth lightly over it.

"Oh," Bridget cried softly at the caress. "Oh, Sam."

He had lifted her dress up over her thigh, halting at the lower curve of her derriere, but now he bunched the fabric in his fist and pushed it higher still, over the silky panties hugging her bottom. And as one hand rose, the other fell, until both were cupped over the elegant contours of her fanny. Instinctively, the lower half of Bridget's body surged forward with the contact, thrusting her against that part of him that had grown hard and heavy in response.

She gasped at the depth and swiftness of his reaction, and he covered her mouth with his, thrusting his tongue inside. Bridget's hand on his chest convulsed at the contact, then moved to join the other in divesting Sam of his jacket, which fell to the floor at their feet. Feverishly, she went to work on his buttons next, pushing each through its hole with a deftness that belied her nervousness about what was happening. Sam tore his mouth from hers, only to move it to her jaw, her neck, her cheek, her temple, driving his hands upward again, over her waist, her rib cage, to just beneath her breasts.

And then his hands were on her breasts, palming them through the fabric of her dress, first coddling then ravaging them before reaching behind her for the zipper. He had it down in no time, and was pushing at the garment to lower it over her waist and hips, and then her dress, too, was heaped on the floor at their feet. Bridget hadn't bothered with a bra or stockings tonight, so she stood before Sam in nothing but black silk panties and high heels, and there was something so acutely erotic about that, about him still being nearly fully dressed while she was nearly naked. She felt vulnerable, something she normally didn't like to feel. But she trusted Sam implicitly, and somehow, that made her embrace her vulnerability.

And then he was pushing at her panties, too, pulling them down, and Bridget was stepping out of them. She started to kick off her shoes, too, but Sam said, "Don't. Leave them on." The huskiness of his voice when he said it told her that he was every bit as aroused as she.

His order sent a thrill of something electric and wholly erotic through her. And she nearly burst into flames when he covered her mouth with his again and began to run his hands all over her naked body. He raked them up over her legs and hips, to the insides of her thighs, across her belly and ribs, along her bottom and back, tracing her spine and her collarbones and down over her breasts, where he held one reverently in each hand. And all the while he kissed her, passionately, deeply, until Bridget didn't know where her body ended and his began.

His shirt was hanging open by now, thanks to her nearly incoherent actions, over a broad, muscular chest covered with dark hair that seemed to be tipped in gold in the firelight. Bridget tore her mouth away from Sam's long enough to gaze down upon him, the sight of their bodies pressed together sending a thrill of heat rocketing through her. Like his, her body, too, seemed to glow in the warm illumination of the fire, and she felt herself grow warm from the inside out. She glanced past Sam then, toward the windows of the living room that looked out on the front yard.

"The windows," she hissed. "Someone will see us."

"No, they won't," he told her as he palmed her breasts. "There's not enough light. And the street is too far away."

"But—"

"Don't worry, Bridget," he told her. And then he lowered his head to one breast and traced its sensitive peak with the tip of his tongue, before opening his mouth over it and sucking it deep inside.

And then all Bridget could do was say, once again, "Oh, Sam."

After that, Sam took control of the situation, and Bridget eagerly surrendered to him. For long moments, he sucked on her breast, laving it with the flat of his tongue, teasing it with the tip, then switching to the other and treating it to the same delight. Bridget wound her fingers tightly in his hair and thrust herself forward, offering him freer access, even though he was taking what he wanted already. As he held one breast and pleasured it, he skimmed his other hand downward, over her torso and between her legs. Instinctively, she parted for him, knowing she was already dewy with her anticipation of his touch.

And touch her he did, dipping his fingers gently into the damp folds of flesh, caressing her, stroking her, exploring her and finally penetrating her with one long finger. Bridget cried out again at the invasion, but she moved her own hand down over his, guiding him in his exploration. Slow, then faster, soft, then hard. And deeper. Oh, so much deeper. *Yes, like that… Oh, Sam, yes… Yes…*

Together they brought her to her first climax, her entire body shuddering as she cried out her completion. Sam paused in his attentions to let her orgasm run its course, then, when her body relaxed some, pulled her more fiercely against him. He kissed her again, more deeply than before, then swept her up into his arms. Bridget closed her eyes and trusted him to take her wherever he wanted, knowing that no matter where it was, she would want, too. She wanted Sam. More than she'd ever wanted anyone. More than she'd ever wanted any*thing*.

She told herself the realization should terrify her. But somehow, it only made her feel very, very good inside. So she rested her head against his shoulder and didn't open her eyes again until he cleared the final step. Even in the darkness, she could tell he was smiling down at her, an errant strand of dark hair falling down over his forehead, just like Rhett Butler. He carried her to the bedroom he'd been using himself, finding his way through the darkness to the bed with no problem. There, he carefully laid Bridget upon it, then leaned over her and kissed her, long and hard and deep.

"I'll be right back," he said softly.

And then he was gone, and all she could do was wish him back. In the meantime, she fumbled with the bed-spread, sheets and blankets until she'd turned the bed down, and stretched herself out on her side. Her body was still humming in the wake of his earlier caresses, her skin so sensitive that even the cool kiss of the sheets aroused her.

Hurry back, Sam, she thought. *I miss you.*

As if her silent plea had summoned him, he appeared in the doorway, carrying the two lit candles from the mantel. "I was going to bring the music, too," he said, "but I didn't have enough hands."

Oh, Bridget didn't know about that. A few moments ago he seemed to have plenty of hands. "That's all right," she told him. "All I need is you. Please, Sam. Make love to me."

He strode across the room to place the candles on the dresser, then turned to look at Bridget, who patted the mattress beside her in invitation.

He smiled. "You still have your shoes on."

She smiled back. "I thought you wanted me to keep them on."

"I do. You look sexy as hell lying there."

"There's barely enough light to see me."

"Oh, believe me, I can see you just fine. And you look sexy as hell."

"You're not so bad yourself. Except for still being dressed."

He glanced down at his clothes, which, admittedly, were in a state of disarray, but were still on his person. "So I am."

"Take them off," she instructed him.

He grinned. "Yes, ma'am."

She grinned back. "I like the way you say that."

"Then I'll have to say it a lot."

"Which means I'll have to give you lots of orders."

"Which I will happily obey."

"Good. Take your clothes off. Now."

Without hesitation, Sam reached up to unbutton his shirt, realized belatedly that it was already unbuttoned, and shrugged it off. It glided to the floor soundlessly, and Bridget could only gaze upon him in wonder, at the generous thatch of dark hair that covered his torso, thinning as it speared into the waistband of his trousers. Muscles corded his abdomen and chest, and veins striped his shoulders and arms, bunching into noble ridges as he settled his hands on his waist.

Wow, she thought. That was all. Just…wow. "More," she told him.

Sam reached for the fly of his trousers and deftly, swiftly, unfastened it. Slowly, he peeled the garment down his legs, kicking it off when it reached his ankles. Then he straightened again and tucked his thumbs into the waistband of his boxers, on each side of his body. Bridget held her breath as he bent to skim those off, too, sucking in a sharp breath when he straightened. In the pale glow of the candle, he was magnificent, his lower body as firm and muscular as his upper body, his legs kissed with the same dark hair that decorated his torso. And there, at his center…

Oh, my.

She caught her breath at the sight of him, because that part of him was even more magnificent than the rest of him. And only then did she realize just how far over her head she had gotten with Sam Jones. Because he was way more man than she was used to dealing with. Physically, intellectually, emotionally, spiritually. And the thought of joining her body, her self, to his and to him just then was…

Oh, my.

She gulped in another breath, hoping it might slow the rapid-fire beating of her heart, but it came out sounding like a gasp. Which, when she thought about it, was maybe what it really was. Because he'd taken her by surprise, her Sam. And now he would take her even further.

When he heard her response, Sam grinned again, proudly this time. "I'll take that as a sound of approval," he told her.

She nodded slowly, but couldn't seem to form any words, as her mouth had gone completely dry and her brain had gone completely slack. She grew even more agitated as Sam began to walk toward her, striding across the big bedroom with utter confidence, clearly unconcerned that he was completely naked and thoroughly aroused. He halted by the bed and reached for her, his hand covering her breast possessively. Just like that, without preliminary or permission, as if he were simply claiming something that belonged to him.

And Bridget realized then that she did want to belong to Sam Jones. She'd been kidding herself earlier when she'd thought she could couple with him on a superficial, physical level and then just walk away. Because there was nothing superficial in her response to him. And it went way, way beyond the physical. *Take me,* she wanted to tell him. *Make me yours.*

And then she wanted to laugh at herself. She was already his, and she would remain his forever, whether he took what she offered him or not.

As if she had spoken her desire aloud, he lowered his body to the bed and lay beside her, the hand on her breast moving to her shoulder, urging her onto her back. And then he covered her, insinuating his thigh between hers, pressing his chest to her breasts, tangling his fingers in her hair as he covered her mouth with his own.

For a long time, they only lay there, Bridget supine with Sam's hot, heavy body atop hers, their mouths joining in the way their bodies soon would, exploring every inch of each other that their hands could reach. Heat shot through Bridget everywhere Sam touched her, every feverish sensation finding its way to her heart, where it gathered steam and exploded again, sending fire to her every extremity. And then Sam was pushing himself up and away from her, kneeling before her, one hand on each of her hips, gazing at her as if he had some serious plans for her.

Bridget bent one leg and started to hook it around his waist, but Sam caught it in his hand, circling his fingers firmly around her ankle. Then he reached for her other ankle and grasped it, too. The sight of her black high heels among their naked flesh aroused her all over again, especially when Sam moved her legs to his shoulders and began to lean forward again. As he drew nearer, he shifted her legs again, so that her knees were bent over his shoulders. But he moved in a way that lifted her hips from the bed, and he tucked his hands beneath her, catching her bare bottom in both hands. Then Sam was tasting the sensitive skin of her belly, and flicking his tongue over the indentation of her navel, making Bridget sigh in both delight and agitation. But no sooner did she start to enjoy her new position than Sam moved his hands between her legs, against the insides of her thighs, and pushed them open wide.

At first, Bridget didn't understand what he intended to do. And when she finally did, she tried to push her legs closed again. It was far too intimate a thing for him to do. She wasn't ready. She'd never...not with any man. But Sam halted her efforts.

"Let me do this for you," he murmured.

"Sam, no, it's too—"

"And let me do it for me, too," he added, grinning.

"Sam, no, I—"

And before she could utter another word of objection, he dipped his head between her legs, opening his mouth over that most sensitive part of her. He traced a lazy circle against her with the tip of his tongue before tasting her more deeply, then penetrating her. And then he did it all over again.

Bridget went absolutely still at the thrill that bolted through her when he began to savor her. She knotted her fingers in the pillow above her head, instinctively thrusting her hips upward, higher off the mattress. When she did, Sam caught her buttocks in both hands again, delving his fingers into the delicate cleft that separated them, penetrating her with one swift, deliberate finger. She jerked at the intrusion, then relaxed against him, unable to do anything but enjoy the feel of him against her and inside her. Again and again he tasted her, entered her, caressed and delighted her, until Bridget wasn't sure where she ended and Sam began.

She didn't know how long he continued his relentless pleasuring of her, only knew that eventually he moved back up her body, dragging openmouthed kisses all along her flesh as he went, pausing at her breasts to enjoy them as thoroughly as he had the rest of her. He moved away from her long enough to roll on a condom—and she was so incoherent by then that she didn't even care where it came from or that he'd had one ready, as if he'd expected this to happen all along. Then, vaguely, she registered him moving behind her, pressing his long body against hers from her shoulders to her calves. He opened one hand over her breast, the other over her belly, spreading his fingers straight enough to bury them into the soft thatch of curls between her legs. And as he pressed his mouth to the side of her neck, he pushed himself into her from behind, going deep inside, stretching her, filling her fuller than she'd ever felt before. And only then did Bridget realize how empty she had been before he came along.

"Oh, Sam," she murmured. "Oh, you feel so good."

"So do you," he murmured back.

And then words became unnecessary, because Sam began to move against her, inside her, going even deeper than before. He started with a lazy, even, confident pace, pulling out only far enough to propel himself in again with more force. Gradually, he increased his rhythm, doubling it, tripling it, the friction of their bodies moving against each other generating heat and so much more. A hot coil began to tense in Bridget's midsection, winding tighter and tighter until she feared it would explode. Just when she thought it would, Sam pulled out of her completely. She started to cry out an objection, but he only turned their bodies so that she was on her back, and he was covering her again. He braced one muscular arm on the mattress beside her, drawing her leg around his waist with the other. Bridget clung to him, curling her fingers around his nape, hooking her leg across his back.

He entered her again, faster this time, wilder, deeper. Again and again he joined his body to hers, until both of them were delirious with their hunger, their need. And as Bridget felt that coil inside her explode, Sam hurled himself against her one last time. Together, they cried out at the pleasure rocketing through them, then they collapsed against each other, panting for breath.

For long moments, they only lay there, each coming to terms with what had happened. It was Sam who finally moved first, pushing himself up onto his elbows to gaze down at Bridget's face. His gaze flew over every feature, as if he was mentally cataloging the way she looked just then. He seemed to want to tell her something, but he only shook his head slowly and smiled. Then he pressed his mouth to hers in a fierce kiss.

"That was incredible," he said.

And Bridget had to agree.

"I'll be right back," he added, rolling away from her.

The condom, she thought as she watched him walk toward the master bath. He had to dispose of that tidy modern convenience that had prevented pregnancy and the spread of disease. Too bad it hadn't prevented her from falling in—

Too bad it hadn't prevented her from caring so much for Sam Jones, too, she hastily amended.

Bridget closed her eyes and lay quietly on the bed, marveling at how very good she felt inside, in spite of the fact that she was already regretting what they had done. It was only going to complicate the investigation, she thought. It wasn't going to help anything at all.

Still, she thought as she began to doze off. She did feel very good....

When Sam eased into wakefulness in the twilit darkness of early morning, his first thought was that he felt very, very good. That must be because it was Saturday, he decided, and he didn't have to go to work. So since he felt very, very good and didn't have to go to work, he might as well go back to sleep. But then as he inhaled a deep, satisfied breath, reality hit. It wasn't Saturday. It was Friday. And the reason he felt so good was because he was holding a woman's breast in his left hand.

What the...?

And then he was wide awake.

Bridget, he remembered then. They had made love last night. Oh, boy, had they made love last night. And he had been the one to instigate it. All three times.

He waited for the crash of foolishness that was sure

to rain down upon him at the realization of what he'd done—what he'd allowed to happen. Waited to be overcome by the idiocy, the carelessness, the dereliction of duty. But really, all he felt was a sad sort of regret. Regret that he had succumbed to a simple weakness he would just as soon have pretended he didn't have— humanity. Or, even more specifically, masculinity. He was a man who had wanted something—someone—and he hadn't been strong enough to resist her. And now that he had enjoyed the pleasure of her company…

Well, truth be told, he wanted to enjoy it again. And again. He wanted to wake up this same way tomorrow morning. And the morning after that. Because as he lay there waiting for his thoughts to come, Sam realized that he didn't just feel very, very good. He felt excellent. Extraordinary. Sensational. Better than he could ever recall feeling. Waking up to find Bridget Logan in his arms, her warm, soft, naked body curling so naturally, so trustingly, into his, and remembering how the two of them had turned to each other during the night, and how incredible that had been… Well. Sam just found himself wanting to wake up that way every morning. For the rest of his life.

Which meant he had no choice but to end this now.

He had sworn he would never get involved with another rest-of-his-life thing again. One time had been more than enough for him. He refused to set himself up again for the same sort of treatment he'd received from his ex-wife. He might not be soured on women after that, but he *was* soured on lifelong forever-afters.

And even if he could find his way to lose the bitterness and risk his heart again, Bridget Logan wasn't the one who would be responsible for it. She could never be part of a lifelong forever-after with him. Not necessarily because he didn't *want* to include her in his life—though, really, this thing was still too new for him to know if that was true or not. But his opinion on the subject was immaterial. The fact was Bridget Logan didn't want to be part of his life. Yes, last night had been amazing. And yes, he was reasonably certain that she cared for him, too, because no two people could have responded to each other the way he and Bridget had last night without there being at least some small amount of affection involved.

But she'd made it clear she wouldn't be hanging around Portland any longer than it took to haul in whoever was trying to bring down the organization her family held near and dear. Hell, the only reason she was even in Portland was because the FBI had dragged her here against her will. As soon as they wrapped up this case, she'd be hitting the road again, and she wouldn't stop until she was at least a continent away, back in D.C., where she'd been living since she left home to go to college. And if she had her way, she'd end up even farther away than that, back in Europe, or some other exotic destination, where she could pursue the dream of her career.

Bridget Logan might be a Portland native, but she wasn't a Portland girl. And Sam hadn't been exaggerating when he'd told her Portland was in his blood. He was a fourth-generation Oregonian. Leaving this state would be like leaving a piece of himself behind.

So he'd have to leave Bridget instead. Or, at the very least, watch her go.

As if he'd spoken the thought aloud, she began to stir next to him then, waking even more slowly than he had himself. The soft squirming of her body against his made Sam go hard all over again, but the reminder of his decision put his arousal to a swift end. Still, she did feel very good lying against him, soft and warm and sweet-smelling....

She went utterly still, and Sam knew she was making the same realization that he had already made himself, that the two of them were lying naked in bed together after having spent the night coupling in the most basic, most erotic way two human beings could. And he couldn't help wondering if her other thoughts were mirroring his, too, about how this had to be the first and last time something like this happened, because there couldn't possibly be any future in it, and to pursue it might be enjoyable for now, but it would only hurt them both in the long run.

Sam made himself roll away from her, to give her what little space he could, then he lay on his back on the opposite side of the bed, staring up at the ceiling. "Good morning," he said. But his voice came out sounding flat, lifeless. Probably because that was how he was suddenly starting to feel inside.

She didn't say anything at first, only continued to lie silently with her back to him, and Sam wished like hell he knew what she was thinking. On second thought, maybe he didn't, he hastily amended. It would probably only make things that much more difficult.

"Morning," she finally said.

It didn't escape Sam's notice that she'd left off the "good" part of his greeting. Yep, he definitely didn't want to know what she was thinking. Especially since she still had her back turned to him. They lay there in stilted silence for a few more moments, until Sam couldn't stand it any longer. They couldn't lie here forever, hoping neither would notice the other was naked or remember how they'd spent the night. Might as well just get it over with.

So he said, "You okay?"

He glanced over at her and saw her nod. Sort of.

"Yeah," she said softly. "I'm fine."

"Wanna talk about it?"

"I guess we should," she conceded.

"You first," he said, shamelessly bailing out of his responsibility, since he was the one who'd brought it up. Uh, no pun intended.

She hesitated another moment, then finally turned to look at him. But where Sam was lying with the sheet down around his waist, feeling unmindful, really, about the fact that he wasn't wearing any clothes, Bridget tugged both sheet and blanket up over her shoulders before lifting her gaze to his face.

"I didn't dream it then, did I?" she asked.

He gave her what he hoped was a reassuring smile. "That good, was I?"

She smiled back and chuckled once, but the sound was nervous, anxious. "It was very nice," she said.

Okay, so she wasn't going to be emotionally scarred for life, he thought wryly. Still…*very nice?* That was all it was to her? "Then I guess I wasn't that good," he translated.

"No!" she said, sounding distressed now.

"That bad?"

Finally she laughed, and it sounded almost genuine. "No, I didn't mean 'No, it wasn't very nice.' I meant, 'No, that's not what I meant.'"

"Then what did you mean?"

She expelled a heavy sigh and smiled again, a little more convincingly. "It was wonderful," she told him.

That's more like it, Sam thought.

"And it was magical," she added.

Damn straight.

"And it was unlike anything I've ever experienced before."

Ditto.

"But Sam," she said, sitting up a little straighter and bringing the sheet and blanket with her, "it can't happen again."

Right.

She hurried on before he had a chance to comment. "It's just that I don't think it's a good idea with things the way they are. I mean, we're working together, and it's an important case, and we need to focus on that. Not anything else."

He nodded. "I agree."

He thought she'd be happy and relieved to hear him say that, but her expression fell, as if that hadn't been what she'd expected him to say at all. Or had hoped he wouldn't say.

"This case is too important to screw it up," he said, still agreeing with her. "And what happened last night…" This time Sam was the one to sigh heavily. "Well, hell, Bridget, I don't know why it happened."

Which was a lie, of course. He knew damned well why it had happened. Because Bridget had looked beautiful and desirable, and ever since that night of the symphony—no, long before that, even—he'd wondered what it would be like to make love to her. He'd relived that one kiss they'd shared so often—in both his conscious and unconscious mind—and every time, he'd allowed himself to carry it further than it had actually gone. He'd made love to Bridget dozens of times in his head. And he'd wanted, for once, to let the rest of his body know what it would be like.

He'd wanted her. It was that simple. And last night, for some reason, he just hadn't been able to resist her.

Now, though, what he said was, "I guess both of us have just been a little high-strung lately, worrying about the case. And when tensions rise that high, they have to be released somehow. And if they can't be released by making progress on the case, then they have to find another outlet." He met her gaze levelly. "Do you agree?"

She didn't respond for a moment, then slowly nodded her head.

"This undercover operation stonewalled before it even got started," he continued. "We haven't seen much progress. After three weeks of posing as Mr. and Mrs. Samuel Jones, we have very little to show for it. And that's frustrated us both."

"Yes," she said. "It has."

"And speaking for myself, it's been a while since I…with anyone." He arched his eyebrows at Bridget in silent question.

"Me, too," she confessed.

Sam was pleased to hear it, then chastised himself for his relief. It didn't matter how long it had been for her. Or him. They weren't two people in a committed relationship who should be sharing things like this. What had happened had happened. And it wouldn't happen again. It was that simple.

"And I find you very attractive," he further admitted. "And I don't think I'm being immodest to say that I think you find me attractive, too."

"I do," she readily agreed.

"Then what happened last night was unavoidable," he said, though he knew that wasn't really true, either. He could have stopped anytime. If Bridget had given him even one tiny sign that she thought it was a bad idea, too, Sam would have stopped. Or if he'd allowed himself to think about what a mistake it would be, he would have stopped. He just hadn't wanted to. And obviously neither had she. They'd wanted each other too much.

"It was bound to happen sooner or later," he said again.

"I suppose you're right."

"But, as you said, it won't happen again."

"No, it won't."

He expelled another slow, anxious breath and spoke aloud the other thing that had been on his mind since waking: "I think we should call off our part of the undercover operation."

Her eyes went wide at his declaration, but she said nothing.

"We really haven't seen much progress in the case since we joined it." He hurried to reiterate his earlier point. "We've maybe learned a few things that offered insight the FBI didn't already have, but nothing to warrant all the time and work we've put in. It's been three weeks, Bridget, but we don't have visible suspects. At this point I think we'll just have to leave it up to the other agents assigned to the case. Because this thing with you and me just isn't working out."

And oh, he really wished he hadn't added that last line, because it sounded far too personal, as if he were speaking not of their contribution to an undercover operation, but a relationship between a man and a woman. Then again, if the metaphor fit…

"You're right," she said, making him think she was talking about a lot more than the undercover operation, too. "Our part of the sting hasn't been very effective, has it? We haven't stung anyone. We should talk to Pennington about cutting us loose as soon as we go into work this morning."

Her voice sounded wooden as she spoke, Sam noticed, as if she were reading the words from a cue card. But everything she said was valid and true. Just as everything he'd said was valid and true. They'd contributed little to the investigation over the past three weeks. Pennington's idea about adding another bogus couple looking to adopt into the mix had seemed like a good idea at the time, but it hadn't worked as well as any of them had hoped. Why waste more time or manpower than they already had?

"We can talk to Pennington this morning," Sam said.

Bridget nodded. "That'll be fine."

"I'm sure he'll agree with us that it's time to call it quits."

"I'm sure he will," she conceded. But her voice was still dull, spiritless. Much like her expression. And her posture. And her.

"No need to expend any more time or effort on something that's not working," he added.

"No, you're right."

"We gave it our best shot."

"We did."

"But we just couldn't make it happen."

"No, we couldn't."

"Totally beyond our control."

"Totally."

"That's how it works out sometimes."

"Right."

By the time he finished his lame pitch, Sam felt lousier and more defeated than he'd ever felt in his life. But he was right about all of it. Of course, realizing that didn't make him feel any better. And it wasn't as though Bridget disagreed with him. Not that realizing that made him feel any better, either. But they *had* done their best. Hadn't they? It wasn't their fault if things hadn't gone according to plan.

"I, um, I think I'll just go, um, to my room," Bridget said softly, disturbing the awkward silence. "I'll just… collect my shoes, why don't I?"

Sam squeezed his eyes shut tight when he remembered the way she had looked, stark naked except for those sexy high heels. And damned if he didn't go hard as rock. He had no idea what to say after that. And neither did Bridget, evidently, because she turned her back to him and let the sheet and blanket fall away. He had one last long—and longing—look at her bare back, then she tugged the bedspread up around herself and rose. She wrapped it around herself sari-style, then bent to retrieve first one shoe, then the other, which, for some reason, was way on the other side of the room. God only knew how that had happened.

She made her way silently to the door, and Sam realized he had never in his life felt more empty than he did at that moment. And if he felt that way, he could only imagine what Bridget must be feeling, having to be the one to go.

She turned around one final time at the bedroom door and offered him a tentative smile. And then, very softly, she said, "We did try, didn't we, Sam?"

And even though Sam didn't know if she was talking about the case or about themselves, he nodded. "Yeah,

Bridget. We tried. But when something doesn't work, it doesn't work, and no amount of wishing otherwise will change it."

And hell, Sam should know. He'd been doing a lot of wishing lately.

Ten

Before heading to the Portland field office to talk to Pennington about ending the sting, Sam and Bridget stopped by Children's Connection, because Bridget had something she needed to drop off for Jillian, and the agency was on the way. And since—at least until Special Agent in Charge Steve Pennington said otherwise— they were still posing as newlyweds, Sam accompanied his faux wife into the building instead of sitting outside with the engine running like some impatient husband eager to get on with more important matters. And be- cause—officially, anyway—they were happily married, they held hands, the way Bridget had insisted they do after Sam had told her that newlyweds touched each other constantly.

Sam tried not to think about how he didn't recall even reaching for her hand, and realized he must have done it instinctively, because it had just felt so natural to his subconscious to do it.

He also tried not to think about that business of constantly touching each other. They had certainly touched each other constantly the night before. And they'd touched each other in just about every place they could reach, too. Last night Sam had done things with—and to—Bridget that he'd never done with—or to—a woman before. And, damn, had it been good. He wasn't sure he'd ever experience something like that with another woman again.

Yeah, they definitely needed to color their part of the undercover operation over, he thought as they made their way down a wide, deserted hallway toward the Children's Connection offices. All in all, it had gotten them nowhere. Or, at least, it hadn't gotten them to where they needed to be. Instead, it had gotten them way too deep into places they should never have explored.

She sure did look beautiful today, though, he thought, stealing a glance to his left. He felt like the drab, boring businessman he was supposed to be, walking next to her in his plain gray suit and boring blue patterned tie. Bridget, on the other hand, looked like a bright splash of sunshine. Because the weather had taken an unexpected—and unusual—turn to the sunny side, with the temperatures hovering around seventy, she'd opted for a linen dress the color of a seashell, cut straight, but strangely showing off her curves in a way that Sam found much too appealing. She was wearing her hair back—probably because he'd told her how much he liked it loose, he thought wryly—but instead of the fat braid she usually wound it into, she'd wrapped it loosely in a piece of fabric the same soft color as her dress. But with one deft flick of his wrist, he could free it if he wanted to. She'd draped a pale-blue cardigan sweater over her shoulders to ward off the coolness of the breeze, and completed the outfit with flat little shoes and a flat little purse the same color as the sweater.

It was, without question, the most feminine outfit he'd ever seen her wear, and he wished like hell he knew what that meant. He couldn't help think she was sending him a message of some kind. But damned if he knew what it was.

"Jillian's office is just down there," she said, pointing with her left hand.

And when she did, the overhead lights glistened off the gold of her wedding band, making it wink at Sam as if laughing at him. He became aware of his own wedding ring then, and marveled at how he'd gotten so used to it, he didn't even feel it anymore. It was as if it had become a part of him or something. How odd.

As they approached Jillian Logan's office, another door opened into the hallway, and a man stepped out into their path. Instead of walking in one or the other direction, though, he stood right where he was, gazing at them, as if waiting for their approach. Instinctively Sam assessed him from head to toe. He was shorter than Sam, a couple of inches shy of six feet, with dark hair and eyes. Not bad-looking, but not Hollywood handsome, either. He looked tired, had circles under his eyes, as if he weren't sleeping well, and there was a strange, unmistakable sort of sadness about him.

A quick search of his memory told Sam he had seen the guy around Children's Connection at some point, but couldn't quite place what the circumstances had been. As he and Bridget drew nearer, Sam glanced at the door from which the man had just exited. Accounting, it said. But the clue helped Sam not at all in his identification.

But the man knew them, something that became clear when he smiled at them and said, "Mr. and Mrs. Jones?"

Sam's radar went up immediately, and he and Bridget, as one, drew to a halt. "Yes?" he said, striving for a curious but calm tone. "I'm Samuel Jones. This is my wife, Bridget. What can we do for you?"

The man smiled again, but there was something about the gesture that didn't feel quite right. "Actually, Mr. Jones, it's I who am in a position to do something for you."

Oh, yeah. Sam's radar was on red alert now, fairly humming with agitation. He looked over at Bridget, and although she had a pleasant, vaguely curious expression on her face for the newcomer's benefit, he could see in her eyes that she was feeling as vigilant about this turn of events as he was.

"I'm sorry," Sam told the man, "but you have us at a disadvantage. Your name is…?"

The man made a soft tsking sound. "I'm sorry. Of course. My name is Everett Baker."

Baker, Sam thought. *Baker, Baker, Baker. Everett Baker….* He'd been questioned by one of the other agents working the case, Sam recalled. He'd memorized the list of people who'd been questioned, and Baker was definitely on it. Nothing had come of the interview, however, Sam recollected. Certainly Baker's name hadn't come up anywhere else. He'd been one of dozens of Connection employees who'd been asked perfunctory questions that had yielded no new information.

"Mr. Baker," Sam said now. "I'm sorry, I'm still a bit confused. You know my wife and me."

"Well, I know *of* you," Baker corrected him. He

smiled that not-quite-genuine smile again. "Of course, everyone here at Children's Connection knows *of* you." He turned to Bridget. "Your mother—well, both of your parents—have done wonderful work here."

Bridget smiled a bland sort of smile. *Good girl,* Sam thought. "Thank you, Mr. Baker. That's so sweet of you to say that."

"And your sister, too, is a wonderful addition here." He glanced over his shoulder toward Jillian's office. "You must be going to see her now," he said.

"As a matter of fact, we were," Bridget said. "If you'll excuse us…?" To make it look good, Bridget began to take a step forward, tugging Sam along with her.

"Actually," Baker said, taking a step to his right to intervene, "if I could have a word with you myself?"

Bridget glanced over at Sam, giving him a What-do-you-think-dear? kind of look. She should be up for an Oscar by the end of this thing. "Sam?" she said in a voice that matched her expression.

Sam turned to Baker, arrowing his eyebrows down in what he hoped was a proper CEO frown. "I suppose we could spare a few minutes. Jillian's not expecting us. My wife just had something she needed to drop off for her sister. What's this about, Mr. Baker?"

Everett Baker looked immensely relieved after that. When Sam looked more closely, he saw a faint sheen of moisture on the man's forehead. He was perspiring. That was strange, since, to Sam, the corridor was a bit on the cool side.

"If you could just step into my office," Baker said, "I won't keep you long. And I promise you'll be very, *very* interested in what I have to say."

Oh, man, Sam thought, as a sudden realization

struck him. This was it. This was the contact they'd
hoped would come. Everett Baker was their baby seller.
Sam was sure of it. He'd always had excellent instincts
about people, especially people who operated outside
the law. And Everett Baker, he knew—he just *knew*—
was operating outside the law. He was going to offer
the Joneses a little bundle of joy in exchange for thousands of dollars in cash. They were about to get a
monumental break in the case. Right when they'd been
ready to end it.

But it wasn't supposed to be Bridget and Sam who got
that break. It was supposed to be the *other* agents posing
as husband and wife. Why would Everett Baker approach
them instead? Why would he offer a baby for sale to
Bridget Logan, who was in a perfect position to expose
him? She was a member of the family who had made
Children's Connection a pet project. She would recognize better than anyone a bogus operation within the organization. Everett Baker would have to be nuts to bring
the Joneses into this. So just what the hell was going on?

Sam had no idea. But he intended to find out.

He managed a smile of his own for Everett Baker.
"Of course, Mr. Baker. I always make time for something that could be very, very interesting to me."

And, extending his arm toward the office to indicate
that Everett Baker should go first, Sam and his "wife"
followed the man inside to hear his proposition.

Bridget tucked herself into the corner of the sofa in
her phony living room as best she could and tried very
hard to share Sam's glee. He'd bought a bottle of Moët
champagne on their way home from work tonight and
was, at the moment, trying to wrestle free its cork. To help

facilitate his efforts, he was doing a little dance around the living room, and she found it impossible not to smile.

Why did he have to be so damned endearing?

And why had last night happened?

And why couldn't the two of them make it work?

Especially since it now looked as if the sting operation, at least, had worked after all. Because Everett Baker had told them he knew of a beautiful baby girl whose teenage mother was poverty-stricken and unable to care for herself or her child. The teen wanted to find her daughter a good home, with people who would love her and care for her in a way that she simply could not.

Sam had done a great job playing the wary but excited businessman/potential parent. He'd asked just the right questions, and had adopted just the right amount of skepticism and concern about the matter. Had Bridget not known better, she would have sworn he was the genuine article. She'd let him take the lead in the interview, since Baker had seemed to want to do it on a man-to-man level and had scarcely acknowledged her presence. Obviously she'd played her part convincingly, too, since Baker had expected her to defer to her husband for this situation.

So they'd been a success in what they had set out to do—at least where the investigation was concerned. Unfortunately, Bridget couldn't see any way for them to be a success where their relationship was concerned. Because they did have a relationship now, she thought. After last night, there was no mistaking that. Two people didn't come together they way she and Sam had unless they felt something substantial for each other. But "substantial" didn't necessarily equate to "love." And it certainly didn't equate to "forever."

And although Bridget could safely say in speaking for herself that her feelings for Sam were indeed love, she didn't think his for her even came close. Yes, he cared for her. But it was different for men. Especially men like him. This morning, instead of talking about how the two of them might make things work, he had immediately suggested they call it quits. Instead of telling Bridget he cared for her in a way that might grow into something more, he'd told her they'd given it their best shot, and oh, well. He cared for her as much as he could, she translated now. But it wasn't enough to last forever.

Would she stay in Portland if he asked her to?

Would he leave Portland if she asked him to?

Unfortunately, Bridget didn't really know the answer to either of those questions. Not that either answer mattered, since Sam obviously wasn't going to ask her to stay any more than she was going to ask him to leave. And now she couldn't even let herself think about any of that, because they'd just had an enormous break in the investigation and she needed to focus her full attention on that.

A crisp, wet-sounding *pop!* stirred her from her musings, and she glanced up to see Sam holding a towel beneath the lip of the champagne bottle to catch a dribble of effervescent gold that spilled over the top. He laughed as he completed the action, and something inside Bridget turned over at the sight. He really was wonderful, she thought, on so many levels. He wasn't like any man she had ever met, and she was certain she'd never encounter anyone else like him again. She loved him. She had no trouble admitting that now, at least to herself. And although Sam cared for her, she knew it wasn't love with him.

"We've got him now," Sam said with undisguised glee as he generously filled a wineglass with champagne and handed it to Bridget.

She was about to tell him he should have used a different kind of glass, like a flute or a Marie Antoinette, but feared he would start in with one of his Where-I-come-from speeches again—"Where I come from, we drink champagne out of paper cups…and we *like* it"—and she didn't want to spoil the celebration. She knew better than he, after all, how different the two of them were, and it had nothing to do with where either of them came from. It had to do with how both of them felt.

"Looks that way," she said mildly as she accepted the glass from him.

Sam beamed as he sat down beside her on the sofa, then lifted his glass to her in a toasting gesture. "To success," he said.

"With the case," she couldn't help adding as she clinked her glass against his.

His smile fell some at that, but he echoed, "With the case."

And then, in unison, they enjoyed a sip of the sparkling wine. For a long moment afterward, though, neither said anything. Each only gazed at the other in silence, as if having no idea what to say. Finally, when she couldn't stand it any longer, Bridget broke the silence.

"So what do we do now?" she asked, deliberately keeping the question vague so that Sam wouldn't know whether she was talking about the case, their relationship or both.

"We wait for Baker to call," he answered immediately.

His response pretty much told her all she needed to know. He was thinking only about the case right now.

Which, she told herself, was all she should be thinking about, too.

"So why do you think he approached us?" she asked, still puzzling over the new—and totally unexpected—development in the investigation. "Why would he try to sell a baby to us, when my mother knows how Children's Connection works better than anyone? He's got to realize I'll say something to her. And that she'll know the offer is bogus and we'll go to the authorities. It's like he *wants* to get caught or something."

Sam shrugged, his expression indicating he understood no better than she what Baker's thinking was in the matter. "I don't know," he said. "The criminal mind is a strange thing. Maybe it's arrogance. Maybe it's stupidity. Maybe it's something else entirely."

Bridget nodded, but something about the arrogance still bothered her.

"He promised us he'd call by the end of next week to set up the exchange," Sam continued. He sipped his champagne again, his expression thoughtful. "Boy, he's a real piece of work, isn't he? He was so slick, so glib, when he proposed the whole plan. He actually made a black-market baby sale sound like a legitimate private adoption. No wonder this thing's been going on as long as it has."

Bridget nodded. Everett Baker had indeed been convincing. She wondered who had written his script for him. Because she just couldn't buy an accountant setting up an operation like that all by himself.

"He's working with someone else," she said. "You realize that, don't you?"

Sam looked affronted. "Of course I realize that. There's no way he could be doing all this by himself. If nothing else, he has an associate lining up the babies somewhere. Someone in Russia, for sure, since the Bureau has made that connection."

"But there's someone else, too," Bridget said with certainty. "Someone here in Portland. I don't think Baker's the mastermind behind this. I think it's all being orchestrated by someone else, and Baker's just the face they wear to approach potential clients."

"I agree," Sam said. "But who? That's the question."

"It shouldn't be difficult to find out," she said, "now that we've fingered Baker. Whoever's working the case shouldn't have any trouble now, putting all the pieces of the puzzle together. Knowing Baker's identity is going to make all the difference."

As soon as Bridget and Sam had told the Special Agent in Charge about their meeting with Everett Baker, Pennington had immediately called in the other agents working the case, then had pulled a few from others to give the investigation an added push. With all the technology and knowledge the Bureau had at its disposal, it would take no time to figure out who Baker was working with, at least here in Portland.

"So now that we know what to do about the case," Sam said, "what happens with us?"

His question surprised her. She really hadn't thought he would address the matter head-on that way. She'd figured he would just focus everything on the case and pretend last night had never happened. Or worse, forget it had ever happened.

"I don't know," she replied honestly. "What does happen with us?"

His gaze met hers levelly, but he made no move to touch her. "Well, obviously, we can't call off the under-cover operation now."

"No, of course not," she agreed. Again. She always agreed with Sam, she realized. Except where it most counted—in the way they felt about each other.

"We'll have to keep playing Mr. and Mrs. Samuel Jones," he said, "at least for a little while longer."

"I don't have a problem with that," she said. Because she didn't have a problem playing Mrs. Samuel Jones. What she had a problem with was falling in love with Sam Jones. Though, really, her love for Sam wasn't the problem. The problem was in his not reciprocating it.

He nodded, looking thoughtful again. Then, once again surprising her, he asked, "How do you want to handle the sleeping arrangements?"

She swallowed with some difficulty. They were actually going to talk about this? "I—I don't know," she said, replying truthfully again. "How do *you* want to handle them?"

He dropped his gaze now, staring into the champagne sparkling in the crystal wineglass. "I know what I said earlier," he began softly. Still not looking at her, he continued, "But now I realize I…" He glanced up then, finally meeting her gaze levelly. "I want to keep sleeping with you, Bridget," he told her frankly.

"Just sleeping?" she asked, even though she knew exactly what he was talking about.

"I want to keep making love to you," he clarified evenly.

She started to point out that there was no love involved in what they'd done last night, at least not on his side of things, but she was too chicken. So all she said was, "This morning you said it shouldn't happen again."

He sighed heavily and dropped his gaze back down to his glass. But all he said was, "Well, now I take that back."

She wanted to ask him why. Wanted to know what

had happened to change his mind about it. But she couldn't. Probably because she wasn't sure she wanted to hear his answer. She didn't think she could handle it if Sam told her he wanted to keep having sex with her because, hey, if they were going to be sleeping under the same roof, they might as well be sleeping together. She would have rather heard him say it was because he loved her. And she knew he wouldn't say that.

So what it all came down to now, she supposed, was what *she* wanted to do.

And she realized she wanted to keep sleeping with Sam, too. She only had a few nights left with him. Once they put the cuffs on Everett Baker and his accomplices, there would be nothing to keep the two of them together. And then Sam would go back to his Portland cases, and Bridget would go back to whatever assignment they had waiting for her in Washington. The fact of the matter was that in a couple of weeks, maybe less, she could be thousands of miles away and never see Sam again. So she would greedily take advantage of what little time she had left with him. She loved him. What else could she do? And, hey, maybe if the two of them spent more time together, he might finally fall in—

No. She wouldn't think that way. That wasn't why she wanted to be with Sam. She wanted to be with him because she loved him. That was all.

"I want to keep sleeping with you, too," she said softly.

His head snapped up at that, and his gaze met hers again. His eyes were full of…something. But for the life of her, Bridget couldn't guess what.

"Just sleeping?" he asked, the ghost of a smile playing about his lips.

She smiled back. "I want to keep making love with you," she said.

"You're sure?" he asked.

She nodded. "I'm sure."

He reached for her then, curling his fingers gently around her nape. Tenderly, he pulled her toward him and pressed his forehead to hers. For a moment he said nothing. Then, tentatively, he tilted his head to the side and covered her mouth with his. Bridget threaded the fingers of her free hand through his hair and kissed him back.

And she wondered where the two of them would be in two weeks.

Once they identified Everett Baker as their baby seller, everything in the investigation fell quickly into place. The FBI assigned agents already working the case to run a background check on Baker, and added another agent to shadow him wherever he went. Sam and Bridget, however, remained in place undercover as Mr. and Mrs. Jones. Baker had told them he would contact them again to set up a time where they could meet—i.e. buy—the baby, and once that arrangement was set up, they could arrest the man on the spot. Until then, however, Sam and Bridget had to sit tight. The FBI was playing it very cautiously. They wanted to make sure there were no loose ends, no loopholes, when they brought the hammer down on Everett Baker. They wanted to arrest him in the act.

Sam did stay on top of things, though, and watched the investigation very closely. The background check on Baker revealed him to be not a native of Portland, but a transplant from St. Louis, Missouri. His accounting degree appeared to be legitimate, though he had never been what one might call an exemplary student. Nor did he appear to have been an especially successful accountant, as he had lived as modestly in St. Louis as he did in Portland.

But there was no evidence to suggest he had been involved in any criminal activity before moving west. On the contrary, judging by the information the agents gathered, the man had led a fairly quiet life. His mother was deceased, his father had taken off for parts unknown and he had no siblings. He'd never been married and had no children. He had moved around quite a bit growing up, though, enough to raise a red flag. Still, it appeared that Everett Baker had been a law-abiding citizen before coming to Portland and hanging out his Babies For Sale sign.

He wasn't, however, working alone.

A review of his phone records indicated he spoke frequently with a man named Charlie Prescott, who had once worked for Children's Connection as a custodian. At first glance, the two might have simply been friends who had met at work and who enjoyed each other's company. But the agent shadowing Everett had decided otherwise when he'd seen the two men meet at a local bar. They had appeared anything but friendly and had even gotten into a shouting match at one point. The agent in question had overheard enough of the argument to conclude that the two men were arguing over a "deal" of some kind, and that Everett "wanted out" of some "arrangement" and that there was a "package from Russia" waiting to be picked up.

When Sam added up everything they'd learned over the week that followed his and Bridget's first meeting with Baker, he arrived at an answer that told him Everett

Baker was working with Charlie Prescott and another individual to pipeline babies into the U.S. from Russia. And if Sam and Bridget could just be patient, they'd catch at least one of them red-handed. Though they wanted the whole ring. That was why the FBI decided not to go after Charlie Prescott until they had ironclad proof to tie him to Baker, not to mention more leads that might implicate others in the crimes. The Bureau didn't want to make any mistakes here, so they decided to err on the side of caution for now.

At any rate, Sam figured all he and Bridget had to do now was wait for that call from Everett Baker, the one where he would set up a meeting for them to claim their new baby. Oh, and to pass the man a briefcase in exchange that was filled with thousands of dollars to take care of all the proper "fees." Wink wink. Nudge nudge. *I won't say anything if you don't, since if you don't take this child, it could be years before you find another one.*

Sam just wished he knew when that call would come.

In the meantime, he and Bridget did their best to enjoy the time they had left together. And he wished he knew what to do to make everything turn out all right. But he had no idea how to make that happen. As much as they liked each other and enjoyed being together— and as much as they exploded every night when they made love—Sam just couldn't see any way the two of them could work things out. Not only had Bridget never once said a word about any future the two of them might have together, but Sam, if he were honest with himself, just wasn't sure how he wanted that future to play out. He cared for Bridget a lot. More than he'd cared for any woman. But the last time he'd loved a woman enough to want to build a life with her, that life had crumbled into dust. He just wasn't sure he was a good judge of what to look for in a happily-ever-after. And he couldn't quite convince himself that Bridget wanted one of those, anyway.

It was a pretty difficult week. On a lot of different levels.

Finally, on Thursday evening, nearly a week to the day after they'd first encountered Everett Baker, the call he and Bridget had been waiting for came. Sam scrawled copious notes as he talked to Baker, even though he knew the Bureau was taping the conversation. By the time he hung up the phone, his heart was racing, his adrenaline was pumping and he knew they were very, very close to ending this thing once and for all. But he knew Bridget wasn't going to like the particulars of what Baker had insisted on the phone.

"What?" she asked before he even had the receiver back in the cradle. "I don't like the look on your face."

"You're going to like what I have to say even less," he told her.

She sat on the sofa in the house they would be leaving soon, in her usual relaxing-in-the-evening attire of blue jeans and sweatshirt and socks. Same as Sam, he couldn't help thinking.

But now her eyes widened in shock. "We've been made?"

He shook his head. "Not that bad."

She expelled a sound of profound relief.

"But he wants to meet me alone. Without you there."

She'd started shaking her head before he even finished talking. "No," she said. "I'm in this, too. I want to be there for the takedown."

"I understand," Sam assured her, knowing it wasn't fair to exclude her from the grand finale, but knowing it was essential they play this by Baker's rules. "But he was insistent, Bridget. And he sounded kind of spooked as it was. Between the argument he had with Prescott at the bar the other night, and this, I think our guy's starting to unravel. We can't afford to do anything that might spook him even more. We have to do this his way. If he wants me to meet him alone, then I have to meet him alone."

She set her jaw firmly, her mouth flattening into a thin line.

"Look, I don't like it any more than you do," he told her. "I'd rather have you there, too." And he would. And not just because she was his partner in this thing, either. But because he'd feel safer with Bridget at his side. There wasn't another agent he could think of that he'd rather have at his back.

"I'll be your backup," she said, as if reading his thoughts.

He shook his head. "You can't."

"Why not?"

"Because you can't be anywhere near the meeting place. If he saw you—"

"He won't see me."

"We can't risk it," Sam insisted. "If he saw you, he'd run. He'd know something was wrong, and he'd take off. And we might never see him again."

She inhaled a deep breath and released it on a ragged growl. "Men," she muttered. "You just don't think we women can do anything, do you?"

Sam had to smile at that, even though he figured his amusement would rile her even more. "Actually, I think you can do a lot," he told her.

But he made himself stop before he added, *especially in the dark.* Somehow, he didn't think she'd take the comment in the spirit in which he intended it. Plus, they couldn't afford to get sidetracked right now, and just thinking about what Bridget could do in the dark made Sam want to drop everything and turn the lights down low.

"We have to do this Baker's way," he said again. "And he wants to see me alone. Even if you're not there for the takedown, Bridget, you're as much a part of this investigation as anyone, and everybody at the Bureau knows that."

"I want to be in on the interrogation once we have him," she said.

"You will be."

"I want to help nail that bastard to the wall."

"I'll hand you the hammer."

She sighed again. "And I want you to be careful, Sam."

He was across the room in a half-dozen quick strides, but he stopped before pulling her into his arms the way he wanted to. Things had just been so weird since the night they'd made love that first time. First they'd decided to forget about it and call a halt to both the investigation and any further contact they might have with each other. Then, when they'd realized they would still be working together, they'd decided to be matter-of-fact about what had happened and enjoy what little time they had left. And they had. They'd enjoyed it a lot. Every opportunity they'd had.

But they hadn't spoken of it again. They'd talked about every aspect of the case until they could recite every detail from memory. But even though they'd turned to each other physically every night, they hadn't said a word about those nights on the mornings following them.

Sam had no idea where he stood with Bridget. And, truth be told, he just wasn't sure where she stood with him, either. But now she was telling him to be careful. That had to mean something. Didn't it?

"I will," he told her. "Even if things seem to be unraveling with this black-market baby ring, *this* deal will go down exactly the way it's supposed to. And we'll have him, Bridget. We'll have him."

She nodded, but she still looked worried. "When does Baker want to meet with you?"

"Tomorrow," he told her. "After work. Seven o'clock sharp. He gave me the address, a motel just north of town. He said he'll have a healthy baby girl for us whose mother is a high-school student who can't care for her. He said he's taken care of all the legal fees, that he'll have her birth certificate and a certificate of adoption with him, all signed by the proper authorities. All I have to do is give him the money to cover the fees and to reimburse the mother for her hospital expenses—yeah, right—and our business will be done.

"It will be fine, Bridget," he added. And then he gave in to his impulse and reached for her. He cupped his hand over her shoulder, just intending to give it a gentle, reassuring squeeze. Instead, he pulled her into his arms and wrapped her in a fierce embrace. And where he'd feared she might balk or worse, try to push him away, instead she folded herself into him, roping her arms around his waist, hugging him tightly to herself.

"Baker's an accountant, for God's sake," he murmured into her ear. "And there's no evidence to indicate that he's ever been violent."

"I should be there, too," she said against his chest. "You shouldn't be doing this alone."

"I'll be thinking about you the whole time," he told her. And he knew that he would.

She squeezed him tighter. "Be careful," she said again.

And all Sam could do was promise once more, "I'll be fine, Bridget. I'll be fine."

Everett Baker felt sick to his stomach. He glanced at the clock on the bedside table, then at the sleeping infant buckled into a car seat that sat in the middle of the bed. He and Charlie always used this motel for their exchanges, because it was never busy and the manager didn't seem to care what went on, as long as he got paid. The place wasn't especially accommodating, however, in spite of the sort of establishment it was. A remnant of the Eisenhower era, when state highways were still the way to travel, it sat off the beaten path, well away from the Interstate, and was surrounded by towering pines and a picnic area. There wasn't another building in sight for miles. The interior was clean, if not stylish, the beige paint, brown furniture, green carpet and orange bedspread probably original to the place. Mass-produced artwork of a generic seascape hung over the bed. Ugly, but it met their needs. They'd never had any problems before. Usually everything went off without a hitch.

But Everett was only doing everything Charlie had told him to do. He'd made contact with a couple on the waiting list at Children's Connection, and he'd offered them a child the way he always did, fast-talking it into what sounded like a perfectly legitimate enterprise. He'd called the couple the way he always did and told the husband to meet him at the motel he and Charlie always used, and to bring the usual amount of money to cover the usual fees. Everett was doing what he always did, as far as Charlie was concerned.

He'd just neglected to tell Charlie that the couple in question this time was related to Leslie Logan.

Everett had thought and thought and thought about what he could do to free himself from Charlie's baby-selling operation once and for all, without fear that Charlie would retaliate by hurting—or killing—one of the Logans. Finally he'd realized that the only way he would be able to achieve that would be to ensure that Charlie got caught and sent to jail. And it would be best if Everett himself got away. So tonight, when he finished what he had to do here, he'd be going on the run. And if he never saw Portland again, it would be too soon.

He'd deliberately approached Bridget Logan and her husband and offered them one of the babies Charlie had in pipeline, knowing full well that they—or at the very least, Leslie Logan—would alert the authorities to the matter. Everett was confident that the motel was being watched right now, with—he glanced at his watch—twenty-five minutes to go before Samuel Jones's arrival. Everett only hoped everything went down according to plan. *His* plan, he meant. Not Charlie's.

He glanced at the baby again to find her sleeping like…well, a baby. Whoever was caring for the little ones in Russia seemed to take good care of the children. But then, the children were worth tens of thousands of dollars apiece, so of course Charlie's Russian connection would see to it that they were well cared for. He had to protect his investment.

But Everett had a lot invested in this baby girl, too. And she was about to pay off, with something far more valuable than a briefcase full of cash. She was about to win Everett his freedom from a life of crime that he'd never wanted and had come to despise. He smiled in spite of his anxieties as he watched the baby's mouth work at something she was dreaming about. In her little pink sweat suit and booties, she looked so tiny, so fragile. How could he have been involved in something that would sell her to the highest bidder?

The knowledge of what he had degenerated to made him sick. It didn't matter that this baby would have doubtless had a good life with whatever family bought her, or that they would have doted on her and pampered her like a princess. The end didn't justify the means. No matter how Everett looked at it, he had become someone who bartered in human lives. He was even an accessory to kidnapping. Which made him no better than Lester Baker, the man who had stolen Robbie Logan and ruined Everett's life.

How had he come to this? he wondered as he watched the baby sleep so peacefully, oblivious to the enormity of what was happening to her. All he had ever wanted was to lead a quiet life and be left alone. He'd come to Portland to see his family, not destroy it. Yet thanks to his involvement with Charlie, the Logans had been miserable for months, watching their pet project, Children's Connection, sink deeper and deeper into trouble, and watching their loved ones suffer all manner of misfortune. All Everett had wanted when he'd agreed to Charlie's schemes was to win himself a friend and make a little money. Instead, he'd become a criminal.

He wished he'd never come to Portland. Wished he'd never even found out the truth about his identity. Now that Joleen was gone, he could have made a quiet, decent life for himself in St. Louis. Maybe, eventually, he would have even met a nice woman, someone like Nancy, and settled down to start a family of his own. And how would he feel if someone came along and stole a member of that family away from him forever?

Thinking about Nancy just brought on a fresh set of fears for Everett. Because he realized he *had* met a nice woman with whom he might have settled down to start a family, and he'd blown it by getting tangled up in something he never should have agreed to. In addition to everything else he'd become, he was going to lose the only woman he'd ever loved. Once Nancy found out what he'd been involved in, she wouldn't want anything to do with him. He'd have to see her before he left town, try to explain to her why he'd done what he had and hope she understood. He wished he could try to explain to the Logans, too, but he knew that would be impossible. If they ever found out what their cherished Robbie had become…

Everett shook his head. No, he thought. No. Then, as if it weren't enough to just think it, he said the word aloud. "No."

He wasn't Charlie Prescott. He had a conscience and the capacity to care for other people. And that was why he had arranged this exchange with the Joneses. Everett would stop Charlie's operation right now, and he'd make sure Charlie went to jail for the rest of his life. By now, the feds would have connected Everett to the black-market baby ring, and they'd be investigating him thoroughly. He'd left more than enough incriminating evidence in his apartment for the authorities to find that would connect Charlie to everything that had happened. And maybe, if Everett played it right, he'd escape from the authorities himself and go into hiding someplace where they'd never find him. Maybe he'd even figure out some way to explain it to Nancy and convince her to come with him. Maybe...

Reiterating his decision made Everett feel better about himself. He glanced at his watch again. Twenty minutes until Samuel Jones arrived, and who knew how many law enforcement officials out there watching the motel. He looked at the sleeping infant again, and although he realized he couldn't return her to wherever she had come from, he could make sure she was discovered by someone who *would* know what to do with her. Not wanting to give himself time to change his mind, Everett picked up the phone on the nightstand and punched the zero that would connect him to the front desk. And when the raspy voice of the old woman answered, he said, "This is room twelve. Someone's abandoned an infant here. Call the police right away."

And once the old woman sputtered out that she would do just that, Everett collected the few things he'd brought with him—except for the baby—and bolted through the door.

He was careening out of the parking lot, spewing gravel in his wake, when he saw a big black Mercedes with Samuel Jones sitting in the driver's seat turning into the parking lot. Their eyes met once. Then Everett stepped on the accelerator and squealed away, giving the engine all the gas he could. And because he intended to never look back again, not once did he glance into his rearview mirror.

He didn't dare.

Eleven

At 7:00 p.m., Bridget was at her parents' house, pacing like a caged animal. She'd gone there ostensibly to have dinner with her family, but she couldn't have eaten anything if she'd tried. Her parents and sister and brothers—and the women who loved those brothers— had kept up a lively conversation at the dinner table, but their accounts of work and bits of social gossip had gone in one ear and out the other. Even the charming stories about their children hadn't kept Bridget occupied for long. Nor had the antics of little Cole when he'd tried to lure Auntie Bridget into play.

"I can't now, Cole," she'd told her young nephew-to-be. "Auntie's just got her mind on other things right now."

He'd shrugged in that philosophical way of children and run along. The grown-ups, too, had retired to the den for coffee. So preoccupied with thoughts of Sam and his meeting with Everett Baker, Bridget hadn't been able to sit still, had kept jumping up for one reason or another. Jillian needed more coffee. Her father needed another slice of cheesecake. That pillow on the love seat needed fluffing. That picture over the chintz chair was crooked. And look, is that a piece of lint on the Aubusson? Where's the vacuum? And heck, while she was at it, why didn't she just dust the entire house and do a few loads of laundry? Leslie Logan, the only one present who knew the reason for Bridget's edginess had had to practically wrestle her daughter to the ground to prevent her from scrubbing and waxing the floors and polishing the silver, assuring her that their housekeeper had all the household chores under control.

When the phone rang at seven-thirty, Bridget nearly jumped out of her skin and bowled over her brother Eric to answer it, but it was only a friend of her father's, inviting Terrence Logan to play tennis the following weekend. And when the doorbell rang at seven-forty-five, Bridget bolted to answer it, only to find a trio of Girl Scouts selling cookies on the other side. She scared them so badly with her sudden and zealous—and, doubtless, wild-eyed—appearance that she ended up ordering a dozen boxes of each type of cookie to assuage her guilt. By eight o'clock, when there was still no word from Sam or anyone else at the Bureau, Bridget was fit to be tied. Preferably to a concrete pylon. That was scheduled to be dumped in the Willamette River.

"It shouldn't be taking this long," she told her mother when Leslie came to join her at the living-room window. Bridget stared out into the swiftly falling darkness, seeing not the amber-lighted street outside, but Sam in a suburban motel, crumpled on the floor in a pool of blood. "Something's gone wrong, I can feel it."

"Don't borrow trouble," her mother told her. "Probably, in all the excitement and chaos of the arrest, Sam just hasn't had a chance to call you."

"Then someone else should have," Bridget said. "Someone must know something. Better yet, I should have been there with him. I should have had his back."

"You know you couldn't," Leslie told her. "And I for one am glad you're here instead."

She draped a slender arm across Bridget's shoulders, then turned her daughter to face her. Leslie's eyes were damp with emotion, faint lines fanning out from their edges. Her mother had aged visibly in the last year. Oh, certainly she could still pass for a much younger woman, but the troubles at Children's Connection had clearly had an impact on her.

And it wasn't just the troubles with the foundation, Bridget made herself admit. It was also the upheaval some of her children had seen recently, too, such as David's misadventure in Russia and Peter's marriage to Katie Crosby. Yes, those things had ultimately ended well, but they must have been trying on her mother and father both when they were happening. And now Leslie must be thinking about how her youngest daughter had finally come home, but would only be turning around to leave again soon.

Her parents weren't getting any younger, Bridget thought. And her brothers were all marrying and starting families. She was going to be an aunt so many times over during the coming years. And she and Jillian had become closer over the past few weeks than they'd ever been as kids. It had felt good to be home again, she had to admit. Only now was Bridget realizing how much she missed her family when she was thousands of miles away from them. There was just so much going on here now, she thought. A whole new generation of Logans was on the horizon. The family was growing and blending, and there would be countless new adventures and events to enjoy. But she wouldn't be around to see any of it. She'd be somewhere else, thousands of miles away, and she'd be working.

While her parents grew older and more frail, Bridget would be working.

While her nieces and nephews were growing from babies to toddlers to children to young adults, Bridget would be working.

While Sam Jones built a life here in Portland, probably with another woman who would love him to distraction, Bridget would be working.

And at the end of her life, when she was an old, old woman, sitting in a rocking chair, she'd look back on her life and see that it had been full of working. Not living. Not loving. Not enjoying her family. Not being happy.

Work. That was all Bridget would ever have to show for her life. She'd go to her grave leaving nothing behind but a memory of herself. And that memory wouldn't even belong to her family, because she'd be spending so little time with them. That memory would belong to her co-workers. They'd think about what a great job she did winding up cases. They wouldn't think about how she had changed or affected or enriched someone else's life. They wouldn't think about how she had changed or affected or enriched her own. She Was a Good Worker— that was what Bridget Logan's tombstone would say.

She turned around to survey the room again. Her

brother David sat on one sofa, holding little Natasha in his lap, the baby patting his face with one chubby little hand, David laughing at the sloppy caress. His fiancée Elizabeth snuggled close to him, her arm looped through his, holding on to him as if she never wanted to let him go. Eric and Jenny sat with little Cole between them, Eric laughing good-naturedly as Cole pointed to pictures in a book and deliberately misidentified them in the goofiest ways. And Peter and Katie stood on the other side of the room, gazing into each other's eyes, Peter's hand opened tenderly over her belly where their baby grew inside her. Even her father was gazing at Bridget's mother from his seat nearby, as if he didn't want the woman he loved ever to be out of his sight.

They all had such rich lives, Bridget thought. Because they all had people to share those lives with. They all worked, too, but at the end of the day, they left work behind and came home to their families. And then they lived their lives. They worked so that they might live. They didn't live so that they could work. They'd achieved the proper balance and were better people because of it.

Oh, how could she have been so stupid?

Tears filled her eyes as she pulled her mother close and hugged her as hard as she could. "I love you, Mom," she said. And to her shame, she realized she couldn't remember the last time she had said those words to either of her parents. "Oh, I love you so much."

Her mother seemed taken aback at first, but then she threw her arms around Bridget and hugged her back. "I love you, too, sweetie," she said. "And I'm going to miss you so much after you leave."

"I'm not leaving," Bridget said impulsively. And the

moment she said the words aloud, she realized they weren't impulsive at all. She'd been thinking them in her subconscious for a while now—she must have, otherwise it wouldn't feel so good, so right, to say them aloud now. She'd left home nearly ten years ago because she hadn't thought there was a place for her here in Portland—she'd thought she had to find it somewhere else in the world. Now she understood, though, that everything she had ever needed or wanted had been here all along. Her family. Her roots. Her memories.

Her Sam.

But was he hers? she asked herself. Was he really? The way she had become his? Oh, the two of them really needed to talk. They needed to stop pussyfooting around the things they wanted and just say them outright. She wanted to be with Sam. Forever. She loved Sam. And she would love him forever. She needed him to know that. And she needed to know how he felt about her, too. As soon as she was in the same room with him again, she vowed to tell him everything. How much she loved him and how she didn't want to be without him. How she wanted to build her life here in Portland and how much she wanted Sam to be a part of that life.

Her thoughts and plans were interrupted, however, when her mother pushed her to arm's length but didn't let go of her. In fact, Leslie only strengthened her hold on Bridget. "What did you say?" she asked.

Bridget laughed once, a nervous sound. "I'm not leaving," she said again. "I'm staying here in Portland."

Leslie's mouth dropped open at the revelation. "But what about your work?"

Bridget laughed again, with more certainty this time and less anxiety. "Oh, who cares about work?" she said.

"I've got something so much better than that. I've got my family."

And I've got Sam, she added to herself. Because she did have Sam. Inside her, in the deepest, most secret part of her heart. He was locked there tight, and there was no room for anyone else. Except maybe her family. The family she had now, and the family to come. Because Bridget intended to be around for all of it. She just hoped Sam would be there with her. She hoped he would want her as much as she wanted him. Hoped he would love her as much as she loved him.

She had to talk to him.

Where was he?

And why didn't he call?

The telephone rang at 1:00 a.m. on the dot. Bridget knew that, because she was sitting at the kitchen table in the house she'd been sharing with Sam, nursing a cup of coffee and watching the second hand creep slowly around the numbers, one by one. She'd been watching the clock for three solid hours, ever since coming home from her parents' house without having heard a word about the investigation. She'd called the Bureau before she left, but they'd sworn they didn't have any news for her, that Sam hadn't reported in since leaving to meet with Everett Baker and they'd call her as soon as they knew anything.

Liars, she thought. Somebody down there knew something, whether Sam had reported in or not. They just weren't saying anything to anyone until they had something they could report to the media.

God, how could she have ever thought she could work for such people for the rest of her life? People who put procedure before the person, who thought the work was more important than the people who performed it. How could she have ever thought she was one of them, when she knew it was the people who mattered?

It was one person in particular who mattered most.

Before the first ring was completed, Bridget was snatching the cordless phone from the table and pushing the talk button. "What?" she asked without even greeting whoever was on the other end.

"It's Pennington, Logan," the Special Agent in Charge greeted her.

Bridget swallowed hard and told herself to be calm. "How's Sam?"

"He's gone," Pennington said.

Her heart leaped into her throat. "You mean he's left town, right? Not that he's..." She couldn't even say the word. She couldn't even think it. It wasn't possible.

"Right," Pennington said, and the breath left her lungs in a long, painful whoosh. "Something went wrong with the exchange," he said. "We're still not clear on what. Somehow Baker must have made Jones for law enforcement, because when Jones pulled into the parking lot, he saw Baker pulling out, burning rubber."

"Oh, my God. With the baby?" Bridget asked, praying he didn't have the infant with him.

"No," Pennington assured her. "He left the baby sleeping in the motel room. Called the front desk before he left and reported the child as abandoned. Then he fled in his car. Something must have alerted him to the fact that it was a setup. Or maybe he just got scared. In any event, he left the child where she was and took off. Jones went after him, but Baker got away."

"Dammit," Bridget hissed. If only she'd been there. Maybe it would have gone down differently.

"Actually, I was thinking of a different word," Pennington said crisply. "But it doesn't bear repeating."

"Sam?" Bridget asked, knowing the one-word query would say everything she needed to say.

"At the same time Jones was supposed to be meeting with Baker, we had other agents closing in on Prescott at his apartment thanks to an anonymous tip that thoroughly incriminated him. Baker went there after fleeing the motel, presumably to tell Prescott what was going on, but he interrupted the raid, and when he saw the place crawling with agents, he turned his car around and fled again. Two of our agents followed, but they lost Baker, too."

"What happened with Charlie Prescott?" Bridget asked.

Pennington hesitated a moment, then said, "He's dead."

"Dead?" Bridget echoed incredulously.

"Our agents had cuffed him and were leading him out to a car when Prescott lunged for one of them and unholstered the agent's weapon. He drew on our agent, so another agent returned fire. Our guys are all fine. But Prescott is dead."

"Did you find out who he was working with in Russia?"

"We did," Pennington told her. "Thanks to files we found on his home computer, we've linked Prescott to a man in Moscow who goes by the name of Vladimir Kosanisky. He's a nasty piece of work, with a long criminal record. We've alerted authorities in Russia, and they've taken him into custody there."

"But Baker's still at large," Bridget said unnecessarily.

"We've sent out bulletins about him all over the county and surrounding areas," Pennington told her, "and we've distributed his photo to all the news outlets and law-enforcement agencies, all the bus stations, airports, train stations, you name it. I don't think he'll get far. But for now— What?" he said, obviously speaking to someone in the room with him. "Are you sure? Absolutely. Get right on it. Logan," he said into the receiver again.

"What is it?" she asked. "What's going on?"

"Baker's been spotted at a diner just north of town. He ordered something to go. The waitress had just seen him on the news. She said he was traveling north on a state highway when he left, one that leads right into the mountains. And there's nothing for miles there. No place for him to hide. No place to run. We've got him."

"Who's going after him?" Bridget asked.

"Davis and Jones are right behind him," Pennington said.

Sam. Sam was going after Everett Baker. She wished Pennington had told her it was someone else. But he'd be fine, she reminded herself. He'd promised her he would be.

"Is there anything I can do?" she asked.

"Just sit tight," Pennington told her. "This thing is coming to an end. Finally. I'll call you when I know anything more."

"Thanks," she said. "I'll be right here."

She hung up the phone feeling both better and worse. Baker was still at large, and that wasn't good. Sam was on his tail, and that wasn't good, either, because it meant he wasn't entirely out of danger. But they'd caught the other bad guys. And Baker wasn't violent. Plus, Sam was very good at his job.

He'd be fine, she told herself again. He'd be fine.

They could talk when he got home, she thought

further as she climbed the stairs to her bedroom. As she washed her face and brushed her teeth, she rehearsed all the things they would say to each other. She was too tired to change into her pajamas, so she pulled back the bed-spread and climbed into bed in the clothes she'd been wearing all day. And as she closed her eyes and willed herself to relax, to go to sleep, she found herself smiling.

Home, she repeated to herself. Soon Sam would be home. And she would, too. Maybe home wouldn't be the house they'd been sharing for the past month. But wherever Sam was, that would be her home. And she hoped he felt the same way about her.

They'd talk soon, she told herself. Just as soon as they both got home.

Nancy's apartment building was completely dark when Everett arrived there what seemed like days after abandoning the baby at the motel and driving off with Samuel Jones on his heels. He hugged the brick wall and slunk away from a gash of yellow streetlight that spilled down the alley behind the building, panting hard and trying to get hold of his thoughts. He glanced down at his watch, its luminous dial telling him it was almost four o'clock in the morning.

Nine hours. It had been only nine hours since he'd left the motel. He could scarcely believe it. In nine hours, he'd abandoned a child that had probably been kidnapped from its mother at some point, had run from federal authorities, had been cornered by two of them and had shot at them! He! Everett Baker! He'd shot at FBI agents! He hadn't aimed, of course, and he was rea-sonably sure he hadn't hit anything, but the fact remained that he, a man who could never conceive of hurting anyone, had deliberately put someone's life in danger. It was like a bad dream. But the pounding of his heart told him it was all too real.

But what else could he do? he asked himself as he tried to catch his breath. After leaving the motel, Everett hadn't been able to resist going to Charlie's to see if the feds had closed in on him yet. But as he'd approached Charlie's apartment building, the place had been overrun with people in blue windbreakers with FBI stenciled on the back of them in big white letters and he'd panicked. He hadn't wanted to show himself to the authorities, and suddenly he was stumbling right in front of them.

So he'd turned a block before arriving at Charlie's building, thinking maybe he'd go to Nancy's instead. Tell her what had happened. Try to think of some way to make her understand. He'd been so confused by then, and he'd figured she'd know what to do. She was smart, levelheaded, his Nancy. And she cared about him. She loved him. She wouldn't turn her back on him the way so many other people had. But just as Everett had made the decision to go see her, he'd heard sirens erupt behind him. Someone must have seen him turn, caught a glimpse of his license plate or decided he was suspicious, and they'd come after him.

And that was when Everett had really panicked.

He'd stomped on the accelerator as hard as he could, and his car had shot forward with enough speed and force that he'd nearly driven right off the road. He hadn't given a thought to where he was driving, had only known he needed to get away. He'd run red lights, cut people off, nearly run down a trio of pedestrians. He hadn't cared. Hadn't even noticed. He'd just driven.

And he'd kept driving until he left the city limits. But the car following him had stayed with him somehow.

At last he felt sure he'd lost his pursuer, and he risked stopping to buy something to fill his empty stomach. But not long after leaving the diner he'd braved a look in the rearview mirror and had seen an ordinary black sedan, the kind used by federal law-enforcement officers, following him again. And the next thing Everett had known, he was driving into the mountains, and there was nothing for miles but trees and trees and more trees.

Even though he'd known it was useless, that there was no way he would lose them, he'd turned onto a dirt road and kept driving. Higher and higher into the mountains, farther and farther from Portland. And still he hadn't been able to think clearly, still he had simply reacted to the panic and terror that were, by then, overtaking him. He'd finally stopped his car and jumped out. But not before grabbing the gun that Charlie had given him so long ago, and which Everett, repulsed by the ugly thing, had stuck in the glove compartment and forgotten about. He'd started to run into the woods and he'd fired over his shoulder as he ran.

He'd run farther into the woods after that, until he'd feared he was well and truly lost, but had stumbled back out on the edge of the highway just after dark. He'd risked accepting a ride from a trucker, figuring since the man was driving toward Portland, he couldn't have seen any of the local news reports yet. But he'd still asked the man to drop him off on the outskirts of the city. From there Everett had jogged the half-dozen miles to Nancy's apartment.

He couldn't have hit anyone, he tried to reassure himself, recalling again the way he had fired blindly at the agents. He hadn't even been looking where he was pointing the damned gun. And FBI agents always wore bulletproof vests, didn't they? He couldn't have hit them. Couldn't have hurt them. He didn't think he'd be able to live with himself if he found out he had. It was going to be bad enough having to deal with the things he'd already done.

Oh, please, God, don't let me have hurt anyone. Not any more than I already have...

Everett squeezed his eyes shut tight and sent the silent plea up into the dark night overhead. But when he opened his eyes again, he saw that the clouds were so thick and black above him that he wasn't even sure his words had reached the place he wanted them to go.

Nancy, he thought again as he gazed up at the big brick building. He needed to talk to Nancy. She'd know what to do. She'd take care of him. She was a good woman. Everett really didn't deserve her. But he hoped, after he told her all the things he needed to tell her, that she'd at least try to see beneath it all to the man he used to be, the man he could have been, if only things had been different. Maybe she'd even come with him when he left Portland, which he knew he had to do. Tonight.

He waited a few more minutes to gather his thoughts, to make sense of what he wanted to say to her. But there was so much, so many things he needed to tell her, and he wasn't sure he'd be able to make her understand. So in the end, he just decided to start at the beginning and do his best to figure it all out as he went. With one final deep breath to steady his irregular pulse, Everett smoothed out his rumpled clothes, straightened his wrinkled tie and wiped the perspiration from his brow with the handkerchief he always kept in his pocket. And then, squaring his shoulders, he circled the perimeter of the building to the front and entered it.

The short walk down the hall to Nancy's front door seemed to take him forever to complete. Even when he arrived, he stood there for a moment, just looking at the tarnished brass number affixed to it. Finally, though, he lifted his hand and knocked. Once, twice, three times, four.

After a moment, he heard a voice on the other side, Nancy's voice, soft and sweet, call out, "Who is it? Who's there?" But she sounded scared, obviously concerned about who would come to her door at this time of night.

"Nancy," Everett called out, loud enough for her to hear, but quietly enough so as not to rouse any of her neighbors. "It's me. It's Everett. I need to talk to you."

"Everett?" she repeated, her voice full of concern now.

But he heard her slip the chain from its groove and then open the two bolts that kept it locked. When she opened the door, he could see that he'd woken her from sleep. Her short brown hair was messy, a little flat on one side where she must have been sleeping on it. And her hazel eyes were squinting at him, as if unused to even the scant light of the hallway outside. She wore a plain white cotton nightgown and had thrown a blue plaid robe over it. But never had Everett seen a more beautiful sight.

"What is it?" she asked quietly. "My goodness, Everett, you look like the hounds of hell have been snapping at your feet."

Close, he thought. That was close to what he'd experienced today. Too close, in fact. "I need to talk to you," he told her without preamble. "It's important."

She nodded. "About what?"

It all came crashing down on Everett then, everything that had happened to him since leaving St. Louis. And

even before that. Joleen's confession about his real
identity. His struggle to get through college. His trouble
in high school. His sadness and loneliness as a child. But
most of all, everything he had done since meeting
Charlie Prescott. How could he explain? he wondered.
How could he tell her and make her understand? How
could she still care for him once she knew?

"There's so much, Nancy," he said helplessly. "So
much I need to tell you. I scarcely know where to begin."

She still looked concerned, but she smiled tentatively
and reached for his hand. "Just start at the beginning,"
she told him. "And it will be all right."

Everett wasn't sure that was true, but he held her
hand tightly and lifted it to his mouth for a brief kiss.

"Come in," she said, tugging him inside. "I'll put on
some coffee and then you can tell me everything."

Bridget was jolted to a rude awakening by the rapid-
fire chiming of the doorbell. Squinting at the clock
through the gray light of morning, she saw that it wasn't
even six o'clock. She'd slept for less than four hours,
and only fitfully at that. No wonder she felt so groggy.

Then it hit her. Someone was ringing her doorbell
before 6:00 a.m. That couldn't possibly mean they had
good news. Leaping from bed, she hurtled herself down
the stairs and pulled open the front door without even
bothering to see who was on the other side. And when
she saw that it was Special Agent in Charge Steve Pennington—without Sam—it was all Bridget could do not
to fall to her knees and weep.

"Sam…?" she said.

Pennington met her gaze levelly, his mouth grim.
But all he said was, "I'm sorry, Bridget."

No, she thought. No, no, no, no, no. "Where is he?" she demanded. He couldn't be... He must just be injured. Maybe unconscious. He wasn't... "What hospital is he in?" she asked.

Pennington's eyes closed for a moment, then opened again. But he remained stone-cold steely when he said, "He's not in the hospital, Bridget. He's dead."

No! No, no, no, no, no!

The words wouldn't leave her mouth, though, just kept ricocheting around in her head, burning her every time they hit. She shook her head, slowly at first, and then more adamantly. No. He wasn't... He couldn't be... He was supposed to be coming home. They were supposed to talk. They were supposed to be together. Forever.

For God's sake, she *loved* him! He couldn't be... He couldn't.

"He and Davis caught up with Everett Baker about an hour north of town," Pennington continued, even though Bridget was barely registering what he had to say. What difference did it make how it had happened? Sam was... And nothing would change that. "When Baker realized they were following him, he pulled to the side of the road and jumped out of the car and started running toward the woods."

Pennington paused there, seeming to realize Bridget wasn't really listening. "Bridget?" he asked.

"What?" she said numbly.

"Baker was armed," Pennington continued. "He shot at our agents. He hit Sam. I'm sorry. I wish I could give you better news. I know you and Sam... Well, I know you two became friends during the investigation. I'm sorry it ended this way."

Bridget nodded, grateful for the encapsulated

version. *Friends,* she repeated to herself. Right. "I'm sorry, too," she said.

"There is some good news, though," Pennington added.

Oh, goody, Bridget thought sarcastically. Whatever it was, it was sure to take the sting out of Sam's death.

When she said nothing in response, Pennington continued, "Thanks to our investigation of Charlie Prescott's computer records, we have all the information we need about how the black-market baby ring operated. Prescott kept meticulous records of every illegal transaction that incriminated not only himself and Kosanisky, but Everett Baker, as well. We'll have no trouble at all putting things to right again. And when we catch Baker—and I promise you, Bridget, we will catch Baker—we'll have enough evidence to put him away for a long time, whether he cooperates with us or not."

Bridget nodded. Yay. Hooray. None of it brought Sam back. Nothing would do that.

"Is there anything I can do for you?" Pennington asked when she said nothing. "Is there anything you need?"

Oh, boy, what a question, she thought. "No," she said. "Nothing." Without Sam, Pennington could give her everything, and it would still be nothing to her.

"I wanted to tell you in person," Pennington added. "Before you heard about it on the news. We're holding a press conference at six."

"Is anyone making arrangements for Sam?" Bridget asked.

"Already taken care of," Pennington told her.

Of course, she thought. His family would see to that. His real family. Parents, brother. The family with whom he'd once had a home. The family who loved him, and who'd told him he was loved.

"Sam's family has indicated it will be a small, *private* service," Pennington told her.

The way he emphasized the word *private,* she knew he meant that it would be for family only. In other words, not Bridget. Because she wasn't part of Sam's family. And no amount of wishing it was different would change that.

"Bridget?" she heard Pennington say again. But his voice seemed to be coming through thick gauze, from very far away. "Is there anyone I can call for you?" he asked. "Your parents? You probably shouldn't be alone right now."

She had to swallow the lump of despair that rose in her throat at his words. No, she shouldn't be alone right now, she thought. She shouldn't ever be alone again. She should be with Sam. But thanks to Everett Baker, she wouldn't be. Instead, she'd be alone—right now, and forever more. Because Baker had killed Sam. And Sam was the only person Bridget had ever wanted to build a life with.

She shook her head. "No, I'll call my parents myself," she said. And then she realized that, from now on, she'd be doing everything herself.

From now on, she'd be alone.

Twelve

Bridget knew her mother and sister were waiting for her in the hospital cafeteria, and she knew they'd worry about her if she was late, but she couldn't bring herself to leave the stall in the women's room into which she had escaped just shy of making it to her destination. She understood that her mother and Jillian were only trying to take her mind off Sam when they invited her to lunch. She knew her mother was growing concerned about the way Bridget had shut herself up in her childhood bedroom at her parents' house. But it had been less than a week since Sam had… And Bridget just didn't want to see her mother and Jillian right now. She didn't want to see anyone. She just wanted to be left alone, with her whys and what-ifs, and wallow in self-pity for the rest of her miserable life.

Why hadn't she told Sam she loved him when she

had the chance? Why hadn't she taken more advantage of the short time they'd had together? Why had she wasted so much of it fighting her feelings for him, when deep down she'd known almost immediately that she cared so much for him? And what if she'd made her feelings for him known? When she thought back to the last time they'd seen each other, she recalled how he'd seemed to be waiting for her to tell him something, but at the time she honestly hadn't known what. And he'd seemed to want to tell her something, too. In hindsight, she wondered if maybe, in a way, they'd both been trying to tell each other how much they loved each other. But neither had said a word.

Because they'd both been much too professional to do something like that.

Would it have changed anything? she asked herself now. If she'd told Sam she loved him then, would he have stayed here in Portland with her instead of going after Everett Baker and Charlie Prescott? Would she be snuggled in his arms right now instead of trying to hide from the entire world?

Why...? What if...?

Oh, Sam...

She wouldn't cry, she told herself, not here, in a public place, where anyone might wander in and intrude on something eminently personal that she herself was just beginning to understand. But she did allow herself some sniffles, and she didn't begrudge herself the few tears that managed to escape her eyes and tumble down her cheeks. Again and again she pulled a tissue from her purse, dabbing at her eyes and nose, until the little plastic package was empty. She really wasn't going to cry, she promised herself. Just another sniffle or two, that was all. And then she'd find her mother and Jillian in the cafeteria, and she'd tell them she wasn't staying for lunch. She wanted to go home, back to the bedroom she'd had as a little girl, because it was the only safe haven she could think of right now. She wanted to be somewhere safe right now. And she wanted to be there be alone, with her memories of Sam. They were still too precious to share with anyone else.

Just as she was starting to pull herself together, though, she heard the soft whoosh of the rest-room door as it opened, followed by the muffled sound of rubber-soled shoes as someone crossed the floor. Bridget peeked out from beneath her stall and saw white nurse shoes and pink scrub pants.

She decided to wait until the newcomer had left—or at least ventured into a stall of her own—before emerging from hers, knowing she must look a mess after all the not-crying she'd been doing, and she didn't want to have to explain her appearance, even to a total stranger. But whoever had entered the rest room evidently wasn't going to leave for a while, because as Bridget sat there listening for sounds of retreat, she heard instead the sound of someone bursting into tears—quiet, hopeless, heart-wrenching tears much like the ones she had been trying to keep inside.

Realizing that whoever was out there wasn't going to be leaving anytime soon, Bridget unlocked her stall and pushed the door open, then ventured out into the rest room proper. A young woman about her age was standing in front of one of a half-dozen sinks, her scrub top spattered with images of Disney princesses, her curly brown hair just barely contained in a bun. She started visibly when Bridget emerged, clearly thinking she had been alone until then. A quick glance at the name tag pinned to her top told Bridget the other woman's name was Rebecca Holley, RN.

"Oh, I'm so sorry," she apologized when she saw Bridget, glancing quickly away. She lifted a tissue to dab first at one eye, then the other. "I didn't think there was anyone in here." She looked at Bridget's face full on then, and must have noticed that Bridget was in a state similar to her own, because she smiled, albeit a bit sadly. "Guess there's something going around, huh?"

A quick glimpse of herself in the mirror told Bridget she was even more pink-nosed and red-eyed than her companion. Good thing she hadn't let herself cry, otherwise she *really* would have been a mess. She sighed heavily, lifting one shoulder and letting it drop. "Sometimes," she said wearily, "life just throws you a curve you didn't see coming, you know?"

The nurse nodded at that. "You said it. And sometimes it's a beanball that smacks you right in the head. And all you can do after that is see stars."

Bridget laughed lightly, thinking it was the first half-decent feeling she'd had in days. "Or those annoying little cupids in diapers," she said, forcing a smile, thinking that was a more appropriate symbol of what had caused her own dizziness over the past few weeks.

The woman didn't smile back, though. Instead, her eyes filled with tears again, and she lifted her tissue to her nose. "I'm sorry," she said again. "You've caught me at a bad time."

Bridget's instincts told her to reach out to the other woman, but she held herself in check. They were total strangers, and Rebecca Holley, who seemed friendly enough, might not be the sort of person who welcomed an extended hand. There had been a time when Bridget was like that, too, but since meeting Sam, that had changed. It had changed, in fact, that first night he'd reached out to her, literally and figuratively. One touch, that was all it had taken. And it was a touch that Bridget would replay in her mind over and over again for the rest of her life. She had so few memories of Sam, thanks to the brevity of their time together. So she would take them all out every day, and she would enjoy them again and cherish them and hope that maybe that would be enough to sustain her.

Why…? *What if?*

"Are you okay?" Bridget said, not knowing why she was prolonging an awkward situation but just wanting to do something to ease the other woman's distress if she could. It was kind of eerie the way the two of them, total strangers, had ended up in the same place at the same time, feeling the same way. It created a strange sort of bond between them that defied explanation.

Rebecca Holley nodded a little jerkily, then, countering her words, she lifted her tissue to her teary eyes again. "I just got some bad news a few minutes ago, that's all," she said. "Nothing I can't handle, though," she hastened to add. "Eventually. I'll be fine, though. I always am." She smiled sadly as she lowered the tissue and squared her shoulders. "Eventually."

Bridget nodded. She knew how that was. As horrible as it had been to hear about Sam's death, she knew she was strong enough to handle it. Eventually. Probably. Someday. If she drank heavily and mired herself in denial and split herself into twelve distinct but individual personalities that lived lives separate from hers, and renounced completely the one that went by the name of Bridget Logan. That might work. Eventually. Probably. Someday.

"Me, too," she told the other woman. "The bad news, I mean," she amended, thinking that the being-able-to-handle-it business might not be as easy to come by as it obviously would be for Rebecca Holley.

This time it was Bridget who lifted the tissue to her eyes in an effort to stop fresh tears.

Rebecca noted the gesture and asked, "Are *you* okay?"

And even though Bridget was thinking she'd never be okay again, she nodded. "Yeah. For now I am." And that much, she thought, was true. Because in that moment, at least, she was okay.

Moment by moment, she told herself. That was how she was going to have to live from now on. Get through this moment however she could—whether it meant commiserating with a total stranger in a women's rest room, or lying in bed curled in a fetal position, crying her eyes out. And then, when the next moment came, she'd deal with that one, too. And then the next. And the next. Eventually, the moments would turn into hours. And then the hours would turn into days. The days would turn into weeks, and the weeks would turn into seasons, and the seasons would turn into years. And then someday, Bridget would be an old woman, sitting in a rocking chair, watching her great-nieces and -nephews cavorting around the yard.

But even then she knew, she would still be thinking about Sam Jones and wondering, *Why...? What if...?*

Sam's house in the working-class neighborhood where he'd grown up was small but cozy-looking, Bridget thought as she stood across the street from it.

She still didn't know why she had come here. Instead of returning to her parents' house after her run-in with Rebecca Holley, she'd found herself driving in the opposite direction, until she'd ended up here instead. She'd just wanted to see Sam's home, the place where he had grown up, the place where he lived now—or, rather, where he had lived until he…

She'd just wanted to see his home, that was all. And now that she saw it, she realized it was exactly the sort of place she would have expected him to occupy. The brick bungalow with the broad front porch was earnest and down-to-earth, firmly built and no-frills. It looked solid and safe, strong and secure. Like Sam. Just like Sam. It was the kind of house where a person could be happy knowing she had everything she would ever need close at hand.

Bridget lifted her hand then, the left one, and studied the wedding ring she still wore. For some reason, she hadn't been able to bring herself to remove it. She shouldn't have it on, should have returned it to Pennington. It belonged to the Bureau. But it had given Bridget some small comfort to have it on; it had preserved a link to Sam. Maybe she'd see if Pennington would let her keep it. She'd pay the Bureau back. It was, after all, a very pretty ring. She turned it slowly around her finger—a distracted sort of habit she'd developed over the past few days—and glanced up at Sam's house again.

She saw movement beyond one of the windows.

Heat filled her belly, and she squeezed her eyes tightly shut, certain she must have been mistaken, that the sunlight had just glinted off the glass and made it look as though there was someone inside. Then she remembered that it was cloudy today, as it so often was in Portland and had seemed to be even more so since Sam had... She opened her eyes again and fixed her gaze on the same front window. For a moment, nothing happened, then...yes, there it was again. There was definitely someone inside Sam's house.

It must be a family member, she decided. His brother, probably, there to go through some of Sam's things and take stock of his belongings. She battled an urge to go to the front door and introduce herself as one of Sam's friends. It only now occurred to her that in spite of the month they had spent together, and all the intimacies they'd shared, she knew so little about Sam's family and his childhood and youth. It might be nice to hear more about him from someone who'd known him since childhood.

But his family was grieving, she reminded herself, and might not welcome the questions of an outsider.

But she was grieving, too, she thought further. And it would bring her comfort to talk about the man she loved. Surely his family would feel that way, too.

Before she could reconsider what she was doing, Bridget glanced both ways and crossed the street. The neighborhood was quiet in the middle of the day, most of its inhabitants at work or school. Off in the distance, she heard the steady metallic sound of factory machinery humming, and, closer by, the sound of a radio playing a top-forty tune. A trio of birds fluttered overhead and landed in a tree in the front yard of Sam's house, chattering loudly at each other. The driveway was cracked in places, loose gravel spilling from the crevices, and one step on the front walkway was chipped. The scars only brought more character to the place, though, Bridget thought. Made it seem that much more real, that much more human. Like Sam, she couldn't help thinking.

When she reached the front door, she hesitated, feeling a little buoyant for no reason she could name. Because she was about to meet someone who had a tie to Sam, she realized, and even that small connection to him made her feel better.

She rapped swiftly three times on the screen door and waited. Although she heard what sounded like the creak of a hardwood floor on the other side of the door, no one came to answer it. So Bridget knocked again, harder this time. Her only response, though, was silence.

She was almost sure someone was inside. Striding to one end of the porch, she leaned over the railing and looked at the garage, which sat back, detached, from the house. There was a car parked inside, she could see through the glass in the door. Of course, that could simply be Sam's car, not the car of some visitor. But somehow, she knew there was someone inside the house.

She went back to the door and knocked again, this time punctuating the gesture with what she hoped was a breezy-sounding, "Hello? Is anyone in there?"

She cocked her head to one side and listened. There. Again. The definite creak of a floorboard. Bridget moved to one of the front windows and tried to peek through the blinds but they were closed too tightly. "I'm a friend of Sam's," she called out further. "I just wanted to…"

But her voice trailed off without finishing the statement. Just what did she want to do? she asked herself. The truth was, she had simply wanted to feel closer to Sam in whatever way she could. And how did she explain that to someone Sam had probably never even mentioned her name to?

Accepting the fact that she had probably only made matters worse by coming here—and convinced now that she must have just imagined or wished that someone was inside the house—Bridget turned and made her way down the front steps. Sam was gone, she told herself, trying very hard to come to terms with that. She would never see him again. As much as she loved him, it wasn't enough to bring him back.

No sooner had the thought formed in her head, however, than she heard the sound of the front door unlocking behind her. By now Bridget had cleared the porch steps and reached the front walkway, and the sound made her stop in her tracks. She couldn't bring herself to turn around, though, certain she was once again imagining things. But then she heard a bolt sliding back and a chain dropping from its casing and swinging against the wooden jamb. And then…

Then she heard the door opening.

Her heart began to pound madly in her chest. But still, she couldn't make herself turn around, couldn't let herself believe what she wanted so desperately to believe. That it was Sam opening the door, that he wasn't dead, that he was right behind her. That he was waiting for her to turn around so he could tell her that there had been a terrible mistake and that he loved her and wanted her to stay here with him. Forever.

"Bridget."

She closed her eyes at the sound of his voice speaking her name. Her mouth went dry, her knees went weak, her heart very nearly stopped beating. Slowly, oh so slowly, she began to turn around. But her head moved faster than her body, and as she glanced over her shoulder, she saw that it *was* Sam standing in the doorway. He was dressed in the way she had preferred to see him, in faded jeans and a gray flannel shirt, his feet bare, his hair mussed, as if he'd been dragging his hands through it in agitation.

Sam. Her Sam. But…not. Because how could he be here?

She told herself to say something, anything, but there were too many thoughts ricocheting through her head just then, and she couldn't grasp even one of them long enough to let it fully form. She could only stand there stupidly, staring at Sam—or his ghost, or her imagination, or whatever it was—and wonder if, in all her grief, she had well and truly lost her mind.

When Sam saw Bridget standing at the foot of his front steps, it was all he could do not to run down there and sweep her into his arms and carry her back into his house. But Pennington would kill him if he did something like that.

Then again, Pennington had already killed him, hadn't he? Sam thought wryly. So what difference did it make?

Days. It had been days since he had seen Bridget. Nearly a week. Nearly a week since he had touched her. Enjoyed the sweet, feminine scent of her. Tasted her. And now here she was, looking like a bright splash of sunlight in an otherwise gray day, her pale-yellow dress fluttering in the breeze like a butterfly's wings, her hair dancing about her shoulders, just begging for a man's hands to bury themselves in the silky tresses.

How would he have felt if things had been reversed, if she had been the one to go after Baker and the Bureau had told him she was dead? What if he'd had to face the prospect of never being able to hold her again? Of never being able to talk to her again? Or dance with her? Or make love to her? Or even just sit in a room reading a book and having a beer with her?

How could he have let them tell her he was dead? How could he have done that to her?

"Sam?" she said, her voice soft, fragile, incredulous. But she said nothing more, only shook her head slowly, as if she simply could not believe her eyes. "Is it you? Really? You're not...?"

She couldn't even say the word, he realized. Which meant that on some level, she had known he wasn't really dead. Probably the level that loved him. At least, that was what he hoped. That Bridget loved him. Because he'd had a lot of time to think about things over the past week. And it hadn't taken him long to figure out how deeply he'd fallen in love with Bridget Logan.

"I can't come out there," he told her. "If Pennington even saw me standing in the door, he'd have my head on a plate. You have to come up here. Please, Bridget. So I can explain."

He didn't have to ask her twice. But she didn't move very quickly, and he hated to think why that might be. Slowly, her eyes never leaving his face, she made her way up the stairs and across the porch, until she stood mere inches away from him. Then, tentatively, she lifted a hand and reached out toward his face. She halted, though, before touching him, as if she were afraid he might melt away on contact. Sam caught her hand in his and pulled her gently forward, over the threshold and into his house. And then he pushed the door closed behind her, hauled her up against himself and covered her mouth with his.

Oh, God, it felt so good to have her in his arms again. How had he lasted a week without her?

For a long time he only kissed her, first her mouth, then her cheeks, then her jaw and her temple and her hair. Then he wrapped his arms around her and tucked her head under his chin and just held her. He felt her heart thumping against his own and the warmth of her soft body beneath his fingertips. He inhaled deeply, savoring the sweet, flowery scent of her, and he heard a soft sigh escape her in response. And he knew without a doubt that he could never let her go again.

"I love you, Bridget Logan," he said.

He hadn't planned to speak the words so baldly out loud that way—at least, not yet. He hoped he hadn't startled her or scared her or put her on the spot with his frankness. But he had to say it now, before something happened to separate them again. She had to know how he felt about her, what he wanted for both of them. He had so much he wanted to say to her, and he needed to get it out *now,* before anything else job-related interfered.

"I love you," he said again, pulling her even closer. "I don't know when exactly it happened, or even when I realized it, but I know it without a doubt now. This week without you has been hell. I don't want anything to come between us again. I know you don't want to stay in Portland, but I don't want to stay here, either, without you. I came home to get a few things—Pennington about had a cow, but the safe house was making me crazy— and I realized this place doesn't even feel like home anymore. And the reason for that can only be because you aren't here. That house we shared, when we first went into it, I'd never felt more uncomfortable somewhere in my life. But by the time Baker called, I felt completely at home there. Because you were there, Bridget. That was why. I realize now that wherever you are, that's where I want to be. Because wherever you are, that will be my home. So when you leave Portland, I want to go with you. And I want us to be together forever."

When she said nothing in response to his impassioned plea, Sam started to feel a little uneasy. He'd said too much. Spoken too quickly. Been too fierce in his convictions. He *had* startled her and scared her and put her on the spot. She didn't love him back, didn't want to be with him forever, and now he'd made it impossible for her to tell him that gracefully.

Swallowing hard, he eased his hold on her, skimming his hands down over her arms to set her a few inches away from him. She was looking down at the ground, not at him, and his heart sank straight to the darkest pit in his stomach when he realized it. She didn't love him. Not the way he loved her.

"Bridget?" he said softly. But try as he might, he couldn't push any more words out of his mouth—out of his heart—than that.

Slowly, she lifted her head to look at him, and when she did, he saw that she was crying. Oh, God, had what he'd said been that bad? He hadn't meant to make her cry.

Then she laughed, a nervous little chuckle, and smiled.

Afraid to hope, Sam smiled back anxiously. He said her name one more time, still too scared to say anything more. "Bridget…"

"Oh, Sam," she replied, laughing in earnest now. "I love you, too."

His relief was palpable. "You do?"

She nodded. "I'm laughing because everything you just said to me is exactly what I was rehearsing in my mind to tell you after you went after Baker. Before Pennington told me you were…"

Oh, yeah. Definite relief happening now. "It is?" Sam asked.

She nodded again. "Except for the part about you going with me when I leave Portland."

His smile fell. Okay, relief-o-meter crashing down again. "You don't want me to come with you?"

She shook her head. "No."

"Oh."

"Because I'm not leaving Portland, Sam."

Zing. Back up into the Major Relief Zone again. "You're not?"

She shook her head. "I'm staying here. With you. And my family. My other family, I mean. In addition to the one I'll have with you. I hope. Someday. When we're both ready."

"Just say the word, sweetheart," he told her, pulling her close again. "And between now and then, we can just keep practicing. No offense, but I'd just as soon do it our way, and not bother Children's Connection again."

"For now I just want us to be together," she told him. "I'm selfish that way and I want you all to myself. But no matter what happens, I want us to stay together. Forever." She pulled away from him, but only far enough to lift her hand to his face again. This time she didn't stop before making contact, though. This time she cupped his jaw in her palm. "I love you so much. When Pennington told me you were dead, a part of me died, too. I didn't think I'd be able to go on without you. Why?" she asked. "Why would he tell me such a thing? Why would you let him?"

This part would be easier to explain, Sam thought, if no more palatable. "If I'd known in advance what he was planning to do, I never would have let him tell you what he did. He told me after the fact what he had done, and why he'd done it..." He blew out an exasperated sound. "He did it for my safety, Bridget. I know that doesn't excuse it, but there it is just the same. He told my parents and brother the same thing."

"But why?" she asked again.

He ran a hand restlessly through his hair. "Because while I was working undercover with you on the Children's Connection case, we had some major developments on another case I worked on a few months ago. Organized crime," he told her. "Long story short, we hauled in a couple of very big fish, and I'm going to have to appear as a material witness for their trial, which is scheduled for next month. And because I'd received a couple of half-assed death threats—"

"Death threats?" Bridget gasped.

"Half-assed," Sam said again. "They were lame, Bridget. No one's going to come after me. But Pennington, being the alarmist he is, thought it would be a good idea for me to lie low between now and the trial, in case someone got the bright idea to carry out those threats. And in his infinite wisdom," Sam continued sardonically, "he thought it was a good idea to make the goons involved think I was already dead. When Everett Baker took a couple of shots at me and Davis, Pennington decided he had a nice, neat way to kill me off temporarily.

"I, in turn, wanted to kill him when he told me what he'd done," Sam continued. "I wanted to call you and tell you what had happened, but by then... I don't know. I guess I figured the damage was done. With you and my family. But I want to tell them now, too. Pennington be damned. I won't have the people I love thinking I'm dead. I'll still play the part to the outside world, but...you and my family are too important to me, and you don't deserve this."

"Why didn't you call me as soon as you knew Everett Baker had escaped?" Bridget asked. "Before Pennington had a chance to reach me?"

"It was the middle of the night," Sam said. "I thought you'd be sleeping, and I didn't want to wake you. Not like that. I figured I'd go ahead and write up my report, then come home to you, sneak in and slide into bed beside you." He ducked his head, suddenly feeling uncertain for some reason. "I planned to wake you up in a much nicer way than a phone call in the middle of the night."

"Oh, Sam…"

"Instead, I almost ended up losing you."

"You never would have lost me," she said.

"If I'd let you go on thinking I was dead, you would have left Portland and forgotten all about me."

She laughed again, totally uninhibited this time. "Oh, no, I wouldn't. I would have stayed right here. To be close to your memory, if nothing else. Why do you think I came to your house today?"

"I don't know," he said.

"Because I wanted to be with you in whatever way I could," she told him. "I came to the door because I thought I saw someone inside, and I thought maybe it would be your brother or a friend or someone I could talk to about you. I just wanted to be close to you. However I could be. And now that I know you're alive…"

Tears filled her eyes, but she continued to smile, as if she'd just been given a gift she didn't have enough ways to say thank you for.

Sam's heart turned over when he saw the way her face changed. "I am so sorry you ever had to think I was—"

She covered his mouth with her hand before he could finish. "It doesn't matter," she told him. "All that matters is that you're here now. And I'm here with you. And both of us will be together forever."

He pulled her close again, looping his arms loosely around her waist, pressing his forehead to hers. "You sure you want to stay here in Portland? Not go gallivanting around the globe looking for terrorists?"

"Actually," Bridget said, "I overheard Pennington talking about a new counterterrorist task force the FBI is putting together for the Portland field office."

"Really?"

She nodded. Or maybe she was just rubbing her forehead affectionately against his. Whatever. Sam didn't care. As long as she was here. With him. Forever.

"And you know, I'm trained in that sort of thing," she said.

"By HQ, no less."

"I think I'd be a great asset to a counterterrorist task force here."

"And here I've been thinking you have a great a—"

"Sam?" she interrupted, grinning.

"Yes?"

"Will you marry me?"

He smiled and lifted his left hand, still sporting the ring Pennington had dropped into his palm that first day of the assignment. Even though Sam hadn't needed to wear it since going after Everett Baker, he hadn't wanted to take it off. He still didn't. But now he wanted very much to make it legitimate.

"I thought we were already Mr. and Mrs.," he said playfully.

Bridget held up her left hand, and he saw that she was still wearing her wedding ring, too. "In everything but name," she said.

"Easily rectified," he pointed out.

"We could elope," she said. "To Vegas. Just like Mr. and Mrs. Samuel Jones did."

Sam thought about that. "Vegas, huh? You know, that could be a really good place to lay low for a month or so, until I have to report for the trial. I'm sure there must be a safe house there."

"But it might be a good idea if you have a federal agent assigned to keep an eye on you twenty-four-seven. Just in case, I mean."

"Good idea," Sam told her. "And you know, I bet there's a lot of things for newlyweds to do in Vegas."

"But you'll have to lie low," she reminded him. And then she smiled. "Good thing for you, someone told me that newlyweds tend to disappear for a few weeks after the wedding."

Sam knew exactly who that someone was, too. And he remembered the rest of the spiel. "Because they want to enjoy each other for a while. In private. Get to know each other. Intimately. Discover all the things about each other that they never knew before."

"We have a lot to learn about each other, Mr. Jones," Bridget said, tilting her head to the side for another kiss.

Sam nodded. "And we have all the time in the world to learn it," he agreed.

Which was true, he knew. Because if he had his way, he and Bridget would be newlyweds—or at least acting like newlyweds—for a long, long time to come.

* * * * *